HOUGHTON MIFFLIN HARCOURT
CHILDREN'S BOOK GROUP
BOSTON :: NEW YORK

ADVANCE READING COPY

IMPRINT: Harcourt Children's Books

TITLE: Lost Voices

AUTHOR: Porter, Sarah

ILLUSTRATOR:

ISBN: 978-0-547-48250-7

PUBLICATION DATE: 07/04/2011

PRICE: $16.99 / Higher in Canada

TRIM: 5-1/2" x 8-1/4"

PAGE COUNT: 304

AGES: 12 and Up

GRADES: 7 and Up

These are uncorrected galleys. Please check all quotations and attributions against the bound copy of the book. We urge this for the sake of editorial accuracy as well as for your legal protection and ours.

Reviewers may reprint cover illustrations to accompany reviews with the following credit:
Courtesy of Houghton Mifflin Harcourt Publishing Company

To obtain an electronic image of the cover of this book,
please visit www.hmhbooks.com.

Please send two copies of your review to:
Jennifer Taber | Publicity Department
222 Berkeley Street | Boston, Massachusetts 02116

Lost Voices

SARAH PORTER

HOUGHTON MIFFLIN HARCOURT
BOSTON   NEW YORK   2009

Harcourt is an imprint of Houghton Mifflin Harcourt
Publishing Company.

www.hmhbooks.com

Text set in TK

LIBRARY OF CONGRESS CATALOGING-IN-PUBLICATION DATA
TK

Manufactured in the United States of America
TK 10 9 8 7 6 5 4 3 2 1
45XXXXXXXX

For Maggie Cino,
who wandered with me on the beach,
singing back to the mermaids

There's always a siren singing you to shipwreck.
(Don't reach out, don't reach out, don't reach out, don't reach out.)
Steer away from these rocks, we'd be a walking disaster.
(Don't reach out, don't reach out, don't reach out, don't reach out.)

Radiohead, "There There"

Lost Voices

"Lucette? Did you even hear the question?"

Luce had been gazing out the window at the darkened sky sinking over the harbor still dotted with rough floating ice, the mountain walls of shadow-colored spruce and rusty boulders under the greenish, glassy dusk of a coming storm. Mr. Carroll's voice jolted her back into the drab classroom with its tan desks and low scarred ceiling, and she noticed with dismay that half a dozen faces were already turning to stare into the back corner where she sat under a tattered map of the world. None of her other teachers ever called on her. Only Mr. Carroll insisted on trying to make her talk. If only he would leave her alone, Luce knew, the other kids would forget her existence completely.

She tightened her body and stared as blankly as she could at the board as the first giggles started up around her. Her stomach began to twist and her hands turned horribly cold. She squeezed them together under the desk to stop the trembling.

"Lucette? You should be on page one twelve of your text-book. The third problem?"

She *was* on page one hundred and twelve. She gaped down automatically at the third problem, and she was sure she knew the right answer. It was obvious.

The laughter got louder and faster. It buzzed around her like angry wasps. Mr. Carroll waved a hand to quiet everyone, but it didn't have much effect. She hated the concern growing in his droopy gray eyes. Luce knew that the quickest way to make them all ignore her again would be just to answer the question. *Parabolic.* She opened her mouth to say the word.

Nothing came out except a kind of faint croak. Everyone could see her now, and almost all of them were giggling. Her hands were shaking so much that she had to sit on them.

Desperately Luce tried to force her voice to shape the word. Just one word and she would be free again.

Her croaking got a little louder. Most of the time she could talk as well as anyone, even if she almost always chose to keep quiet. Lately, though, her voice had developed a habit of abandoning her whenever she needed it most. Someone squealed and threw a wad of paper at her, clipping her on the side of her head.

That was enough to knock Mr. Carroll out of his trance. His wobbly eyes spun away from Luce. His huge round cheeks blushed scarlet, though there was no reason why *he* should feel embarrassed.

"Amber?" Mr. Carroll yelped, too loudly, to a girl sitting all the way at the front. It was almost a shout. It was as if he thought he could cancel out the ugliness of what he'd done, drawing all those eyes down on the skinny dark-haired girl who huddled in the back of his class, struggling with the loss of her voice.

"I have *no* idea what the answer is to this stupid problem, Mr. Carroll," Amber twittered in her happy voice. "Nobody does except you." The shrieks of laughter that followed were strangely excited, and Mr. Carroll took advantage of the shifting mood, clowning as he worked out the problem on the blackboard. Even now he couldn't leave it alone, though. He kept shooting Luce guilty looks, pinching his lips together, and of course everyone noticed. Every time he glanced her way, a few more pairs of eyes flocked after his. Luce kept her face down, drawing a thicket of black hatched lines in her book until the ink became so dense that hardly any white shone through.

When the bell finally rang Luce felt sicker than ever. The other students grabbed up their backpacks and raced out, eager to get to the cafeteria for lunch. *Lunch.* Where in that bright blocky room would she ever be able to hide? Mr. Carroll tried to catch her attention as she slipped past him, but Luce pretended not to notice.

"This is, like, eighth grade already," a boy hissed in her ear. "You act like some freaked-out ten-year-old." Luce kept her face blank and unresponsive, even when he prodded her arm.

She slunk after the other students, staying close to the walls. A crack of thunder smacked against her thoughts. It was terrifically loud. The lightning must have struck very close to the school.

Not today, Luce thought, and all at once she remembered the date again. Her stomach seethed, and she knew that the storm wouldn't just blow over. She'd have to spend the afternoon watching the rain lash down outside and listening to the windowpanes clashing like cymbals in the wind. It would be exactly the way everything was a year ago today: the day her father's boat hadn't come home.

There was one good thing about the storm, anyway. It was a distraction. Kids huddled in the cafeteria, pretending to be terrified of the booming thunder, screaming and grabbing each other. The windows near the ceiling of the tall room looked almost black, and the rain rattled rock sharp against the panes. It was a small space compared to cafeterias Luce had seen before, but even with students bused in from every village within thirty miles, it was always half empty. Lightning ripped through the darkness and the windows flashed blinding white and then went dark again. Everyone was too busy chattering about the violent weather to think of her. She slipped off to her usual spot at the side and sat alone with her back to everyone, and closed her eyes.

* * *

It wasn't a storm at all, then. Hot sunlight glared through the van's open window and burned her cheeks. A bright golden blob of sun curled on her palm like a kitten. A sign flashing by outside welcomed them to Missouri. Her father laughed and gunned the motor.

"You know they just don't make cops smart enough to catch up with me, don't you, baby doll? *Look* at that. Over the state line already, and they still don't know what hit them!" She smiled back at him, shy as always, and he beamed at her and twisted a lock of her long hair around one finger. Then he squinched his lips and shot her a look. "I mean, I guess I have to admit that maybe they could have caught me, once or twice"—he drawled it out playfully, and Luce knew he was faking his reluctance—"if I didn't have you to help me with *strategy*. You're my secret weapon, honey. You've got the mind of a great general. And not a one of them ever suspects it." Luce was already giggling when her father launched into the sluggish, moronic voice he always used to mimic policemen and judges. "You don't mean to say that that *sweet* little wisp of a thing could be the diabolical mastermind behind this incredible theft, do you? No, I'll never believe it!"

Luce knew he was only kidding. About the most she ever did to help was to stand lookout while her father loaded stolen chemicals or electronics into the back of their van. Even so, she loved hearing him say it. "You and me, we've got them all fooled, don't we? Now, as soon as we hit St. Louis I'll take you to the best bookstore in town, and you can pick out a whole damn stack. *And* for a hot fudge sundae. You've most certainly earned your share of the spoils."

Luce's bare feet were already propped high on piles of books and the duffle bag holding her clothes. Her gawky knees poked up in front of the dashboard. She could feel her right leg starting to get sunburned, but she didn't bother moving it. The rest of the van was stuffed with the weird-looking lumps of equipment her father had swiped from his last temporary job, this one doing maintenance work in a huge dry cleaning plant. Even the wind swirling across the front seat couldn't completely get rid of the sharp chemical stink. Sometimes her father wrinkled his nose into a ridiculous doglike snout and then gave her a sideways grin to let her know the smell bothered him, too.

The smell changed in Luce's nose. Now it was the greasy stench of Tater Tots and gluey fried chicken. That moment in the van had happened almost three years before, and the memory suddenly seemed stale and cold, as if she had used it to comfort herself one too many times. Her eyes were still shut tight, but she knew that if she opened them she wouldn't see the bright sunshine on the highway anymore.

"Come back come back come back," Luce called silently to her father. She tried to make the words powerful and wild, so that he would hear them wherever he was. "It's been a whole year!" There was no answer. Just the giddy shouting of the kids roughhousing at the tables behind her and the piercing soprano of a teacher who was screaming at them. Luce kept arguing with her father anyway. "It's my birthday tomorrow. You can't miss it twice in a row!"

It didn't work. She couldn't see anything but the dark, red insides of her eyelids. She was all alone in this horrible school, with noplace to go but back to her uncle's tiny brown clapboard house two miles outside of town. She could disappear into the woods on days when it wasn't raining too hard, but that carried its own risks. Her uncle tended to get irritable if he didn't find her at home, and after a few drinks he might express his irritation by slamming her into a wall.

When the bell rang again, she realized that she hadn't touched her food.

* * *

After lunch the storm turned so violent that the kids stopped joking about it. It was just like last year. Some of them had fathers out on the sea, and with the weather this ferocious there was always a chance that not all the boats would make it back home. Even the teachers seemed nervous. The thunder boomed, and the fluorescent lights looked dim and sick. No one was all that surprised when, halfway through seventh period, there was a shattering burst of lightning and the power went out completely. Kids shrieked and banged into desks in the darkness. Mrs. Dougherty yelled for quiet, but she sounded so hysterical herself that no one paid any attention to her. Luce sat tight at the back of the room, and in the faint greenish light coming in through the windows she could see the tumult of kids fighting to get to the door. A girl named Crystal got knocked down, hit her head on the wastebasket, and started sobbing.

Luce stayed where she was, listening to something she could hear under Crystal's sobs; there was a new kind of silence, prickly with expectation. But what did she think was going to happen?

Then the door swung open, and the beam of a flashlight streaked across the room. Mr. Carroll, again. "Everyone, please, form a line. We don't need to make things any worse. One line, that's right. We have emergency lighting working in the cafeteria. Once everyone's quiet I'll lead you there. The buses will be coming in a few minutes to take you home." His voice was steady, and the students finally started calming down. Luce wanted to stay where she was, but she knew it would only attract attention if she didn't move. Reluctantly she stood and gathered her books while Mr. Carroll helped Crystal off the floor. "Are you all right, Crystal? Do you need to see the nurse?" Suddenly Luce knew that Crystal wasn't crying because of her head.

"What about the boats?" Crystal was barely whispering, but somehow Luce heard her anyway. The flashlight was pointing toward the windows, and Mr. Carroll's face was too dark to see. But when he spoke his voice was very soft.

"Well, the last news we had was half an hour ago. But the word then was that all the boats were just fine. Don't worry. They're all heading home."

Luce knew the idea that came to her then was childish, but she couldn't completely suppress it and her heart started pounding. She pictured the boats sliding into the harbor, and following behind them was an extra, unaccountable boat, so battered and patched that it looked almost ghostly behind the gray veils of the rain. Everyone would scream in amazement when they recognized the *High and Mighty* returning after a whole year lost, maybe having been trapped in the ice somewhere, where the men had survived by hunting seals and fishing . . .

"You should know better than to fret when I'm late, honey," her father said in her thoughts. *"Life has a way of turning crazy on me sometimes. But you know I come back just as soon as I can."*

Luce nodded in her mind, trying to drown out the suspicion that this was just a cowardly way of avoiding the truth. After all, he'd come back before. When she was eight he'd been sent to jail for a while—something to do with writing checks that didn't belong to him—and she'd gone into foster care. But then on her ninth birthday the faded red van was waiting outside her school, and she'd looked up to see him grinning at her through the open door. They couldn't go back to Texas after that because the police thought her father had kidnapped her. That hadn't made any sense to Luce; how could you kidnap your own daughter? After a while he'd stopped trying to explain. "Just put it down as one of those things that don't make good sense, doll," he'd told her. "Lord knows there are plenty more where that came from."

It seemed like a very long time before the students were finally lined up and sent out to the waiting buses. Too long and too quiet, without any of the fights and shrieks there'd been during lunch. The storm boomed louder than ever. Outside, the raindrops popped all over the sidewalk in tiny bright explosions. Even in the heavy rain she preferred to walk home; anything to keep away from those stares. Below her was the harbor, the high trembling sea, while on either side rags of mountains dense with rain-blackened spruce jarred steeply upward, their darkness giving way to spills of cold, white ice halfway up. Cinnamon-colored rock outlined each base. It was early April, and the brutal darkness of the winter had yielded to days almost as long as the nights, but even so, the days were white or deep gray, rain-slashed and somber. Luce had lived in Alaska for only the past fifteen months, and she still wasn't used to any of it: the pale summer nights, winter days where the air seemed to be permeated with coal dust, the endless cold, the antlered shadows of huge elk suddenly appearing in the middle of the roads. Everyone said it had been an unusually warm winter, and Luce could barely imagine how that could be true. She stopped for a while at the edge of the cliffs, feeling the icy rivulets coiling around the side of her neck and inside her jacket while she gazed at the seethe and dip of the waves far below. Ice floes still jostled each other in places. To Luce they looked like greenish sheep nosing through the water.

By the time she got home every power line in the village seemed to have been knocked out. She sat in the small pea green kitchen, her feet on the patch of raw wood where the linoleum had peeled away. There was a good chance her uncle Peter would stay away until early morning, she knew; the anniversary of his brother's disappearance was a perfect excuse to go out drinking, and her uncle wouldn't want to pass it up. She ate crackers with peanut butter and read by candlelight until she fell asleep with her head on her arms.

* * *

What woke her wasn't a knock. It was more of a flapping noise at the kitchen door, wet and sloppy. Luce jerked awake and listened. The candle had gone out. All around her the house was dead quiet, apart from the thrashing of the waves outside. Even the rain had stopped now, and the windows were dark gray with early dawn. She knew at once that her uncle hadn't come home. And she knew that she'd better keep out of his way when he did. Anytime he stayed out this late it meant he'd be coming home roaring drunk.

The flapping noise came again, and now Luce was awake enough to recognize the sound. "Gum!" Luce called in relief. She ran to let him in. He was squeezed up under the door frame, his shapeless little face bright and anxious. Cold wind rushed through the open door. "You know it's my birthday, Gum? I'm fourteen." He cooed in a way that made her think he understood her, and she smiled at him. It was as close as she was going to get to hearing "happy birthday" from anyone.

Luce didn't know if it made sense to call Gum her friend, exactly, when he was more than three years younger than she was and what they called mentally disabled. He could barely talk. At least he couldn't seem to say anything that made sense. He spoke in a mixture of gibberish and seagullish moans. But she felt safe with him, and she knew he was always happy to see her, too. His pale silky hair swirled in the wind as he clung to the door frame. Gum's mother was still alive, unlike Luce's, but his father was long gone. His mother struck Luce as coarse and venomous, but then in her opinion most adults were. She couldn't understand why all the kids she knew were in such a hurry to turn into them. People whispered horrible things about how Gum's mother treated him, and it wasn't too unusual for him to turn up at strange hours like this.

He bounced on the balls of his feet and hopped back from the door, flapping his hand at her. She hesitated for only a second. It would probably be better if her uncle Peter came home to an empty house. He'd be angry, of course, if he checked her room and she wasn't there. But then he'd fall asleep, and by the time he woke up he'd definitely have forgotten all about it. Luce looked into Gum's shining eyes and sighed.

"Hold on while I get my jacket, okay?" Gum bobbled and trilled on the grass. Behind him she could see the slow roll of the meadow breaking off suddenly where the cliffs plunged down into the crashing waves. The sea was still wild from the storm, and even from here she could see how the waves arched high into the bitter air before they fell like toppling buildings. Luce shivered.

Gum couldn't stop squeaking as she tied her sneakers and squeezed into her old silvery down jacket. She'd grown so much in the past year that the sleeves ended halfway up her forearms, but she could still get it to zip as long as she didn't wear a sweater. She took Gum's clammy hand in hers so he wouldn't fall, and they walked down the path that traveled along the top of the cliff. On their other side white wooden staircases zig-zagged steeply upward through the darkness of the spruce, heading to tiny-windowed board houses tucked among the trees. Cold and dark as the morning was, Luce felt her heart leap with happiness as she felt the sweet, free wind rush across her face. If she hadn't had to worry about Gum tumbling off the edge she would have started to run.

A hundred yards from her uncle's house there was an incline where, by half clambering and half sliding, they could get down to a broad pebble beach at the bottom of the rocks. Tiny avalanches skittered away under their feet, and when Gum almost lost his footing Luce made him sit down and slide with her until they reached the spot where a tangle of dead roots gave them a handhold. Luce jumped the last two feet onto the pebbles, then turned and caught Gum in her arms to help him down. The tide was about as low as it could go, which was a good thing, because the waves were enormous. Luce couldn't help feeling anxious as she looked at those iron gray walls of water and the strange lace patterns of the foam where they crashed and slid back. Any one of those waves could easily pick her up and sweep her far away. Then no one would ever see her again. The idea was frightening, but what scared her even more was that, if she was honest with herself, she was horribly attracted by the idea of drifting away with the sea.

"Gum!" He was eager to run off to the tide pools, and she had to catch him back and grab his head to make him look at her. The morning was a little brighter now. Gum's face was glossy with mist and it shone in the silver light. "Gum, you need to stay *way* back from the water today, okay? You understand me?" Adults never got tired of warning them how dangerous the sea was here, how fast and unpredictable the currents could be. It wasn't even safe to wade. Just last fall a fifth grade boy had been grabbed right off the rocks by a rogue wave. He'd vanished while his friends watched helplessly, and two weeks later some fishermen had found his body in their net.

Gum squeaked and ran a few steps, then turned and hopped in place, obviously daring her to chase him. He spun around and leaped along, pounding deep hollows in the pebble beach. Luce ran after him, but she went at a deliberately lazy pace, giving him the thrill of outrunning her. She'd put on more speed later, catch him suddenly and swing him through the air. But then he veered down the steep slope of the beach: not all that close to the water, really, but close enough to make Luce nervous.

"You promised to stay back!" Luce called after him. He showed he understood her by shooting a sheepish look over his shoulder and thumping clumsily back up the grade, flopping onto one knee before he scrambled up again.

The wind cried in her ears, its whistle curling wildly up the scale. There was something disturbing in the sound of it, Luce thought: a very subtle undertone, like a voice drifting from the far side of the earth. It was too alluring, too sweet, as if that vast oblivious expanse was calling her to join it. Vaguely Luce felt the percussion in her own legs as she stepped closer to the sea. A tongue of water drenched her sneakers, so icy it stung, and Luce started.

What had she been thinking? It was terribly irresponsible to let herself space out like that while Gum raced on alone. The wind was just wind. That was obvious now. There was noth-ing unusual about it.

She went after him, calling his name, but he had a good start on her. He was already almost to the cliffs that closed off the far end of the beach. There were tall spiky rocks sticking out of the beach down there, forming a kind of maze, and as Luce ran Gum dashed behind a rock and disappeared. The pebbles rattled under Luce's pounding feet and the cold wind slapped at her face.

"Gum?" she called. She'd finally reached the place where she'd seen him duck behind the rocks, but he was nowhere in sight. "Where *are* you?" There were round dents in the smooth beach that showed the way he'd run, and she followed them, weaving between huge crags. The waves crashed in a little closer now. The tide was coming in. If she didn't find him soon they'd both be in danger.

"Gum, it's time to stop playing like this! You need to get back here." Then she heard a soft sobbing sound, and turned a corner. Gum was curled in a tight ball, bobbing on his toes and crying. She couldn't see his face. A huge clump of wet brown seaweed spread out in front of him.

Luce crouched beside him and gently put her arm around his shoulders. The waves were getting much too close, and she had to soothe him enough that he would be ready to come with her. "Gum, it's okay. I'm sorry I didn't keep up with you, but it's all okay. Let's go home now." He finally looked up at her. His eyes were red and his face was slick with tears and snot.

"Fish girl!" Gum moaned. Then he started sobbing harder than ever. Luce couldn't believe it. It was the first time she'd ever heard him say anything that made any sense at all.

"Do you mean me, Gum? Am I the fish girl?" Gum squealed and rubbed his wet cheek against her jacket. With one shaking hand he reached out and pointed across the heaps of rubbery seaweed, to the place where a pale *something* lay half covered in brown tangles. Luce stood up to see it better. Then she gasped and grabbed Gum, pulling him up and wrapping her arms around him protectively.

A little girl was lying completely naked in the seaweed. Her eyes were closed, her skin was a milky greenish color, and her mouth hung open. She couldn't have been any older than two. Her bare chest didn't move at all, and Luce knew at once, with absolute certainty, that the girl was dead.

2

The Face in the Water

Luce managed to herd Gum back up the cliff, but it wasn't easy. He kept trying to twist away from her and run back to the dead girl. When they reached the pebble slope she practically had to push him, and at the top she looked back to see the waves already encroaching on the jumble of tall rocks. They didn't have much time, Luce knew, before the waves would seize that tiny cold body and swirl it away. Now that they were safely back at the meadow, she couldn't understand why she hadn't picked the body up and carried it up the slope herself. The idea that the girl might be lost forever sickened Luce. Maybe the girl's parents didn't even know what had happened to her, and now maybe they would never find out. It would be unforgivable if that happened because Luce was too afraid to touch a corpse. She could run to Gum's house and call the police, but it was obvious that by the time they came it would be too late.

Gum suddenly feinted, trying to jerk free of her grip on his hand, but she caught him back. He was keening now, shrilling out a single high, unbroken note.

"Stop it!" Tears were pouring down his face as he gaped at her. "Gum, I'm going back for her! It's going to be fine! But you *have* to let me get you home first." Gum stared and his squeal weakened to an uncertain whimper. "If you keep fighting me it's going to make me too late, okay? Come on!" Gum still looked confused, but he let her tow him along as she raced across the swaying grass to his lavender house with its ratty satin curtains. She was dashing so quickly that he stumbled, jerking down on her arm before he regained his footing. She had to slow down, but every second of delay might be one too many.

Luce threw open the door of Gum's house and almost propelled him inside. Mrs. Cooper gawked at her from the kitchen doorway, ashy burn marks in her scraggly blond hair and a cigarette flopping on her crackly lower lip.

"And what do you think you're doing running off with my son at this hour?" The voice was a shriek.

"You need to call the police. Tell them to come to the beach!" Luce didn't want to waste any more time explaining, and she slapped the door closed right in Gum's wild face and charged back the way she'd come. At least now she could be fairly sure that Gum wouldn't follow her, and that was something. She slid down the eroded slope on her back, not even noticing when the snarled roots tore her sleeve, and hit the beach so hard there was a sharp tweak in her ankle. The uneven ground made the pain worse, but still Luce pushed herself to run faster. From here the tall rocks at the end reminded her of a house where no one had lived for years. Gray water tumbled between its walls.

The rising waves had already narrowed the beach by at least five yards.

"I have to *save* her," Luce heard herself whisper between her panting breaths. "I have to make sure she gets home." She knew the urgency that possessed her was irrational; nothing would bring back the dead. Still, the idea that the girl's parents might never hold her again while her soft small limbs were gnawed by crabs seemed impossibly cruel. She couldn't accept it, even though she could tell that water must already cover the place where they'd found the body. Luce darted around the first outcropping of rock and straight into a miniature whirlpool. It spun as high as her knees, tugging on her, before it fell back again. She was left standing on pale froth and crushed shells.

At least all the rocks here broke the full force of the waves. And she might be able to catch on to one if a wave grabbed her. As a fresh influx of icy, biting water rushed up her legs, she forced herself to calm down and try to remember the route Gum had taken. The stone walls around her were blank and gray, but she was sure she remembered that golden tuft of grass arching out of the one to her right.

She made her way between the rocks always sloping downward. Now that she was moving more slowly she had time to become aware of her fear. Each wave that lashed in twirled as high as her thighs before spilling out and sloshing ankle-deep. Luce had to hold the rocks each time to keep her legs from being jerked out from under her. They were already going numb.

It was right around the next bend, Luce told herself. *Only a little farther.* She just had to concentrate on being brave. There was a sudden dip in the beach as she turned, and a huge swell lunged at her. There was a paler blob racing along inside it. Luce staggered as the pale shape hurled straight into her chest with a rubbery thud, and for an instant that unseeing childish face hovered just below hers. A few traces of milky hair pranced in the water. Luce just had time to scream in horror at the realization that the waves had thrown the corpse against her before the outrushing water lifted her up. Her mouth flooded with salt.

Her flailing left hand caught something soft and cold, and then her leg banged a pinnacle of rock. Somehow she managed to hook her knee around it and groped in the same direction with her right arm, clinging fiercely as the water drained away. She was gasping and trembling so violently she wasn't sure how she could keep her grip, but she had been lucky. She was halfway up a crag of rock with angled sides and, she saw, a decent number of wide handholds. She could climb up without too much trouble. The only problem was the body dragging from her left hand. She had it by the ankle; its pale skin was too soft, like slime-filmed silk, but even so, her fingers were digging into it. Luce tried not to look at it as she inched her way farther up the crag, using her knees to grip and her free hand to pull herself, the baby's limp form flopping against her leg like some revolting and terribly heavy doll. She tugged the body higher, so that it was resting on a small ledge. In the distance someone was screaming.

Luce was afraid of slipping if she turned too much, but by craning her head she managed to catch a sideways glimpse of a few figures, one of them wearing something long and golden, standing above her on the cliffs. Mrs. Cooper was up there yelling at her, Luce realized with relief, next to Gum and some other adult she didn't recognize. Awful as Mrs. Cooper was, even she would have probably called the police by now. All Luce had to do was hold on. She began shivering as the wind wrapped around her soaking clothes. The waves kept reaching up her legs, coaxing her to surrender to them again.

She felt the sharp edges of the rock digging at her thighs and face, felt her own heaving lungs and the sickening thing clutched in her hand. At one point a wave came in and knocked the small body off its perch, and Luce barely managed to keep her grip on it.

She made the mistake, then, of looking down at the lifeless thing she could have died to save. The dead girl's face was a blind rush of white inside the gray-green water, and between her parted lips there was the hollow, haunted darkness of a soundless moan.

Still, she'd succeeded. The girl would get back to her family, and Luce told herself that was all that mattered.

* * *

"I don't even know how to start with how foolish that was," the policeman told Luce. His face was only slightly less gray than his hair, and he curled his hands on his rounded gut. She was sitting on a plastic chair in the corner of a cramped office, an old down comforter bundled around her. A foam cup of instant cocoa warmed her fingers. "I don't imagine anybody would've been too pleased about swapping a live girl for a cold one. The common-sense thing to do would've been to call us and sit tight till we got there." No one would have cared at all if she'd vanished, Luce thought, but she didn't say it. The man talking to her had been lowered down the cliffs in a rope harness, lifting the girl's body and then Luce back to safety, but it was really Gum who had saved her. He'd screamed and pulled on his mother until she'd followed him back to the cliffs, but it was purely chance that Luce's crag had been visible from the particular spot where they'd been standing. That was when Mrs. Cooper had finally called the police on her cell phone.

"You *couldn't* have got there in time," Luce murmured, almost too softly for him to hear. They'd already contacted the school to excuse her for the day and then insisted, over Luce's objections, on trying to reach her uncle at work. Peter had called in sick, but he didn't pick up at the house either. Luce was hoping he'd unplugged the phone so he could sleep off the booze undisturbed. She couldn't let herself even imagine what he'd do to her once he heard about this, but maybe she'd find some way to keep it a secret. "Did they find out who she *is* yet? Did they find her parents?" She'd asked that so many times already that the policeman raised his eyebrows.

"And why is that such a big thing to you?" Luce couldn't answer that, even to herself. That cold little face had just looked so heartbroken. "What they were telling me when I went for your cocoa was that no little girls even close to that age been reported missing anywhere near here. Not since last year. So my next thought was it had to be she fell off one of the cruise ships, though you'd think we'd have heard something, but that didn't check out either. Can't tell you any more than that."

Luce swayed a little. She'd done something crazy to bring that girl back to the people who loved her, but maybe there wasn't anyone like that. Maybe the girl was one of the ones no one wanted, just the way she was.

Maybe the right thing to do would have been to leave her in the sea.

The policeman had the phone in his hand again. "Wish your damned uncle would answer sometime." He was shaking his head.

"You could let me walk home by myself," Luce told him. "My clothes are mostly dry, even." It was almost true. Her silvery jacket was draped over the radiator, and tufts of matted down had started leaking from the rip in its sleeve. "I am fourteen."

He stared at her. "You come across younger than that. But I guess you're on the tall side, even for a fourteen-year-old." He considered her for a minute. "All right. But I'm driving you home. Just give me a sec, here." They headed out into the station's main room, with its wheezing coffee machine and gray benches, while the policeman found his coat.

"What do you mean, there was no water in her lungs!" Someone was yelling at Luce's back, and she jumped around. "Baby washes up on the beach, no injuries anywhere, dead an hour or two at *most*. She *must* have drowned. Only explanation there is. There's got to be water in her lungs!" It was the other, younger policeman shouting into his phone. "Would just one little thing about this *please* make some kind of sense?"

The gray-faced man glanced at him nervously and caught Luce's elbow, tugging her out onto the street. Once they pulled up at her uncle's house, Luce ran to the door and turned to wave back at the gray man. He didn't leave, though. He was watching to make sure she went inside.

Luce slipped through the door as quietly as she could and waited just inside the kitchen until she heard the car pulling away. Maybe Peter wasn't even home, but Luce didn't feel like chancing it. He'd wake up with a blasting hangover, and then the last thing she wanted to do was explain why she wasn't in school. The kitchen was warm and dirty, and there was a bottle out on the table that hadn't been there when Luce had left.

After a moment she skimmed silently out the door. Her clothes were still dank and stiff with salt, but it seemed too risky to change them. She'd walk around until after school let out and then try to sneak back to her room unheard.

* * *

Luce followed the path along the cliffs, looking down at the crashing sea; she kept imagining tiny pale faces gazing up at her from the waves, sadness so deep you could drown in it yawning in their wide gray eyes. She sat watching the swirling patterns of foam around the rocks for a few hours, picturing drifting faces and sometimes scanning the horizon for whales, until she felt cold and sore enough that it drove her to walk on.

After a while the open sea bent back and there was the harbor below her instead, its sandbars crowded with lounging sea lions. She reached the town's biggest street, lined with small wooden houses whose overhanging upper stories were supported on posts. There were a few stores here that sold odd foods like sugar-cured salmon and smoked elk meat alongside the canned beans and chips. Everything was made of the same wooden boards, everything was painted dark brown or tan, and the hills were crossed by the same flimsy stairs as the slopes behind her own house. The whole town seemed to be trying to crawl away from the sea. In one spot there was a two-room shack that hadn't managed to escape in time: the shore had eroded beneath it, and now it stood at an awkward slant, abandoned to the gray waves that pawed again and again through its single glassless window.

"If you think you can get away with crawling out of school, I'll teach you to think different!" The voice was bellowing but slurred, and it made Luce stumble a little from shock as it broke through her daydream. She'd come to the stretch with the town's two bars and one ramshackle church, all lined up against the hard ascent of the mountains behind. Her uncle Peter had just slumped out of the Dark Water Inn, and his breath smelled of sour drink and decay as he glared wearily down at her. "If you're too damned lazy for school, we'll see how lazy you can be gutting fish all day! Up to your elbows in the slime of their innards. And you'll see how easy it is for the knife to slip, too."

"They let us out early," Luce said, shrinking back a little. As long as the policeman didn't keep calling him, she could probably get away with the lie. Her uncle would never get around to checking up on her himself.

"Maybe that's all right, then." He looked at her skeptically. "I heard something awfully strange, though. Heard *you* were the one went and found that dead baby on the beach? At dawn today?" Luce was appalled; of course, she thought, of course she should have realized that the news would get back to him. "What kind of business you think you have, sneaking out of the house like that? You think people don't talk when they hear that? Saying I don't keep enough of an eye on you."

"I couldn't sleep," Luce whispered. She could tell by the way her uncle glared at her that this wasn't good enough. "I just went for a little walk?"

"Not trustworthy enough to be left alone," he muttered. "You go getting into trouble all the time, and I have to hear about it from who-knows-who running their damned mouths." Of course he didn't even mention the fact that she could have drowned, Luce thought. Peter had his hand on the back of her neck, and he steered her into the bar. "You're going to sit right down and not cause any more disturbance until I'm ready to go home."

"I can go home by myself! I promise. I'll just go home and do homework."

"You'll do your homework right here," Peter snapped; he apparently hadn't noticed that she didn't have her book bag with her. Luce realized that she couldn't argue with him, not while he was in such a foul mood. He shoved her down at an out-of-the-way table back in the corner next to the broken juke-box. Someone had left a tattered romance novel on a chair, and Luce picked it up just to look like she was doing something. Maybe Peter would get so drunk that he'd forget all about her, and she could slip away. The bartender watched her curiously.

"Didn't know you had one of those, Peter," he observed while Luce's uncle swayed across the dim space toward the bar. Peter slung his heavy thighs up onto his stool and knocked back the trace of whiskey that was left at the bottom of his glass. Daylight floated in through the dusty windows, but most of the bar was already just as dark as it would be late at night.

"Not mine. She's not mine. Just the pain in the ass my no-good brother left me. Leave it to Andrew to keep causing problems even *after* he's dead." The bartender didn't laugh at this the way he was supposed to; his mouth pinched and he shot her uncle Peter a critical look. "She's not mine, that is," her uncle snarled defensively. "But she *should* have been."

Luce hunched down as far as she could, hearing that. The tightness came back in her stomach, because things always went badly when her uncle started talking this way. He'd definitely beat her once they were alone.

"How should it be," the bartender asked, "that the girl *should* belong to anybody? Excepting to the ones who made her?" He had his back to Luce now, fetching out the whiskey to pour her uncle a new shot. He thought of something. "Where's her mother?"

"You remember Alyssa Gray?" her uncle asked. The bartender looked at him sharply.

"Who doesn't remember her? Sweet, bright, funny girl like that. Could make anybody laugh like crazy. And so beautiful, too." The bartender glanced at Luce again, but she kept her head down over her book, even though she couldn't read it very well in the dimness. It was something about the bronze hair and oddly violet eyes of the heroine. The dead girl's eyelids had had a pearly iridescence to them, Luce remembered, almost a shimmer. "You don't mean *that's* Alyssa's daughter?"

"And Alyssa, you seem not to recall, was *my* girl. Talking about marrying me, even, before Andrew dragged her off from here. He just fooled her with all his crazy talk. And he made her a sidekick to his messed-up life of rip-offs and split towns. It was like some kind of obstacle course for them, what with all the places they couldn't go back to." The bartender didn't seem particularly interested in what Peter was telling him now, though. Luce didn't let herself look, but she knew he was still gazing her way.

"I guess that girl *does* look a lot like her mother. Almost as pretty. You just don't see it too easy because the personality's so different. Alyssa would have had everybody cracking up by now." Luce wished they would talk about something else. There was no chance her uncle would stop looking over at her as long as he kept thinking about her mother. "Andrew—he was one of the guys lost with the High and Mighty, wasn't he?"

"Andrew's whole damn life was a shipwreck. The High and Mighty was just the finishing touch for him." Her uncle's voice sounded different now: smeary and vicious, yes, but also choked. "Everybody who got near him went down with his own personal disaster. Killed Alyssa, just by not getting her to the hospital in time. And now you can see what's left of him." Luce knew, without looking, that her uncle was nodding in her direction. "Flotsam spinning around on the waves."

"And you don't think, if Alyssa was alive," the bartender challenged, "she'd appreciate you speaking more kindly of her child?" Peter didn't answer that. He'd turned to gaze off at a spot on the floor, and Luce thought he might be about to start sobbing. The silence felt thick and somehow sticky. After ten minutes of quiet she tried to slip out of her chair, but her uncle's gaze pivoted to fix on her at once.

The afternoon wouldn't end, and Luce couldn't leave. Every time she tried moving even slightly her uncle swung his bleary face and glowered at her. He kept drinking, and every time he looked her way his face seemed bigger and messier, less like a human face and more like a pile of wet garbage, or a plastic bag wobbling around on the sea. She let her head drop on the table and closed her eyes.

She was lying propped on her elbows on a cheap motel bed. They'd stopped on the outskirts of Minneapolis, and the window was white with falling snow. She was half daydreaming and half watching a dance contest on TV while her father paced around the room talking on his cell phone. Sometimes he'd wander back toward the bathroom, like there was something he didn't want Luce to overhear. On the TV a woman in black sequins kicked her leg high and arched her back until her long hair brushed the floor. Luce's own dark hair had just been cropped, short and spiky: what her father called a pixie cut. "It suits your otherworldly beauty," he'd told her, which made it hard for Luce to argue with him. "And besides, this way we won't have to keep messing with trying to get the tangles out."

Now she knew he was talking to his brother, Peter, far away in Alaska. It was one of the few states Luce had never been to, and she'd never met Peter, but she knew talking to him usually put her father into a glum mood. "No, you do have a point there, Peter," Luce heard her father say. "You absolutely do." There was silence for a while. "You think I ever stop thinking about that! Look, I'm well aware—that I could have done better by her mother. I'm well aware. We were a *hundred* miles from the nearest town when the van broke down. You think I should have tried to operate on her myself?"

Luce barely remembered her mother, but it hurt her to hear the ache in her father's voice. She rolled onto her side and watched the dancing snow, how the white swirls almost canceled out the world behind. She could just make out the cloudy shape of the motel's big blue sign.

"No, I am not determined to live my whole life repeating the same mistakes!" There was another silence. "School's a waste for some kids," he snapped. "You should see how fine a job Luce is doing educating her own self. The books that girl reads!" Her father was pacing faster, smacking the mustard-colored walls with his free hand. "Peter, you've made your point. You've already made it. You can stop now, all right? Yeah, and thank you for your offer. It's appreciated."

Luce was relieved to hear the phone snapping shut, but when she looked over at her father she could see how he was still struggling to calm himself. His head hung, and he clutched at the wall. As Luce watched he sighed, carefully straightened himself, and forced his mouth into a big smile. Only when the smile was in place did he turn to look at her. "Baby doll?" he said to her. He was trying hard to sound cheerful, but Luce could hear the crack in his voice. "You ever think it might be time for you and me to try settling down somewhere?"

Luce shook her head. "I like traveling with you." Her father sat down next to her and ruffled her spiky hair.

"Oh, I like it too, doll. And you're a real trooper. But I can't help thinking sometimes that maybe it's not the best life for you." He couldn't keep the smile together anymore, and his voice was so mournful that Luce sat up and threw her arms around him. "Peter's saying he can find me work on the boats this spring. Pays good. And we can live at his place until we save enough to get our own. You know you've never even seen my hometown." He gave Luce a sad smile. "We'll get you going to school as a regular thing. And you should maybe have more of a normal social life than just hanging around with your old dad all the time."

"You hate Peter!" Luce objected. "And he's always so horrible to you."

"I do *not* hate him! He's my brother. That kind of bond goes deeper than, you know, whatever trouble we've had. Just more like there's a personality conflict." He looked at the snow. "He's doing his best to help us, Lucette. It's generous of him. More than I've got any right to expect, after everything." He tried to smile again, but it came out slanted and strange. "Not that any man in his correct mind *wouldn't* have tried to steal your mother. But you know that's not sufficient excuse for how I acted. Not enough to repair Peter's feelings, anyway."

"It's none of Peter's business!" Luce was starting to get angry; she didn't like hearing her father blame himself that way. "Mom *loved* you."

"She did," her father agreed. "She did do that. Gave me more and truer love than any human being can hope for in this life." He was looking away, and Luce knew he didn't want her to see the tears in his eyes. "But the truth is that it would have been a whole lot better for her if she hadn't." He was so upset that Luce didn't try to talk him out of his plan to move back to Pittley, Alaska, where he'd grown up. If she had only argued with him then, screamed, threatened to kill herself, then maybe he never would have gone out on the *High and Mighty* at all . . .

He's dead, Luce thought. She couldn't have said why she was suddenly so sure of this; she only knew that it was inescapably true. *Drowned. He won't ever come back.* And then she felt the sticky wooden table under her hands. There was a sudden crash. She looked over to see Peter splayed on the floor with a barstool tipped across his stomach, his arms swinging heavily as he tried, and failed, to right himself.

The bartender rushed around the counter and helped Peter up to a sitting position. His face was blotchy and swollen on one side. "You okay there?" the bartender asked.

Maybe Peter was trying to answer him in words, but it came out more like a growl. He managed to drag himself onto his feet, but Luce wasn't sure how long he'd be able to stay upright. He was clinging to the edge of the bar for balance.

"I'll get you a cup of black coffee," the bartender said after a minute. "Shouldn't have let you drink so much. Coffee, and then you better get your niece on home. It's a school night." He looked at Luce, and she got up and walked over. "Can you get home okay?"

"It's almost two miles," Luce told him. "And that's if we take the shortcut. Along the cliffs." The bartender tipped his head sideways.

"Maybe you should wait till I can get somebody to drive you, then. Don't want Peter too close to any cliffs, his condition being like this." It was the wrong thing to say. Peter pulled himself straighter and raised his eyebrows in a way that was probably supposed to seem dignified.

"I'm not in need of any coffee," her uncle said with an exaggerated effort to enunciate clearly. It didn't quite work. "And I'm perfectly capable of escorting my niece back home. The way you talk to her, it seems like you don't recall who's the adult in this family."

"I didn't mean anything like that, Peter," the bartender soothed. He gave Luce a funny look, as if she were a fellow conspirator. "Just two miles is pretty far to be walking in the cold, and once my son's off work he'll be happy to give you a ride. Sit down and have a coffee while you wait for him." The bartender checked his watch. "It's twenty past eight now, and he's off most nights by eight thirty." Luce was amazed that it wasn't at least midnight. The day had already dragged on for such a horribly long time. An image of the dead girl's milky greenish face flashed in her mind again.

Peter shook his head. "Get your things, Luce." She stared down; there was nothing to get. The bar was cold enough that she hadn't even taken off her jacket. "When—we—get—home," her uncle said laboriously, "I'll check to see you've done all your homework properly, and if you have you can watch half an hour of TV before bed." Of course Luce knew he was only saying that to impress the bartender. Her uncle had never checked her homework once, and Luce didn't think he was about to start now. He locked one thick hand on the back of her neck and shoved her out through the bar's dirty glass door. He didn't even say good night to the bartender. Luce peered back to see the bartender watching them from the door. His forehead was wrinkled with worry, but when he saw Luce looking he smiled at her and waved. Luce didn't dare to wave back, though. It would only make her uncle angrier, and she was already afraid of what he might do once they reached the house.

The sky above was vast and dark, but the clouds had thinned enough that a yellowish blot showed where the moon must be. Her uncle steered them toward the cliff path while the cold wind buffeted their faces. Neither of them spoke, and the only sounds were the wind in their ears and Luce's fast soft steps alongside her uncle's, which came slower and heavier, grinding the pebbles like teeth. He didn't let go of Luce's neck, and she didn't look at him. Below them a few beacon lights bobbed on the midnight blue harbor.

After a while her uncle wasn't walking beside her anymore, but behind her. He still had his left hand in a hard grip on her neck, and now his right hand curled around her shoulder and stroked her awkwardly. Luce didn't know what to think. Her uncle never touched her except to slap her. She wanted to pull away, but she couldn't take the risk of enraging him.

The path turned and led upward, and the harbor was behind them. Now the cloud-dulled moonlight cast its faint haze on crashing waves some eighty yards below.

They were still walking, but much more slowly. The dream-like darkness filled Luce's eyes, and then she felt her uncle's hands slide down to grab her hips. He pulled her back so she was pressing on his body and rolled himself against her.

She tried to cry out, then. She tried to beg him to stop. Her voice was stuck deep inside her, and the night filled her mouth like a choking gas and she couldn't make a sound, not even when she heard the zipper of her jeans sliding down and felt his thick fingers groping hungrily under the fabric. Her legs shuddered the way glass does in the moment just before it breaks.

He pushed her down on the grass and she started to crawl away, but his hands were on her, pulling her back, digging inside her clothes. She could taste the long grass, feel the jagged stones slicing at her palms. His breath was loud and fast, and Luce gathered all her strength; she was going to at least try to fight, even though he was so much bigger than her. She would rake his eyes out, hurt him as much as she possibly could. Suddenly she didn't care how angry she made him. She didn't even care if he threw her off the cliff. What reason could there be for her to stay alive when everyone who'd ever cared about her was dead, lost forever, and she was so utterly alone? With a desperate wrench of her torso she managed to flip herself over and he grappled with her, throwing one heavy knee onto her stomach. One leaden hand cracked across her face so hard that her head crunched into the stones, and she heard something pop in her neck. Pain swelled in so many parts of her body that she couldn't keep track of it all: a dark confusion of aches.

The clouds tore back from the moon, and golden light spilled across Luce's face. Her uncle Peter had his back to the moon so that all she could see was the black silhouette of his head and shoulders looming over her. His knee was still crushing into her gut, pinning her down, but after a second she realized that he had stopped yanking at her jeans. Luce's heart was racing and her breath sounded like tearing paper. They stayed like that for so long that Luce thought it couldn't be real, that she must have fallen into some other world.

"Alyssa?" her uncle finally whimpered. He sounded babyish, weak. "Alyssa, I didn't *mean* it." He staggered up onto his feet and stood there for a minute staring down at Luce sprawled on the grass, his giant's body wavering as if he wasn't sure what to do.

"I'm not *her*," Luce rasped. She barely registered her own voice, but her uncle obviously heard her; something shifted in the way he held himself. "I'm still—I'm just a kid." She could almost feel the dream ripping away from him, leaving something dull and resentful behind.

"You don't need to be coming back to the house, then. Do you?" His voice squeezed out in a hostile croak. "Unless . . ."

Then he turned away from her and ran, veering crazily up the path.

As soon as he was gone Luce's voice came back in force. She shrieked and wailed, ripping up clumps of grass. No one heard her, no one came to help. She screamed until her throat was raw, and then the tears poured out. But they couldn't wash anything away.

3

Changing

For a long time Luce sprawled there sobbing, feeling the long sharp grass cutting at her cheeks, the icy wind pounding against her trembling back. She could still feel the sore places under her clothes where Peter's fingers had dug into her like hooks piercing a struggling fish. She didn't want to understand what had just happened to her. As long as she didn't let herself understand all the implications of it, maybe she wouldn't have to completely feel them either. But what she couldn't help understanding was that her uncle, the only family she had left, had tried to rape her and then had run off and left her there all alone in this desolate spot high on the cliffs. He'd run away home, but he didn't care that she had nowhere left to run to. The icy night rattled its long grass in her ears until it sounded like the air was full of bones. The cold sank into her body in a way it never had before, not even in the deepest snow. The cold took over her skin, her muscles, her brain, and then at last, with a tiny sigh like something breaking, it took over her heart.

It frightened her to feel the cold bite right through her cen-ter that way, but once it was over, and her heart had truly become as chilled and bitter as the night all around her, she knew it was easier that way. The freezing wind didn't bother her anymore, and a peculiar looseness and freedom began to spread through all her limbs. She started to feel like a wild, shapeless thing: a stray piece of starlight curled up on the grass like a glowing snake or a puddle of rainwater with human eyes. She was liquid, unbound by skin. Suddenly it all seemed funny to her. Maybe she was going to die, maybe this feeling was death, but that didn't mat-ter so much. Why hadn't she understood before? She didn't have to be the strange girl no one wanted, trying to disappear into the corners of her schoolrooms, trying to keep from getting hit by her uncle at home. No one would miss her. She could be a free thing, and spill into places where nobody would ever find her again.

Just for a second Luce knew she did still have a choice. She could go back. Gum would miss her; he was almost as alone as she was. If she only *chose* it, she could pull her body back to-gether, make it into arms and legs again, and go running home to huddle in her tiny bedroom with her heart pounding. Her uncle wouldn't actually lock her out of the house, although he proba-bly wouldn't speak to her either. He was expecting her to come home, in fact, sooner or later. She could still be a regular girl. In a sudden flash she realized that he might even be just the small-est bit sorry.

She could be a girl, but then she'd spend the whole night, and the next night, and the next, sick with dread. Soon enough the time would come when greed or bitterness would overwhelm Peter's shame again. He'd practically told her so. Every night she'd wrap herself in her blankets and wait shuddering for the moment when her door would creak open and his rough hands would crawl all over her, crushing her face against the pillow.

No, Luce said. She didn't have a voice anymore to say it with, but she knew the night heard her anyway. NO! And with that cry she poured herself out on the darkness. She had a sensation of falling very rapidly, and for just a second she realized that she must have somehow slipped over the edge of the cliff. It was hundreds of feet, here, down to the knife-sharp rocks and then the sea. Nobody could survive a fall like that. It just wasn't possible.

So then it only made sense that the absolute violet blackness all around her *must* be death. It was cold and silky, and it went nowhere, and it lasted for a very long time.

* * *

After a while, though, she began to realize that the perfect darkness was moving. It was moving faster than she ever could have imagined possible, swirling past her at amazing speed. If it could rush past her that way, did that mean that she was somehow still alive? Whatever the movement was, she could feel that it was strong and rippling. The darkness wasn't quite so solid anymore either. Once or twice she saw specks of living light like twisting scarlet threads. The lights pirouetted closer and then, with a blink, they were far behind her. *Behind* her,

Luce suddenly thought, and she was so astonished that she almost stopped. Then it wasn't actually the darkness that was moving so quickly. *She* was the one who was moving through the darkness! She gave a kind of squirm, and found that she could control the direction of the movement. She could curve in long, dizzy swoops, shoot up, and even let herself roll over and over. Mostly, though, she kept moving forward. Nothing felt as good as knowing that she could send the darkness streaking out and away at her back, traveling faster than any car she'd ever been in.

One of the red lights swam close to her and opened its hollow mouth as if it wanted to blow her a kiss. Then it was gone. Just a shining little worm.

It wasn't so dark here, really, or anyway the darkness didn't stop her from seeing things in the way it used to. It was a living, leaping darkness, full of shapes that were just as free as she was. Luce knew at that moment that she'd never experienced anything nearly as beautiful as this power and this gracefulness. All of it was hers, a marvelous gift. And at this moment of deepest joy, Luce began to hear the sound.

The closest word for it was music, but it was better than any music. Every molecule shook with soft, sweet excitement. Every note washed around her and covered her in a bath of dancing silk. She thought that the beauty of it must be more than she could bear, but somehow she went racing on and on inside the sound.

People were looking at her, pointing. It was the strangest thing she'd ever seen. They were up above her somehow, waving their arms, but then the sound rose and spun around them, too. Of course so much beauty made them stop their ugly hub-bub right away, which was what Luce wanted. She didn't like being pointed at. It was terribly rude. Instead they stared at her, and then, Luce could feel, the music began to take the shape of their secret hearts. It knew them, it forgave them for every bad thing they'd ever done, and they loved it more than they had ever loved anything in their lives.

Up above, the moon was golden and wide-eyed, and it watched Luce tenderly. Its light gleamed like floating coins all over the tops of the waves, and a slab of shining ice bobbed past. A misty glow covered the smooth side of the cliffs just behind her, and then Luce realized that all those dreaming people were on a ship, and that the ship was coming toward her, and toward the cliffs, as fast as a train driving out of a tunnel. Still the music throbbed on, coating the night with its bliss, while the ship's sharp metal prow sped straight at her forehead.

Luce dove just in time, pushing her way through the deep black water, and still the music that was somehow more than music shook around her, in her chest, in her throat. The only thing that almost drowned it out was the terrible metal shriek when the boat's steel hull sheared in two as it slammed into the rocks. The strange thing was that no one on board screamed. Actually it wasn't so strange, because Luce understood exactly why all those people stayed so calm and quiet. They were still listening to the music, listening so hard that they didn't even care if they drowned.

Luce thought she should be upset, but she found that she didn't quite care either. The deep invasive chill was still in her heart, and it gave her the funny feeling that these were the same people who beat their daughters or left them alone to die on the tops of cliffs. She didn't want to think too much about it, but she almost thought the people on that boat must deserve what was happening to them now. She was still far below the waves, and for some reason she didn't feel any need to try to reach the air.

Huge slabs of ripped and twisted metal began to fall past her into the water. Luce saw things she recognized—hunks of pipes, deck chairs—as well as heavy machine-type things whose uses she didn't know. Then she began to see the people. At first there were just one or two of them off in the distance, but soon the water was full of drifting, sinking bodies. They looked like enormous raindrops plummeting all around her, their arms slowly wheeling through tangles of seaweed. Some of them still seemed completely calm, and sank with drowsy smiles. One man Luce saw seemed actually to be trying to swim for the bottom of the sea. But others had been shocked out of their enchantment by the cold of the water, and they were flailing frantically, trying to fight their way back to the surface. Even though she thought that they must be bad people, even very bad, she still hated to see them so upset and scared.

She looked up. In the moonlight the surface of the water high above her looked like twisting golden foil, and against that gold there were dark frantic shapes splashing crazily away. Some of the people on the boat must have snapped out of their dreaming enough to try to swim for shore. The wonderful music began to fade, and around her more of the sinking people began to panic. An old man's face sank inches away from her own, and she looked deep into his shocked, staring eyes and saw his mouth contort as he choked on seawater. He was struggling horribly to breathe, but water rushed into his lungs instead of air.

How long had it been since she'd taken a breath?

The music came back, but it was different now. It came from a few different directions at once this time, and though the music didn't sound like any normal *voice* Luce had ever heard in her life, she couldn't help thinking the shimmering sound was made of several different voices. Quick curving shapes, as lovely in their movements as living water, began to dart among the swimmers, and Luce suddenly understood that they were *singing*. They were all singing together in voices too beautiful for Earth, and the music began to swell again in her own chest. Above, she could see the desperate swimmers suddenly calming down, settling into the cold waves as if they were going to sleep in their own soft beds at home.

She must have gone deeper without realizing it, because she found herself face to face with the drowning old man again. He wasn't afraid anymore. Waves of satiny, vibrating music poured from Luce's mouth, and the old man was comforted. He gazed at her with his round blue eyes as if she were someone he had always wanted to see, his heart's only treasure, long lost but suddenly returned to him. Even her own father, Luce realized, had never once looked at her with such profound tenderness, such acceptance. Luce knew the old man must be dying, but he was so *happy*. Happy just to be with her, and to listen to her singing. He understood her so well, and the better he understood her, the more complete his love for her became. He was still smiling at her as the silver bubbles gushed up from his mouth and his eyelids sank over his blue eyes. Luce stayed with him, though, even as they drifted deeper and deeper into the smooth dark-ness. No one had ever looked at her that way before, and she wanted more than anything to see that gaze again. Down and down she went, watching the man's quiet face, his wrinkles, and the faint gleam of his white hair.

Too far down. All at once she wasn't sure if she could find her way back to the surface. The water began to constrict her chest and head, hundreds of tons of dark weight squeezing from above. It was too far down because she *did* need to breathe. She knew that now. Her lungs were crying for air, but the air now seemed so impossibly far away, and she was still sinking deeper.

A violent sinuous shape ripped past her, catching her waist in a thin, strong arm as it went. She was moving again, faster than ever before, but now that was because the shape beside her was pulling her along. It was definitely a human arm holding her, but the shape didn't seem to be a person, at least not in the usual way, though it did have a head that looked like it might belong on a girl. Luce couldn't make out the face, though. It was hidden in a storm of fire-colored hair that seemed to have its own light. She tried to tell the shape that she needed air, but the words wouldn't come to her. Parting water ripped around her face as if she were rupturing endless layers of silk curtains.

They were rushing so fast that shapes began to blur in Luce's eyes, and the cry in her lungs became a long, aching scream. The darkness turned narrow and hard, with long stony sides. Where *was* she? She could feel the rising urge to thrash and fight, to claw at the shape holding her and the brutal rocks closing her in. Luce opened her mouth to shout, and at that moment the water broke around her head, and the sweet air flooded into her chest.

Luce heaved hungry lungfuls of air, lying in the cold water with her face on the rocks. She was in a cave with a tall, arching roof and brittle ruffs of crystal sparkling on the walls. Stalactites dripped from above and the rocks gave out a very faint green glow. It was almost totally dark, she knew, but she could still see. Her hearing seemed strangely sharp and vivid, too. She raised herself on her elbows and looked around.

Lying next to her was the most beautiful girl Luce had ever seen. She was about sixteen years old, and gleaming lights stroked like fire along her wet red-gold hair. She was staring straight at Luce, and she was furious.

"Maybe you're some kind of queen back where you came from," the girl snarled at Luce. She was so angry she was trembling, and she spoke with an accent Luce didn't recognize. "But this is *my* territory, and as long as you're here you'll follow *my* rules!"

Luce was too confused to answer, and after glaring at her for a moment the girl continued talking. "So many of us die because of things no one can help! They get tangled in fishing nets and drown, or the orcas . . . I'm fighting all the time to try and keep everyone safe. And one thing I *don't* have time to deal with is one of us almost dying just out of pure stupidity! What were you thinking, going so deep like that?" Around them other heads were breaking through the water. All of them were girls, some very young and some about Luce's age. The red-haired girl seemed to be the oldest one there. She gazed harshly at Luce's blank expression, then thought of something. "Don't you speak English?"

"I do," Luce said. "I just—I don't understand what I did wrong." She also didn't understand where she was now, or even how she was still alive, but she decided it would be better to ask about those things another time. The red-haired girl was tense with rage, almost baring her teeth, and Luce was afraid to make her any angrier.

"You don't understand what you did wrong! Swimming that deep as if you couldn't drown! I could have easily drowned saving you . . . I should have just left you to die there! And bringing down a ship that big by yourself! Have you considered how lucky you are that we were close enough to hear you and rush over to help? You could have broken the timahk!" Luce couldn't believe what she was hearing. It sounded like the red-haired girl thought that she, Luce, had somehow made that ship drive into the cliffs. It was an insane idea, impossible. Even if Luce had *wanted* to do something so evil, she was just a shy, skinny girl barely strong enough to sink a canoe.

And did the beautiful girl think Luce had murdered all those people? The idea horrified her, and she stared around the cave, hoping someone would tell the redhead how ridiculous it was to imagine something like that. The faces of about twenty girls looked back at her from the dimness. All of them were silent, wondering. And, Luce realized, all of them were so beautiful it almost hurt to look at them for long. They had a dark, shimmering quality and a slight greenish tone to their pearly skin.

"I didn't do *anything* to that ship," Luce finally protested in bewilderment. "It just—it came right at me. I barely managed to get out of the way." As she said it, Luce realized how wrong it all sounded. How *had* she managed to get out of the way of the ship as it rushed at her head? Nobody could dive that fast or that deep. But as she thought it over, Luce realized that was just what she'd done: she'd dove at unbelievable speed straight down into the sea, and the ship had slashed safely above her. The water must be freezing, too. It must be cold enough to kill anyone who tried to swim in it for more than a few minutes.

For that matter, what were all these girls doing in the ocean? None of them seemed to want to pull themselves out of the water either. And, she realized, none of them were wearing any clothes. The water lapped around Luce's naked back, and the cold didn't bother her nearly as much as she would have expected.

Somewhere in the cave a girl laughed, in a bright, sweet voice. The redhead glared in that direction and the laughter stopped at once. Then she turned her marvelous face back toward Luce and puckered her lips critically. There was something in her expression Luce couldn't quite make out, though: a shift and slippage of emotions, something alternated with her anger; it might have been anxiety or longing . . . It didn't make any sense and only heightened Luce's suspicions that the red-haired girl was somehow unhinged.

"We follow the timahk here," the redhead said slowly. Her voice had a very hard, bitter music in it, like cracked diamonds. "We won't hurt you, no matter how offensive I find your behavior. But you've already given us enough reason to expel you, if it comes to that. So do you want to leave?" *Leave for where?* Luce thought. She shook her head in sudden anxiety. "In that case we need to get this much straight. *All* the mermaids in my territory obey my rules. No matter *who* they think they are. Do you understand me?"

"All the *mermaids* . . ." Luce repeated. She felt completely baffled. Pale faces stared back at her, and Luce realized they were all just as mystified as she was. No wonder they were so confused. Their leader was an obvious lunatic.

Luce rolled onto her back and strained to lift her legs out of the water. They felt bizarrely heavy all of a sudden and also much too long. With an effort she managed to heave them up out of the sea.

A silvery green tail, halfway between a fish's tail and a serpent's, waved uncertainly in the darkness of the cave. It weighed so much that Luce could barely hold it up, and the cold air made it burn. Luce shrieked and let the tail drop, and salt water spattered across their faces.

The red-haired girl was staring open-mouthed at Luce, and then the laughter came back all around them. Almost all the girls were laughing now, but it didn't sound mean. It sounded like the way people laugh when they suddenly understand something that should have been obvious all along. Luce gaped around in desperation. She could hear a few of the girls repeating another word she didn't know: "metaskaza."

When the redhead spoke again her voice was much gentler, and high-pitched with surprise. "Nobody would have believed, hearing the way you sang . . ." She shook her head and smiled suddenly at Luce, and the smile was so warm that Luce almost felt safe. "You mean, you really didn't know?"

Luce started laughing along with everyone else, but it was too shrill and fast. Hysterical. The redhead let out a kind of soft, lulling hum, and Luce felt her panic receding. She kept humming until Luce calmed down.

"I'm Catarina," the lovely redhead said, still smiling her luminous smile. "I'm queen here. Who are you?"

"Luce," Luce answered, but then that didn't seem like enough of a name when she was so lost. "I mean, I'm Lucette Gray Korchak." She thought of explaining that she lived with her uncle in Pittley, but then she realized how absurd that would sound.

"Not anymore," Catarina said. Now her voice had a hint of that magical singing in it, and Luce started to feel sleep washing through her like waves. "You don't need one of those compli-cated human names anymore. You're just Luce now. And you're one of us."

4

The Timahk

Luce slipped into a velvety sleep, but even as she slept she was somehow aware of the row of girls' heads, all lying like hers on the pebble beach inside the cave. As the tide came in, she let it lift her softly and carry her farther up the beach, and when it went back out her body followed the water. It was effortless. All the girls' bodies traveled with hers in the same way, so that their haunting faces formed a kind of second tide as they slept. Soft echoes washed around them from the waves booming against the rocks outside; she slept in a sonic cradling, a deep bath of rich, whispered sound. Even in her sleep she was surprised by how safe she felt, too. Only now that Catarina was beside her did Luce realize she'd been living for months with a constant undercurrent of fear.

When she finally woke it was just a tiny bit less dark. A few holes in the roof of the cave let down shafts of light that gleamed off the spiny crystals all over the walls. Luce stretched and felt her strange new body twisting out into the water. It was so powerful, so smooth, and the soft lapping of the water thrilled her. It felt like small gliding kisses. Around her in the cave other mermaids were starting to roll and squirm. Some of them even sat up, but Luce noticed that all of them kept their long tails in the water. The tails had different shimmering colors. Next to her she could see that Catarina's tail was a fiery bronze color, almost the same color as her waist-length, rippling, gleaming hair, except that the tail was more golden . . .

Luce sat up and ran her fingers through her own spiky hair. She realized at once that it was all wrong for a mermaid.

"I'm going to let my hair grow long," Luce announced to no one in particular, and Catarina laughed and sat up at her side. Such a wonderful, delicate laugh, even if it was also somehow harsh. Luce hadn't realized Catarina was awake, but hearing her gave Luce a feeling of being wonderfully protected. The night before she'd been too stunned to really absorb everything, but now it hit her: Catarina had actually risked her own life to pull her to safety. Luce turned to see Catarina's warm, sardonic smile.

"Your hair won't grow anymore, Luce. It'll never grow any longer than it is right now." Luce looked at Catarina's moon gray eyes and tried to understand. "That's the bad part. But your hair won't ever fall out either, and it will never turn gray. And your nails won't grow. Not even if you survive for a thousand years . . ."

Luce thought about it. "I don't think I understand." Catarina smiled wryly.

"How old were you yesterday? When you changed?" It was strange, but for a second Luce had trouble remembering. Hadn't there been something special about yesterday? Then it came back to her.

"It was my birthday," Luce explained. "I turned fourteen." Catarina lolled drowsily in the water and splashed her tail a little.

"Then I've got good news for you," Catarina said, a little sarcastically, Luce thought. "It's *always* going to be your birthday. Forever. It will be your fourteenth birthday for the rest of your life. And if you don't do any more of the crazy stuff you tried yesterday"—Catarina smiled—"then the rest of your life could be a very long time. Potentially. Most of us don't make it for that long, though." She watched patiently as Luce absorbed all this new information.

"You're saying we don't get any older? We don't have to be adults?" Luce thought about Mrs. Cooper, her uncle Peter, who wasn't forty yet but already seemed so old. She thought of their miserable, broken-down eyes and sick, dragging bodies, how *pathetic* they all were, how heartless, and how tired they always seemed when they moved . . . Excitement charged through her like an electric current, and her tail gave a huge involuntary flip that sent a wave of salt water splashing over everyone. The other mermaids didn't seem to mind, though. Instead everyone was grinning at her, enjoying her obvious happiness. "Oh, Catarina, that's fantastic! That's the best thing I've ever heard!" Catarina tried to look strict, but then she couldn't help laughing.

"I think so, too," Catarina admitted. "Adult humans are monstrous things. Just disgusting. Foul. And the things they *do* . . ."

Her voice faded, and Luce watched the lovely face turn stone hard and furious. Luce wasn't quite sure which bad human actions Catarina was so angry about, but she wanted to agree with her.

"The things they do to what?" Luce asked, and Catarina looked at her with so much bitterness that her shining gray eyes almost seemed blind.

"*You* ask me that! You ask me! Your revolting uncle kept beating you, but even that wasn't enough to change you into one of us! You didn't change until he actually tried . . ." Catarina was choking with outrage, and Luce was too surprised to talk. She hadn't said a word about what had happened with her uncle; she was positive she hadn't even mentioned him. When Catarina was finally able to speak again the fury was gone, replaced by a dead, flat coldness that was even more frightening than her anger. "I'm talking about the things humans do to their own daughters, Luce. To the little girls who trust them, and who can't escape from them, because they don't have anywhere to go . . ."

"How did you know?" Luce whispered. But even as she said the words, she was already starting to understand. She'd begun to notice something peculiar as she looked around at the other mermaids.

When she looked straight at any of the mermaids all she could see was stunning beauty. Every mermaid was so excruciatingly lovely that her beauty almost seemed like a living thing, like something just a little bit separate from the mermaid herself . . . For the first time it occurred to Luce to wonder if her own face was really that breathtaking now, more striking than any human model's. And every mermaid had a kind of dark shimmering around her, too, like a pulsating glamour.

But whenever Luce observed another mermaid from the corner of her eye, that dark sparkling haze took on shapes. It wouldn't be quite true to say that the darkness formed pictures and that the pictures shifted and told stories. If Luce had been asked to describe what she was seeing in words, that would have been the nearest explanation she could have come up with. But in reality it was more dreamlike, more subtle than that; the darkness *suggested* the story, gathered the story up in itself and revealed it, but in a way that Luce could read as clearly as a book.

Luce tried looking at one of the older mermaids that way: a slightly chubby girl of about fifteen with such pale curly hair that it could almost be mistaken for sea foam sliding over her shoulders, and with pale, exquisite, sea green eyes. As Luce watched she could see how the girl's mother had thrown her from a speeding car, breaking half her bones as she smashed into the asphalt. Even now, there was something just slightly awkward about the way the girl held her rounded, elegant body. It had a barely perceptible twist around the shoulders, as if not all her bones had healed correctly. The girl watched Luce watching her, but she didn't seem bothered by it. "Hello, Luce," the girl said distantly in cool bell tones. "I'm Samantha. You're an amazing singer, especially for somebody new . . ."

Luce looked down, suddenly embarrassed. If she could see Samantha lying shattered by the side of the freeway, then Samantha could see her uncle's crude hands sliding down around Luce's hips.

"You don't need to feel ashamed, Luce," Samantha continued airily. "You didn't do anything wrong. And besides, all of us . . ."

It was true. One girl who seemed no older than seven had been starved almost to death by her foster parents; another had

had a pot of boiling water poured over her head; another had lived with a father much worse than Luce's uncle. Others had simply been abandoned or orphaned or even just unloved, and had turned cold from pure loneliness. And Catarina . . . Luce let the beautiful red-gold head shift into the corner of her vision.

There was a sudden whirl and a smack as something icy, wet, and shining lashed into Luce's face. The blow wasn't hard enough to really hurt, but Luce was still shocked. Catarina had actually *slapped* her, right on the cheek, with her golden tail. Luce cried out and covered her face with both hands.

"I can't believe you hit me!" Luce screamed, even though she knew she might be overreacting. After all, her uncle always hit her much harder than that. But somehow it felt so much worse to be slapped here, and especially by Catarina. Luce had been so sure she could trust her.

Around them the other mermaids gasped and whispered.

"I'm sorry, Luce," Catarina said roughly. "I didn't hurt you much, though, did I?" Luce glared up at her without answering. "I should have explained. You can never look at me that way!" Now Catarina's voice had a wild, piercing sound that made Luce stop scowling. "I don't allow *anyone* to look at me that way! It's just . . . I can't stand for anyone to see . . ."

Suddenly Luce felt horribly sorry for her. It was bewildering to feel pity for anyone so strong, so ferocious, and so lovely, but Luce did. If she'd been sure Catarina wouldn't just get more upset by it, Luce would have hugged her.

"It's okay, Catarina," Luce whispered. "I'm really sorry I tried to look. I promise I won't ever try again to see anything . . . anything you'd rather keep private."

"You don't need to be so nice about it, Luce," Samantha announced in her too-serene voice. "Catarina gets ridiculously sensitive about everything from when she was human. And about some stuff afterward, for that matter. You'll see. But *she* doesn't mind seeing the things that happened to us!" Luce expected Catarina to get angry at this, but instead she just turned her face away from them and rippled her long body, and then disappeared under the water without a splash. A dozen other mermaids flicked themselves and dove after her; they were so fast that it was almost impossible to see them leave.

Samantha shook her head disapprovingly. "Catarina's a tremendous singer," Samantha explained. "Definitely our best. She has every right to be queen here. But she still feels degraded by what happened to her. And no mermaid should *ever* allow herself to feel that way. That's almost like saying we deserved what the humans did to us."

Luce thought she was starting to understand; she felt an ache of tenderness for Catarina as the truth sank in. "That has something to do with why we all changed? Into mermaids?" It felt awkward to say the word out loud, but somehow Luce was sure that she'd hit on the truth. "We changed because of what human beings did to us."

"Yes," Samantha agreed. "That's what we are. They *made* us." Suddenly she gave an awful laugh, sharp and high. "And then the humans wonder why their ships sink! They wonder why so many of them end up drowned! And they never even suspect we're here!" Samantha wasn't calm at all now. She sounded like a vicious baby. "But there wouldn't be any mermaids anywhere in the world if the humans weren't all so evil!"

Luce couldn't help thinking that there must be something wrong with what Samantha was saying, but she wasn't quite sure where the problem was. She felt a little dizzy. There was a soft waving in her head that matched the rhythm of the lapping water. But one thing seemed clear from what the other mermaid was telling her: the ship that had crashed into the cliffs yesterday must not have been the first one ever to sink in the waters near this cave. She gazed around at the dim space with its glowing crystals like half-obliterated stars, listening to its constant resonance as the waves roared outside. Like living in the hollow of a violin, sustained in one endless note . . .

"You mean you sink ships a lot?" Luce asked. Her own voice sounded wrong for a mermaid, broken. The others always seemed so clear and confident, even when they were angry or sad.

"You mean 'we,'" Samantha corrected. She was very cool and stiff now. "You're with us now, Luce. *We* sink ships when we can get away with it, which isn't anywhere near every time we see one. That ship you sang to yesterday—we wouldn't have ever tackled a ship that big if you didn't force us to. There just aren't that many of us, and only a few can *really* sing." Samantha shook her head. "That was impressive work, Luce. I bet Catarina would have been a lot angrier than she was if you weren't so talented."

Luce didn't like being told she was responsible for what had happened to the ship, but she couldn't help feeling flattered. It felt odd and exhilarating to hear the admiration in Samantha's voice. Even so, she didn't think she could let that pass.

"Catarina kept saying that, too—that I sank that ship," Luce objected. "But I didn't do anything. I mean, I heard the singing, and then the ship came straight at me, and it was really just an accident that there was a cliff right there." Luce was trying to remember exactly how everything had happened; it had all been so overwhelming, and her memories seemed to get mixed up. "I didn't even know it was *me* doing the singing. It was just like something I felt, like it came out of nowhere . . ." As she said it Luce wasn't completely sure whether or not she was telling the truth. How could she sing like that and not realize she was doing it?

Samantha looked at her skeptically for a long time, and Luce began to cringe a little. Mermaids flashed away under the water, one by one. Soon they were all alone in the cave.

"Maybe," Samantha finally conceded, but she still seemed doubtful. "Maybe you just started spontaneously singing the perfect song of persuasion, and everyone on that ship went mad for it, and you didn't know what you were doing at all. But that ship definitely went down because of you, Luce. And *we* definitely had to clean up your mess. You still don't realize what a big job that was, do you?"

Luce looked at her in bewilderment. She realized that Catarina had said something about this, too: that it had been stupid to go after such a big ship. She'd said Luce almost broke something, the teemeeka or the teemaya . . .

"What's wrong with it being a big ship?" Luce finally asked. "And what do you mean, 'clean up my mess'?" Samantha just stared at her, first with disgust, then with exasperation. Then finally she burst out laughing.

"I'm forgetting how much you have to learn," Samantha admitted. "You're still metaskaza." Whatever the word meant, Samantha made it sound more than a little insulting. "Let's go find everyone. I bet Catarina's done sulking by now." There was a flick and a flash, and Luce was alone in the cave.

The idea of diving into that dark, surging water frightened her, even though she knew she'd done it just yesterday. But yesterday, after all, she hadn't done it on purpose!

If she let herself hesitate much longer, though, she'd never find Samantha and the others . . . Luce gathered her courage and swung her head around toward the sea. Her tail seemed to move by itself in a single whipping motion, and suddenly Luce found herself slicing through black water.

She had such force, such speed. She'd almost forgotten how magnificent it felt, this rushing power, the clear water parting around her shoulders, the sting of salt on her tongue. She could see a slightly brighter blot in the darkness, and she knew that must be the underwater tunnel Catarina had dragged her through the night before. With a sudden burst of delight Luce let her tail spin out, driving her faster. She hurled through the tunnel so quickly that she almost knocked her head against a bend in the rock.

Then she was in the open sea. It was vast, silvery, and treacherous, full of drifting life. Ice floes drifted and bucked in the distance. She started at a moaning, coughing sound that shivered through the water around her before she realized it was only the barking of seals. Luce was afraid to go any farther alone—what if she couldn't find her way back to the cave? A giant reddish octopus pulsed by, and farther off there was the sinuous dipping of a small group of porpoises. She pushed her way to the surface and looked around at a lonely expanse of peaked water and craggy rock walls, an overcast sky, feeling her body rise and fall rhythmically with the swells. A chill wind whistled in her ears,

and she began to feel something of the sickening, icy abandon-
ment she'd felt that night on the cliffs. How could they all have
gone off and left her on her own when it was all so new to her
and she had no idea which way to go?

The whistling became brighter and sweeter, too musical
for wind, and Luce realized it wasn't whistling at all. The mermaids were calling to her from a place just around a zigzag in the
coastline. It was something else they could do with their voices,
Luce suddenly understood: disguise them as wind, just in case
any humans were close enough to hear. As she listened, Luce even
recognized the voice: it was Catarina. Carefully, experimentally,
Luce tried to make the same sound in reply.

It came out in a long, beautiful gust. And it was much
more powerful than she'd intended: a luxurious rush of sweet,
high sounds. Luce was so delighted she laughed out loud and
dove again.

She understood how it worked now. She still needed to
breathe, yes. But a single breath was enough to last her for a very
long time.

She found them in a skinny, pointed beach squeezed between
high rock walls: a beach no human could ever get to without a
boat, where protruding crags would block the view of anyone
who chanced to pass by. The mermaids were cracking mussels on
the rocks and sucking them down raw. Luce's stomach roiled with
nausea at the sight, but then the nausea turned into hunger.

"Hey, Luce! I was just about to go back and look for you
when we heard you answering." It was Catarina, who looked
more beautiful than ever in the pearly daylight. She was perched
out in the middle of the inlet on a wide underwater crag shaped

almost like a sofa, lolling back against an outcropping of rock, and Luce joined her there. Luce was surprised by how cheerful Catarina sounded now, and also by the intense joy she felt at the sight of Catarina's welcoming face. She almost didn't care what the other mermaids thought of her, Luce realized, just as long as Catarina liked her. "You really have a wonderful voice," Catarina added, and this time Luce heard something a bit resentful in her tone. And wasn't there something strange in the way Catarina looked at her, something hungry and suspicious at the same time? Luce's sudden worry must have shown too clearly, because Catarina laughed, and when she spoke again all the resentment was gone. "Do you want help getting breakfast? I bet you're not used to cracking your own this way." She took a mussel from her stash on the rocks and bashed it open. Luce accepted it uncertainly. This was a new start for her, after all, and Luce was very conscious that she couldn't afford to make a bad impression. It hadn't lasted long, but even so, her experience that morning of finding herself abandoned to gray, rocking emptiness still lingered, its cold pressure filling her chest. She made an effort and gulped the mussel down.

It wasn't bad at all, actually. It was chilly and smooth and salty in a way that felt right to her. She ate more, and then she swam to the beach and tried some rubbery leaves of brown seaweed. The other mermaids were very entertained by the diffident way she bit into the first leaf and then by the changing expressions on her face as she chewed. She was introduced to more of them: Kayley, who was eleven, with an Inuit tint to her skin and beautiful tipped-up eyes and who had sleek black hair; Miriam, who was the same age as Luce, but had been a mermaid already for more than seventy years and had lived with other tribes along the coast. But as they ate and talked there was something that was starting to make Luce uncomfortable.

The mermaids on the beach ranged in age from five or six up to about sixteen, and they chattered and giggled like any young girls. But at the farthest edges of the group and out on the water, there were a few smaller, softer heads that bobbed and stared or suddenly popped out of nowhere like the heads of seals and then vanished again. Some of them didn't even have hair. They watched Luce in a sad, yearning way that made her feel a little queasy.

Samantha saw her looking. "Larvae," Samantha explained, although that didn't help Luce understand much. "Don't pay any attention to them, okay? It only encourages them to hang around more." Then Samantha failed to take her own advice, and shot a look of distaste at one little head that had floated up too close. "And besides, they attract sharks."

Luce didn't know what to think of that. She was just starting to understand how much she didn't know, how many questions she would need to ask before everything made sense to her. Larvae?

"Are they mermaids?" Luce finally asked, and Samantha grimaced. Kayley nudged Samantha and shook her head to say that it was time to change the subject.

"She does need to know these things," Samantha snapped at Kayley. "We have to talk about it sometime." Then she turned back to Luce. "*Technically*, yes. Technically they're mermaids." Her bell voice was colder, more emotionless than ever. "That is, the timahk protects them." *That word again*, Luce thought. "You can't ever hurt one, no matter how much you want to, and you're not allowed to drive them away. But they're not, not *proper* mermaids. They can't even talk, and they just make these awful squeaks when they try to sing . . ." Luce couldn't help thinking of Gum. She realized she missed him, and she glanced around at the bobbing larvae curiously.

Babies, Luce suddenly realized. Toddlers. What happened when someone hit a baby girl or left one in a Dumpster? They turned into these mermaids that weren't quite mermaids, and they could never get any older, never learn how to talk or act right . . . Luce shuddered. She was starting to understand why the other mermaids were so repulsed by the larvae, but at the same time she felt sorry for them. They had such sad, mushy, helpless little faces, and they stared at her with such longing in their wet, wide eyes.

"Couldn't we try to take care of them?" Luce hazarded, and saw the disgusted looks the other mermaids flashed at each other.

"That's a really terrible idea, Luce," Kayley snapped. "We told you. They attract sharks. It would be a lot better if we *could* drive them away, but the timahk . . ." She shook her head angrily. "Anyway, there's no point getting attached to one of them. They can't swim that fast and the orcas just gobble them up all the time." She made another grossed-out face. "But there are always more of them. They just keep coming."

Luce realized that it wouldn't help to talk about it more now. She was just making the other mermaids angry. Maybe later she could try to talk to Catarina.

Catarina was right there suddenly, leaning on one elbow. She'd swum over from her rock so smoothly that Luce hadn't even noticed her arrive. Now that she was here, though, her presence was so elegant and so forceful that Luce had to make an effort not to stare.

"It just occurred to me," Catarina announced. "We still haven't explained the most important thing to Luce. She doesn't know what the timahk is."

The other mermaids stopped chattering at once. Their faces turned severe and solemn.

"What is it?" Luce asked. "Everyone keeps saying that word." Catarina reached out and lightly, tenderly, touched Luce on her left cheek, right where the golden tail had smacked her earlier that morning.

"I almost broke the timahk myself today," Catarina admitted softly. "If I'd slapped you even a little bit harder . . ." There was a low murmuring among the other mermaids. "If I'd actually *hurt* you, Luce, I would have deserved expulsion from my own tribe. That's the penalty for breaking the timahk. And a mermaid who's thrown out on her own like that . . ." Catarina didn't have to finish the sentence. The grim looks on the faces all around her were enough to let Luce understand the truth: the ocean was full of dangers, and a mermaid swimming off on her own probably wouldn't survive for very long.

Luce couldn't bear the idea of that happening to Catarina. With a small start Luce realized that she already loved Catarina, and not only because she was so grateful for the risk the older mermaid had taken in rescuing her. If only she had had a sister like her, so powerful and clear and fair, maybe being human wouldn't have been so hard at all.

"It's our code," Catarina said. "The timahk is the code of honor for all the mermaids in the world. Breaking the timahk is the worst thing that can happen to a tribe. It would be better if we were all killed than if we lost our honor that way. That's why a mermaid who violates the timahk has to be expelled. It's to preserve the honor of her tribe."

Luce began to grasp how serious this was. She straightened herself, and her voice turned so cold and strong that it surprised her.

"What do I have to do?" Luce asked. "To obey the timahk?"

There weren't very many rules, really. The most important rule was that no mermaid could ever hurt another. No mermaid could ever be banished from a tribe either—unless she broke the timahk first. Anyone who came would be automatically welcomed into the group. And if you saw another mermaid in trouble, you had to do your best to help her, unless it was a situation where interfering could get you killed, too. Luce agreed in her heart with these rules. It all sounded much better to her than the way people on land treated one another.

And then there were the rules concerning humans. These were harder for Luce to accept.

"No contact with humans," Catarina said firmly. Luce was upset by that; she'd already been thinking about swimming back to Pittley to visit Gum, though she wasn't sure which direction would lead her there. She had the vague impression that she'd swum a long, long way after she fell off the cliffs the night before. But if she found her way back and called to him, maybe he'd scramble down to the beach.

"That just means we can't be friends with them?" Luce asked. She had to suppress an impulse to ask *why* she couldn't have human friends. She understood that questioning the timahk

wouldn't go over very well. Catarina was already scowling at her.

"*Friendship* with one of those creatures is *unthinkable*,"
Catarina snarled. "Friendship! No *contact* means much more than
that. It means you never *speak* to a human, and you never *touch*
one. No interaction at all. You can sing to them if you feel like
it," and here Catarina's smile turned cruel. "But then they have
to die. That's the last rule. That's the rule you almost broke last
night, Luce." Catarina's voice was bitter now and merciless, so
that Luce felt a little scared. "No human who hears a mermaid
sing can ever be permitted to remain alive. *Ever*. And that means
you don't sing to a boat, unless you can guarantee that there
won't be a single survivor."

Luce was so shocked that she couldn't restrain herself now.
"Why? Why shouldn't they get to live? At least the good ones?"
Her voice had turned pleading, and Catarina's tail flicked out of
the water; it waved urgently for a moment, drops flying from its
golden scales. She was obviously fighting a desire to smack Luce
for real this time.

"*Good* humans? Luce, haven't you learned *anything*?"

Luce couldn't answer. She was thinking of her father's
warm voice, his sidelong, playful smile. But if she tried to explain about him to Catarina, she'd have to tell the truth: that
her father was a crook and a liar. Almost anyone would judge
him to be an extremely bad man. Luce was perfectly aware of
that. He was a thief, a scoundrel, a cheat, and he was also the
best and kindest person Luce had ever known . . .

So maybe that proved Catarina's point in a way.

"You saw how they acted last night, anyway," Catarina

added in the same savage tone, though at least she'd put her tail back in the water. "As long as you do a good job singing, they *want* to drown. It makes them happy. Happier than they've ever been in their rotten human lives! They're so disgusted with *themselves* that they'd rather be dead. We just help them, really."

There was silence for a moment. Luce was thinking about the face of the drowning old man when Catarina added something, a little reluctantly. "But it's hard for any mermaid to keep too many humans enchanted at once. Even the best singers can only handle so many at a time . . ." Then Catarina shot a vindictive glance at Samantha. "*Some* of our singers can barely even deal with one human."

Samantha's face buckled with humiliation, and Luce knew this was revenge for what Samantha had said back in the cave: that Catarina was too sensitive about her past.

Luce tried not to let the personal drama distract her. She needed to understand. "And that's why you won't try to sink a ship that's too big? You wouldn't be able to . . . to make completely sure . . ."

"Exactly." Catarina nodded. "We can't risk losing control of the situation. Just think of what they'd do if they ever found out we're here! They'd poison the whole *ocean* if they had to just to kill all of us." A snarl came back in her voice. "They already *do* poison it. Such filthy things they throw in here!"

Luce was still brooding over all of this. She didn't like the idea of killing anyone. But on the other hand, everything Catarina had said was obviously true. Humans did do terrible, unimaginable things, to one another and to the whole world. They'd done something awful to every girl here.

"But what do we do about kids?" Luce asked at last. "If there's a kid on one of the ships . . ."

Catarina flashed a callous smile, and stroked Luce's hair with her long, cool fingers.

"Oh, but they're just going to grow up, aren't they?" she said.

5

Wondering

After the painful explanation of the timahk, though, the after-noon turned wonderful. The mermaids swam out into the open sea and taught Luce tricks: ways of swimming upside down, of turning underwater loops so fast that the flying bubbles made their long bodies look like giant silver rings, and how to use a quick corkscrewing movement of her tail to shoot straight up out of the waves. They took turns twirling up into the air and then splashing down again, and Luce laughed so hard she felt breathless. It was a pale gray day, the clouds above glowing like soft lamps, and around her the water pleated aluminum white and dull dark green together. The crisp salt smell excited her, the rhythm of lift and fall became a kind of music ringing inside her chest, and the gulls wheeled and screamed above. Once in the distance she spotted the sweeping shape of a bald eagle.

It was so easy to tread water now. She didn't even need to use her arms. Just a tiny circling movement with the broad, sensitive fins at the end of her tail, and she could stay in one place with her head above the water for as long as she wanted, riding the swells. It still felt a little strange, but Luce was becoming aware of just how much she loved having that forceful tail. It was infinitely stronger than her legs had been; it was stronger than any human legs, even a marathon runner's. And then the color of it was so beautiful, a brilliant silver glimmer over soft jade green. It was perfect for her, exactly the color she would have chosen.

They were all so friendly to her, so much fun. Luce had barely ever had real friends in her life. She and her father never stayed anywhere for more than a few months, so even the rare friends she had made were always left behind as soon as her father told her it was time to pack up again and the red van rumbled off down the next highway. But Luce had been enrolled in different schools a few times, and the other kids had never treated her like this, with so much warmth and acceptance. Luce was starting to realize that a lot of the other mermaids actually admired her, even though she was the one who was new and strange. It was an incredible stroke of luck, she thought, that she'd found them all. Luce still didn't like what her new friends did—sinking ships, drowning people—but it was hard to think of them as evil when they were being so nice to *her*.

Luce did an especially high twist up into the air, then at the top she somersaulted and curved down again into the sea. Silver water flashed in her eyes, and when she came up into the circle Catarina beamed at her delightedly. "That was incredible, Luce! And when you're still getting used to your tail. You're really a natural at this." Again Luce thrilled at Catarina's warm golden smile, and the sweet moonlight glow of her gray eyes set in their thick fringe of auburn lashes. She was sure now that Catarina *did* like her, very much. Luce was just grinning back when she caught sight of another dark, disquieting flicker in Catarina's eyes.

"She's *such* a natural," Miriam agreed. While most of the mermaids had a slightly green or golden cast to their skin, Miriam's was just faintly blue, her tail inky, and her eyes were smoky black above high, fragile cheekbones. She seemed very small for her age: fourteen, like Luce. "I've been in the water for longer than any of you, and my singing's nowhere near—" Miriam broke off. Luce understood by now that singing was a touchy issue, and also that it might be the reason for the awed glances some of the younger mermaids gave her.

Something else kept bothering Luce, though. Just the ghost of an unbearable idea, always hovering at her back. Maybe if she ignored it for long enough, it would eventually go away.

"Catarina! You know what you should teach Luce?" Samantha exclaimed. "Some of those singing tricks you can do. Like that one where you make your voice into a ball, kind of? I bet she'll be great at them." Luce thought that sounded fantastic. She loved how it felt to use her voice now, and also she wanted something to distract her from that needling, half-formed idea. She turned to gaze excitedly at Catarina, expecting to be met by her shining smile.

Instead Catarina looked tense, sullen. The happy sounds of the chattering mermaids faded as they all noticed Catarina's darkening mood. She looked around at them all with her brows drawn together, her lips pursed. The silence lasted much too long.

"Singing can't be taught," Catarina finally announced in her coldest voice. Hearing it, Luce felt like the back of a steel knife was being drawn along her skin. Was her singing the reason why Catarina watched her with shadows stirring just behind her eyes? "You know that, Samantha. Maybe it's possible that someone could get better by practicing on her own, though I can't say I've ever really seen that happen . . ."

Samantha and Kayley exchanged a look that was much too obvious. It was like they were daring each other to say something. Luce wasn't completely sure what was going on.

Kayley was the one who took the chance. "Do you even hear yourself, Cat? Everyone can tell you're just afraid. You think if Luce was that good while she's still just metaskaza . . ." Luce was dismayed. Catarina's lovely face was crumpling with pain and anger, and Luce had the awful feeling that she was about to be stuck in the middle of a fight. Whatever this was really about, she didn't want anything to do with it.

"I don't want Catarina to teach me anything about singing," Luce lied firmly. "I'm not sure singing even interests me that much. I'd rather learn more about swimming." Kayley shot her a look of open disbelief, but Catarina's tension finally dissolved.

"I'd love to teach you more about singing, Luce," Catarina said, and the falseness in her tone was apparent to everyone. "Just like I wish I could help *everyone* here . . . It's just that it can't be done. It's a gift; we each have to accept exactly how much we've been given. But you shouldn't let that stop you from enjoying it. Believe me, we're all very glad to have another singer as talented as you are. I've been doing much more than my share of the work."

Luce looked around. Suddenly the sea looked much too silvery, too empty, and too huge, and she wondered if she could suggest going back to the cave. They'd been playing in the water for so long that the afternoon light was shading into a soft gray gloaming. As she gazed farther out she saw something black arch up out of the water, a tall bladelike fin defining its movement as it sleeked back into the waves. It was up again too quickly, and it seemed to be heading their way. Luce realized there were a few of them.

"Orcas," Kayley said. Luce couldn't understand why the other mermaids didn't seem more worried. "They're pretty far off still. And we can outswim them, easy." Luce looked around and saw that a few of the larvae had caught up with them, along with a few curious seals. It was hard to tell the drifting heads of the larvae apart from the heads of the seals unless you watched for a while.

"We can't just leave the larvae out here," Luce said anxiously. "Won't the orcas eat them?"

"They eat them all the time," Kayley agreed. "Like potato chips. That's why *we* should get out of here." Mermaids were already flashing away under the water. "Come on, Luce!" Kayley's black glossy head blinked under a wave, then Catarina's red-gold hair formed a sudden streaking torrent, just for a second, as she dove away.

Only Luce hesitated. One of the larvae noticed her looking and tentatively wriggled in her direction. They really couldn't swim very well, Luce realized. They were hopelessly clumsy, uncertain in their movements, and their tails were soft and stubby. She suddenly remembered that she hadn't seen any of them inside the cave. Probably they couldn't dive well enough to get through that deep underwater tunnel.

Didn't the timahk require her to at least *try* to help them?

The soft larval mermaid nosed up to her and gently butted its head against Luce's shoulder. It was about two years old, Luce thought, maybe three. Just about the same age as that poor little girl she'd found on the beach.

"Who'z zat?" the larval mermaid warbled at her through its pink baby lips. It had such lonely blue eyes that looking in its face made Luce almost nauseous, but at the same time it reminded her of Gum. Nobody had ever wanted to take care of him either, just because he couldn't talk right. "Who'z zat?" The shining black curves of the orcas rose and fell much closer now. Looking around, Luce counted at least five of the larvae, and realized she couldn't possibly save all of them.

She hooked her right arm around the gibbering larva next to her and dove. A second later something dark and huge streaked near her, and the water in her eyes filled with dark red. Blood unraveled through the water in smoke-shaped curls. Luce spun her tail in a corkscrew, hurling as fast as she could, but she hadn't had enough practice swimming to keep her course straight with the larva dragging on her arm. The awkward weight threw her movement off, and Luce curved around to the right before she could stop herself. A wall of glossy black filled her eyes, and she dashed head first against the side of an orca that was practically erupting up out of the water, then rolled over its back as the momentum of the leap sent it hurtling past. The blow and the tumbling rush left her disoriented in a cloud of spinning bubbles. For a moment she couldn't tell which way was up.

The larval mermaid wasn't in her arm anymore. Somehow the impact had knocked it away, and now as she swirled in place she couldn't see it anywhere.

A wave of displaced water sent Luce pitching sideways, and again the sea turned crimson. It was like looking through red rippling glass. Luce spun in time to see a single small hand floating by, its palm upturned. To her horror, she realized that some of the bloody water had seeped into her mouth; she could taste the poor little mermaid's sour, metallic death . . . Panic finally seized her. She lashed out her tail, and now that she wasn't trying to pull the larval mermaid along with her, she found her body streaking away from the carnage at terrific speed. After just a few seconds the water in her eyes was dusky gray and clean, truly clean. Silver fish whipped out of her path. Luce spun through the waves in a frenzy, sure that her skin was still streaked with blood. She swam on and on until her lungs began to hurt, then flung herself toward the surface.

She came up suddenly in an expanse of empty twilit sea, under cliffs she didn't recognize, and gasped for air. Her head was spinning. Seals moaned, forming disorienting streaks of black as they parted around her. At least, Luce realized, she was still near the coast, so as long she followed it she'd find the cave eventually. It was pure luck that she hadn't sped farther out to sea in her panic.

But even so she didn't know if she should follow the cliffs to her left or to her right. Right, she decided. Her movements were strangely wobbly and, now that the adrenaline was ebbing from her system, she began to feel exhausted.

Why had she let go of that poor larval mermaid? Somewhere far behind her the waves were bright with blood, and the foam was pink. Luce swayed in the water, and darkness blurred her vision. She thought she might faint. She pushed her way to a crest of projecting rock and wrapped her arms around it, her tail trailing out behind her and dark fog growing in her eyes. If she rested for a while it might be easier to find her way back home.

Home, Luce thought. It was strange to realize that that dark, jagged cave was the first real home she'd ever had apart from her father's red van. She'd definitely never thought of her uncle's house that way, not even when her father was still alive.

The terrible idea that had kept bothering her all afternoon came back. Luce was relieved that oblivion was flooding into her mind now and drowning her suspicions in darkness.

* * *

"Oh, Luce!" It was Catarina's voice, but Luce couldn't open her eyes at first. Everything ached. "Luce! Wake up!" At least three pairs of hands were holding her, lifting her off the rock, and Luce finally pulled herself out of the dark half-dream and looked around. It was night, and a group of the oldest mermaids was holding her. A search party, Luce decided.

They actually cared enough to come looking for her, then. She almost couldn't believe it. They really *cared* if she disappeared. Luce was flooded with gratitude, with a sense of finally having found someplace she belonged. After her father's disappearance she'd come to believe that she would stay lost forever; yet here was Catarina staring at her with furious tenderness. Catarina's face flickered between different expressions: anger and relief and happiness. "Luce, are you determined to get yourself killed? Why didn't you come with us?" They started swimming slowly now, Catarina holding her on her left and Samantha on her right, so that all their heads stayed above the water.

"Look at that," Miriam said behind them. "She's covered in bruises. What was she doing?"

Luce was finally conscious enough to talk. "I'm okay. I just tried . . ." Luce shook the red, bubbling memory away. "Thank you for coming to look for me."

"Of *course* we came." Catarina sounded indignant. "Am I going to have to rescue you every day? Luce, you need to be more careful. It's like you don't understand how dangerous it is here, even though I keep on trying to get that through your head. When are you going to start listening?" Catarina was nagging her like a worried mother, Luce realized, and she couldn't help smiling to herself. Samantha glanced over just in time to see the smile.

"I think she likes making you save her," Samantha sniped in her cold, ringing voice. "We could get home a lot faster if she's ready to dive."

Luce plunged under the water, but she couldn't swim as fast as usual. Her body was too sore. The others zipped ahead, but Catarina stayed beside her, rippling along at a deliberately languorous pace, and Luce knew Catarina was looking after her. Making sure she made it home safely.

If the cave was her home, Luce decided, then that must mean Catarina was her family. She wouldn't judge Catarina any more than she'd judged her father. How could you consider someone you love bad, no matter what anybody else might think? Catarina kept glancing over at her as they swam. It was different this time, though: as if Catarina were calculating something, adding up numbers only she could see.

When they came near the cave's entrance Catarina caught Luce's hand and guided her to the surface. They floated upright facing each other in a spot where the shore bent close around them. A few enormous stars flared through a gash in the clouds, and their light leaped in white sparks on the jet black water. Catarina's gray eyes were so close to Luce's that she felt like she was falling into a twisting, gleaming pool.

"We need to talk, Luce," Catarina said. "Before we go back in. I need you to be honest with me." There was a shiver of music in her voice; it made Luce want to tell her everything, and Luce fought it. There were some things she could *never* say. She waited. "Luce, were you *trying* to die? Tell me." The question shocked Luce into a new, cold wakefulness. Why would Catarina think that Luce was suicidal?

"No! Catarina, I wasn't . . . I'm really happy to be with you, really, but there were all those larvae out there, and you told me that the timahk . . . So I was trying to save one of them." Luce was ashamed to admit what had happened. She hadn't swum well, and because of that the larva had died. "Somehow I couldn't swim straight while I was holding her, and then the orcas were right there. I slammed into one of them . . ." Luce couldn't bear to tell the rest of the story, but it was clear from the strain on Catarina's face that she could guess what must have happened next.

"The timahk does *not* require you to endanger yourself, Luce." Catarina sounded much gentler than Luce would have expected, and also relieved. "And there's really no point trying to save larvae. I know it's a painful thing to accept, but they're not made to survive for long in the sea. It's not just the orcas. If there's a storm they can get thrown onto the beach, for instance, and then they never make it back to the water in time . . ."

Luce was silent, thinking of the dead little girl she'd found. Her closed eyelids had been faintly iridescent, like mother of pearl . . . Suddenly she thought of something: none of the mermaids ever seemed to let their tails leave the water for more than a few seconds. And there was a cold, painful burning in her own tail whenever the air touched it. Even leaping into the air, the way they'd done earlier, had sent a stinging prickle through her scales.

"What happens then?" Luce asked. "I mean, to a mermaid who can't make it back to the water?"

Catarina winced and rubbed one hand across her forehead. Apparently this was a difficult subject.

"It's awful, Luce. What happens when one of us gets stuck out in the air like that. I hope you never have to see it." Her eyes were still turned toward Luce, but there was a seething blankness in them that told Luce she was thinking of something else now. Then Catarina focused again with an obvious effort and flashed Luce a slow, aching smile. "So, do you promise to start taking better care of yourself? We don't want to lose you, you know." Catarina kept her voice light, but Luce could hear how seriously she meant it.

"I promise," Luce agreed, and Catarina smiled. "I'll be way more careful, and I'll listen to everything you tell me. From now on." It had been so long since anyone had asked her to promise anything; it felt wonderful to say those words. "But, Catarina? I really need to know what happens. Before we go back in. You need to tell me what happens to a mermaid who gets washed up." Catarina stared at her. She was wavering between rage and concern, and odd unfinished expressions darted across her face.

"Luce, do you have a good reason for asking me this?" Luce stared back at her, and Catarina must have recognized her urgency, because after another moment of hesitation she continued. "Well, they almost always die. Not absolutely always. At least that's what I've heard. But the pain is unbelievable. Just try holding your tail out of the water sometime, and you'll see what I mean right away. You won't be able to stand it for long. It's so terrible that the mermaids who go through it die of shock. The pain stops their hearts . . ."

Luce couldn't help recognizing that Catarina was holding something back, so she decided to ask her outright. "Do we turn human again? Catarina, is that what happens? As our tails dry out . . ." From the flash in Catarina's eyes Luce knew she'd guessed the truth. "I found a dead little girl on the beach right before I changed. And her skin looked like ours, with that green shine. And they said she hadn't drowned, that there was no water in her lungs at all, and they couldn't understand where she'd come from." The words rushed out now. "I keep thinking that she must have been one of us, or a larva anyway . . ." Then Luce remembered what Gum had said. *Fishgirl.* He'd seen that little mermaid before her tail changed back!

"It *killed* her, Luce," Catarina murmured. "She died in unspeakable agony. And she didn't even get to die as a mermaid, but just as one of those . . ." She grimaced and looked off, and Luce wondered if it was really the larval mermaid Catarina was thinking of. "Let's head back to the cave. It's better if we don't keep talking about this."

Luce knew enough to let the subject drop. She remembered what Samantha had said: that it wasn't just her human past that Catarina couldn't stand to be reminded of but also some things that had happened to her after she'd changed. Luce thought of Catarina's slight, delicate accent, and wondered where she'd come from originally. And was this her first tribe, or had she lived in other places before, like Miriam?

They dove together, down through the underwater tunnel, and Catarina seemed remote and somber, though she still glanced over now and then with that brooding look on her face. An inexplicable idea occurred to Luce: Catarina *needed* her, in a way that she didn't need any of the others. Then Luce told herself that she was just being conceited, thinking something like that. Catarina must care equally about all the girls in her tribe. After all, she was their queen.

* * *

But Luce almost forgot all her tangled thoughts when their faces broke through the water of the cave. Samantha and Miriam had already brought the news that Luce had been found alive, and they were all waiting to welcome her. She was surrounded by girls who laughed, and swirled over to hug her, and to tell her how crazy she'd been. They fussed over her bruises and agreed she should rest for a day or two.

And then they rolled apart, to make room for her to sleep next to Catarina. It seemed to be understood now that she and Catarina belonged together. Gratefully Luce curled up next to her friend, and after a moment she leaned her head over to nestle against that smooth gold-white shoulder. Luce gazed up into the darkness of the cave, watching the soft green phosphorescence; an isolated star gleamed through one of the holes in the roof.

She couldn't sleep. The mermaids around her didn't breathe steadily in the way sleeping humans would, but every now and then Luce would hear a single deep inhalation from somewhere in the darkness.

She couldn't sleep, and the intolerable idea that had nagged at her all day suddenly took over her mind. It insisted on blotting out all her other thoughts and refused to let her look away.

The *High and Mighty* had disappeared somewhere out here. Not a trace of it had ever been found. Maybe the violent storm that day had shattered her father's ship, drowned all the men.

Or maybe the storm had had some help. Maybe one of her new friends had sung into her father's desperate face until he forgot all about the daughter waiting for him back at home. Sung to him in her sweet, wild voice until death was the only thing he desired . . .

Maybe *Catarina* had. And Catarina's shoulder was pressed like cold silk against Luce's cheek.

Luce sat up and looked around her. The mermaids' faces shimmered softly in the darkness. They looked so innocent, all sleeping together that way. Any human, Luce knew, would look at them with wonder, with helpless adoration. They were simply too lovely to be real.

Luce closed her eyes, and then slowly, stealthily, she raised her tail from the sea. It was still heavy, but she had much better control of it now. An icy draft blew down from the roof, licking the drops from her scales.

At first the burning sensation was almost pleasurable. It was a shivering mixture of heat and chills, and Luce began to wonder if Catarina had told her the truth. Catarina hated humans so much that it wouldn't have surprised Luce if she'd lied just to make sure that Luce would never try to change back.

Then the pain bit into her. A million burning teeth gnawed at her tail, slashing razors made of pure sun cut her, and light began to flash in Luce's eyes. It took all her strength to stop herself from screaming, and with a gasp she let her tail fall again. The pain was so stunning that for a while all Luce could do was lie trembling in the lapping water while hot tears welled in her eyes.

There was truly no going back. Not even if she'd had any place she could go. Not even if this wasn't the only place on earth where anyone cared about her at all.

To survive, Luce thought, she needed to make some rules for herself. She needed her own personal timahk.

She could still think about her father, Luce decided, though it might be better if she didn't let herself think about him too much. It wouldn't be fair to expect she could forget everything about being human.

But she could never again allow herself to wonder about one thing, and that was the way her father might have died.

6

The Last Kiss

For the next few days they all insisted that Luce stay in the cave. She was too bruised to swim as well as she should, and if any predators came it wouldn't be safe. They brought her food and sometimes one of them would linger and talk for a while, answering her questions or telling her stories. They didn't ask her much in return; she hadn't been a mermaid for long enough to have anything to say about that, and Luce found out quickly that it was considered rude to ask another mermaid about her human life, at least beyond the glimpses you could see by just looking sideways. They knew about her uncle, of course; they could see that much. But no one ever asked about her parents, and she never said anything about her wandering life in the red van before she'd come to Pittley. Luce was glad that she didn't have to explain too much. She'd made a decision to keep everything about her father as secret as she could.

Luce found out, too, that she was happy to be left alone sometimes, in the cool and the darkness. It was hard to think clearly with so many chattering girls around, and then so much had happened to her over the last several days that she wanted some time just to wonder about all of it. She swam slow circles in the calm water of the cave, skimming along just above the pebbles at the bottom and watching the fragile, milky, long-legged crabs whose bodies were transLucent and whose tapering feet looked almost like pink glass. There were tiny drifting medusas, too, with crystalline gelatinous frills around cobalt blue hearts, and dagger-thin fish that sometimes hovered in place and sometimes sliced away from her. She loved everything, watched everything.

There was another reason Luce was glad to be left alone. She couldn't forget the splendor of the song that had coursed through her the night she'd changed. Her longing to merge with that music again was so intense that Luce felt a bit embarrassed at the thought of anyone noticing how much it meant to her. She hadn't forgotten either how edgy the mention of singing always made Catarina; it might be better to keep any singing she did strictly private.

So when everyone was away and she was fairly sure they wouldn't hear her, she began to practice.

It was hard to control it, Luce found. Her new voice, after all, was magic, and singing was a little like taking the pressure off a coiled spring. When she sang her voice took on a volatile aliveness, an urge to expand and rip through water and rock and sky. It was hers, but she didn't entirely own it. It might even be stronger than she was.

Learning to sing, Luce thought, meant learning to tame the voice that was living in her. She would begin with a single note and hold it, doing her best to keep it low and soft as it struggled against her, full of yearnings to rip and surge. Once it settled down a little, she would let it lift a step and hold it again. Sometimes it got away from her and took over the cave with a high, liquid throbbing where impossible notes raced and fused together, and she would have to bite her lip as hard as she could to stifle herself, or lift her tail from the water until the pain stunned her voice into submission.

On her third day in the cave Luce floated on her back in the dark water watching a palm-shaped blot of violet sky that shone through the roof, and tried a little run of notes. It was the first time she'd deliberately ventured on a melody, and her voice seemed pleased. It didn't fight her nearly as much as usual. The melody spilling from her was so lovely, Luce thought: a piercing lilt that hovered for a while, and then a long cascade of tones like something falling . . .

It was a whole song. Other notes took her voice, and carried it where they wanted to go. And, Luce realized with a shock, it was a song she'd heard before.

She'd *sung* it before, straight into the face of the old man she'd drowned, and he'd gazed back at her with rapture as he listened. Luce let out a little cry right in the middle of the song, and heaved her tail up to force her voice to be quiet. After a few seconds the first jolts of pain started, and the song dimmed in her throat.

Once Luce was sure it was completely gone, she allowed herself to lower her tail back into the water. Pain still jarred and sparked for a minute, then gradually slipped away. She'd let her voice run free, just for a few notes, and immediately it had turned into a song whose only purpose was murder! And yet sing-ing it had exalted her. Her heart was pounding now from joy as much as horror.

But after all, she was all alone in the cave. There were no humans around to hear her, no chance that she was luring some-one to die. Why shouldn't she let herself feel that song moving through her then, when it had such a powerful will to live and its life made her so happy?

She let her voice rise again into the sweet high note that had started it all. The song hesitated, just for a second, but then it was back in her throat. Music spilled down the worn stairs of a farmhouse outside Pittsburg—Luce had forgotten that house until this moment, but now she knew it belonged to an old friend of her mother's—then the single note split into a thrumming chord, and she wept, and soft arms picked her up off the floor and cradled her. A rain of dark hair brushed against her face.

Of course people were ready to die in exchange for this song, Luce thought. She would joyfully die for it herself if she had to. She would drown again and again, only to find herself in this tor-rent of living music.

There was a slight pitching disturbance in the water around her. Luce ignored it. She was following the song now as it ran down a glittering sidewalk toward a tall young woman in a black sundress. Luce had done something wrong, but the woman forgave her completely . . . Minutes passed as Luce flowed inside her own unthinkable music.

"Luce." It was Catarina. Her hair ran out like flames across the dark water. Luce's singing shattered into the dark of the cave and the red flickering web around Catarina's golden face. Luce gaped at her in sudden anxiety, and she was only partly relieved when Catarina gave her a sly smile. Maybe she'd misunderstood, and Catarina didn't care at all if Luce sang to herself? Luce watched the gray eyes nervously; wasn't there something heated in their gaze that didn't quite go with the smile, with the casual friendliness of Catarina's tone? "I came to see how you're doing. How does swimming feel now?"

In fact, Luce felt much better, but she wasn't ready to talk yet. Her voice only wanted to leap out in wild notes, and she almost couldn't stand the thought of limiting it to dull, small words.

"There's a Coast Guard boat a few miles off," Catarina continued, and Luce began to focus more. "We could take it without you, but if you're well enough we'd certainly appreciate your help."

Luce had known this might happen sometime, but she wasn't ready to hear it now. Her body dropped into the water and eddied there in confusion, and she couldn't meet Catarina's eyes. Catarina didn't understand. "Your bruises *look* almost healed," Catarina said, and there was a harsh edge to her voice, "but if it still hurts you that much to swim . . ." Luce was still emerging from the dream of her own singing, but she clearly recognized the quickening eagerness in Catarina's eyes, the impatient swishing of her movements. It was so confusing; Luce had imagined that Catarina resented her singing, but now her friend's long golden body rippled with terrible desire. No matter what she claimed, she'd be furious if Luce refused to come with her. And in spite of herself, Luce felt a surge of the same shivering desire: to be out in that wild sea, devoured by her own much wilder song.

"I'm ready to swim," Luce stammered. "I just—I'm so new—I don't think I'm ready to sing to anyone." Catarina's tail flipped up behind her and lashed the water into a nervous froth. Her eyes flared.

"You think I didn't hear you just now? Luce, you're second in command! I'll lead the ship in, and you cover from behind. You have to watch out if they try to lower the lifeboats . . ." Luce was wide-eyed with dismay, and Catarina finally checked herself. "Just swim out with us, then." She gave Luce a long, uncomfortable stare, examining something in her face, and her mouth twisted into a wicked smile. "You don't have to sing if you don't feel like it. I promise. All right?" And without waiting for an answer, she caught Luce's hand and dove.

Luce went with her. The mouth of the cave opened onto a glorious view. The ocean was stained green and golden, laced with writhing threads of light, and Luce realized it was the first time she'd swum through sunlit water. She'd been inside the dark cave for so long that she now swept her tail in excitement and raced through the delirium of sun, Catarina still holding her hand. Shine streaked over Catarina's flying hair and lit the bubbles churned up by their swimming. Luce's happiness was so bright and brash that she could almost forget her anxiety about what they were going to do.

She wasn't going to do it, Luce corrected herself. Catarina had promised that she wouldn't have to sing. Luce would keep her voice shut deep in her chest, where it couldn't hurt anyone. It wasn't like she could have done anything to stop Catarina either; Luce had seen the ravenous eagerness in her friend's face. Nothing would have held her back.

Then the shoreline was just a low gray band wrapping the horizon on one side, and the tall white Coast Guard boat skimmed along in front of them. Behind it drifted a pack of mermaids, all waiting for Catarina. As long as they kept their bodies vertical in the water, with their tails pointing straight down and their chins tucked against their chests, they were almost indistinguishable from seals. Luce knew the sailors could look directly at them and never suspect a thing. Only Catarina's fiery hair might cause some concern, and she stayed just below the surface until she'd made sure everyone was ready. Then her pale face rose in the center of a green glass wave.

"Fan out," Catarina commanded, and Luce could see how the mermaids all thrilled to the order. Their bodies dipped and flicked as they spread out to surround the ship, Catarina in the lead; Luce couldn't help thinking of wolves closing in on a much larger animal, an elk or a moose. Luce stayed where she was, centered in the V of the ship's wake. She wanted a place as far from Catarina and the others as possible. Even though Catarina had said it was all right for Luce to keep quiet, the other mermaids might resent it if they noticed she wasn't helping.

On the deck a tall young man with caramel-colored skin and dark curly hair was busy with some complicated task involving an electric drill. Luce couldn't quite make out what he was doing, but the bright sun formed pale branching shapes on the blue shoulders of his uniform as he bent over whatever object he was repairing. Luce fought a sudden impulse to call out, to try to warn him, though she knew that wouldn't help.

A light breeze blew, and then something about it shifted. The sound of the breeze became more alive, more golden. The young sailor kept on with his work, but a soft inward look stole into his eyes, as if he were amazed to find himself alive on such a beautiful day. The tone of the breeze flexed and curved, becoming just a bit richer, tinged with a thickening music, and the caramel-skinned boy smiled to himself and switched off the drill. He straightened and gazed off into the distance as the boat began to turn. Luce had to speed up to maintain her position in the wake.

Luce couldn't believe how skillfully Catarina sang. The enchantment rose so slowly, so sensuously, that time and place softened and liquefied. It was different from her own singing, Luce thought. Her skin warmed as she listened to it, and blood began to pulse in her temples.

The prow swung drowsily around on the sunlit sea. Soon the boat wasn't running parallel to the cliffs but nosing toward a bare island half a mile farther out: an island that was nothing but gray rocks jutting high up out of the waves, with tufts of silvery grass and white roosting birds along its sides. Other voices began to spread their music under the gathering power of Catarina's song.

Luce understood what Catarina was planning. After the boat cracked apart people would come to examine the wreckage and try to figure out what had happened. Catarina was heading toward the island rather than the cliffs, because she didn't want any of the investigators coming too close to their cave.

The young sailor gently turned his head and gazed straight into Luce's eyes as she swam along behind. He didn't seem at all surprised to see her there, just happy and a bit perplexed, as if he couldn't understand how he'd forgotten the name of someone he'd known and loved for so long. He gave her such a sweet smile and waved peacefully. Luce hesitated, then waved back at him. That didn't count as breaking the timahk, did it?

The boat was speeding up now, and the mermaids' song flowed over the sky until every breath of air, every grain of sunlight was awake and alive. Luce felt the song streaming over and inside her body, and then she heard a single high, tremulous note soaring above the curls of music. It tore from her chest and peaked somewhere just under the sun, floated there, and then began a long tumbling descent. The young sailor's sleepy love changed, heightened into a fever of longing. The song entered into his mind, and Luce suddenly understood him. Her quivering song felt his thoughts, and it told her how heartbroken he'd been since his mother's death. They'd been fighting, and he hadn't gone to see her in the hospital as cancer ate through her; he'd stayed away, until it was too late.

She had promised she wouldn't sing, Luce reminded herself. She could still lift her tail into the sunlight and hold it there until the burning forced her voice to stop. But even then the ship would smash apart. Everyone on it was already doomed. And she *couldn't* let the young sailor die, Luce thought, with so much grief still inside him. Her song fell and the note split into a widening chord, and then the young sailor knew that, even as she died, his mother had forgiven him. She'd thought of him with the purest compassion, with gratitude for the years of joy he'd brought to her life.

At least, that was what Luce's song told him. It vibrated with a sense of perfect homecoming, and as Luce sang to him everything broken was mended, and everything lost was restored. She meant the song only for the caramel-skinned boy, but other sailors heard her and they began to crowd around him: almost all men, though Luce spotted a few young women there as well. A row of faces watched Luce, all rapt with tenderness as the music sank into their minds. Some of the heart-chill she'd felt the first night she'd sung came back, bringing the idea that these men deserved whatever happened to them. This time, though, Luce understood that it was just part of the magic of her own voice, a kind of anesthesia that let mermaids kill without caring, and she pushed it away. She didn't want to let go of the warmth she felt for the dark boy staring down at her, not when his smile was so beautiful.

The ship's motors were thrumming at the limit of their strength, and the wake around Luce rose higher, thicker with white foam. She couldn't swim nearly as fast with her head above water, and she struggled to keep up. The ship was only moments away from crashing.

The dark boy couldn't wait any longer, though. He gave a sudden shake as if he couldn't stand to feel his life still holding on to him, and hurled head downward over the side, crumpling as his body hit the water at an oblique angle. And then the other sailors followed him, one by one, their bodies plunging heavily with loose arms flopping around them. They were so taken by the dream in Luce's voice, it seemed, that they couldn't even focus enough to dive properly. White rings of foam spread out around the places where they disappeared.

The boat's hull crunched; shuddered; screamed like a living thing as the rocks tore it apart. It had so much momentum that the metal sides bowed out from the impact, swung upward, and then began to lean back into the water. The sides of this island were steep, Luce realized, the underwater slopes precipitous; the ship would go down quickly. That was another reason Catarina'd picked this spot. She'd known exactly where to go.

It was horrible, Luce thought. But she was undeniably a part of it. Her voice was free and desperate, stretching out of her and pounding through the sea.

She closed her eyes and dove. Down into the cool, swelling gray, where she didn't have to see what she'd done. Down, until her reaching hand brushed something soft, and her eyelids opened reflexively. Dark curly hair. The caramel-skinned boy looked up, his face at most a foot away from Luce's as she plunged. She barely managed to keep herself from running into him. And still her song pulsed on and on, an immense beating heart made of music.

He gazed up at her, his eyes shining with joy. Luce remembered what her father had said about her mother: *She gave me more and truer love than any human being can hope for in this life.* That was the way the drowning boy stared at her, Luce realized, with a fierce adoration that seemed too consuming to belong on Earth. She would never feel lonely again if only he would keep watching her with that glow in his eyes. *More and truer love than any human being . . .*

But that was because she wasn't human.

If she'd stayed human, no one ever would have loved her as much as the caramel-skinned boy did now. And then Luce saw that he was already dead, his brown eyes still locked on her face. His eyes were empty and gentle, watching nothing.

* * *

When Luce broke through the water again the other mermaids were already gathering, swishing their tails with excitement.

"Look at our little metaskaza!" Samantha exclaimed. "Did you see that? She had them actually jumping overboard!" Luce was nauseous, trembling; it took her a second to understand that Samantha was talking about her.

"Even you can't call Luce metaskaza anymore," a blonde named Regan objected. "Not after that! I've never seen anyone do that before." Luce felt choked and her eyes were hot, but she wouldn't let herself cry while they were watching her. She looked around at the white scraps of debris still bobbing on the surface of the water, then up at the grassy crest of the island. There were obviously no human survivors, just as Catarina had said.

But where was Catarina?

Miriam noticed the way Luce's gaze searched the waves.

"There was one kind of stubborn one," Miriam explained. Her eyes were blue-black, gleaming but also somehow sad, and a mist of pearl-colored light clung to her pale, bluish skin. "He almost made it to shore before we noticed. Catarina's giving him some . . . some personal attention. She'll be back with us soon. She took him straight down a little while ago."

As queasy as she was, Luce felt worried by this. "What if she goes too far down? If she's all by herself . . ."

Samantha thought that was funny. "I really wouldn't worry about Cat, Luce. She's better at swimming deep down than the rest of us. And besides, I kind of think she likes to be alone sometimes." Samantha's voice took on a cold, mocking tone, and something about it bothered Luce.

"She always catches up with us pretty soon," Miriam added defensively.

Luce gazed around at the other mermaids. There was an uncomfortable tension to the way they gazed back at her, Luce thought. It was almost like the way people had looked at her when she was still human.

"I'm going to go make sure Catarina's okay," Luce announced, and dove before anyone could stop her.

The sunlit water was full of random trash. There were pillows and diaries, shoes and boxes of cookies: anything that wasn't heavy enough to sink straight down. There was a steep wall of rock just beside her, and a drowned young woman lay on a protruding shelf with her arm over her face, as if the light was bothering her. Below Luce the water darkened, dilating like the pupil of an immense eye.

She couldn't see Catarina anywhere. Luce pushed farther down, and the water turned colder, its sun-flecked green gradually shading to somber dark emerald, its pressure increasing. Luce couldn't justify the icy, unsettled feeling in her chest; of course what the other mermaids had told her was true. It was Catarina, after all, who'd swum to the depth where Luce's own breath had started to give out on her first night in the sea, Catarina who had saved her life.

Then Luce saw something far below: red-gold hair like a single match flaring up in the green darkness. *Too far down*, Luce thought. She spiraled her tail and raced toward it. As she came closer she could hear Catarina still singing, but much more softly than before. It didn't seem like any human could still be alive after such a long descent. Was Catarina singing to herself?

The fire-colored swirl grew in Luce's eyes, and she saw that Catarina wasn't alone.

A tall, black-haired young man of perhaps twenty was clinging to her, his hands circling over Catarina's slender back, caressing her long waist. He must have seized hold of her as she sang, Luce thought, and she waited for Catarina to shove him away. Catarina's song throbbed on in her throat, wild with longing, and a crown of bubbles broke from her and obscured Luce's view for a moment. She was almost level with them now.

Catarina's fingers were tangled in the young man's hair, and her tail snaked and thrashed around his legs. There was another burst of bubbles as Catarina blew her own air into his lungs, the song humming on in her chest, while her mouth . . .

Luce stopped where she was. Her stomach was tight and cold with disbelief. Catarina and the black-haired man were locked in a frenzy of slow kisses, and his hands slid across her pale skin. She was breathing into him to keep him alive for just a little longer. Luce's own lungs were beginning to ache. How much longer could Catarina keep on this way without drowning herself?

How could she do this at all, after everything she'd told Luce? She'd said it would be better to die than to break the timahk! She'd said that if even one mermaid broke it, the whole tribe would be dishonored.

Luce pushed her way back to the surface, deliberately coming up at a distance from the rest of the tribe. Her whole body was trembling, and she knew she wouldn't be able to hide her emotion from anyone who saw her face. She eddied on the surface, unsure what she should do. The sunlight was gone, and the day was dimming.

After a minute Catarina's flame-colored head splashed up twenty yards away, and Luce heard her gasping as she finally breathed in again. She had her back to Luce, and the man she'd held was nowhere to be seen.

7

Forgiveness

Luce watched Catarina swim over to the other mermaids. Their heads were only visible as dots flocking up and down on the darkening sea. She saw them draw close together and confer, then turn to scan the waves. If she didn't go back soon they'd come to search for her.

Luce didn't know how she could stand to talk to anyone, with her stomach so knotted and sick and her nerves prickling with dread. But if they had to look for her they'd get worried and upset, and they'd ask more questions. And Catarina might start to suspect that Luce had witnessed her closed in the arms of a human male.

Luce forced herself to swim back to the group. She pulled her reluctant mouth into a smile.

"Catarina! I was so worried when I couldn't find you!"
Catarina gave Luce one of her long assessing stares. Luce knew

Catarina was trying to read the look in her eyes, trying to guess what she'd seen.

"They said you went to look for me. Luce, that really wasn't necessary. I can take care of myself." Luce carefully brightened her smile.

"You've saved me twice already. I thought it was my turn. But I guess I swam down in the wrong place. You're really okay?" Catarina seemed to relax slightly, though there was still something cautious in her stare.

"Of course I'm okay." She gave Luce a smile that was a little too warm and affectionate. "I'm not the one who likes taking crazy chances. Swimming headlong into orcas!" Luce made herself laugh. "Honestly. For *you* to be worrying about *me* that way. It's ridiculous." She shook her head, and suddenly her warmth seemed genuine. "I bet you're tired after all that. And everyone's starving. Come on!" There was the flick and glint of long tails as the mermaids dove, and Luce went with them.

Sick as she felt, Luce already knew she would never betray Catarina's secret. Maybe Catarina had destroyed the tribe's honor by kissing that young man, but Luce would never be able to live with herself if Catarina was banished. She'd never stop thinking of her friend alone and adrift in a desolate sea. Even the idea of such abject loneliness made Luce want to cry. If she ever had to face expulsion, Luce thought, she might just feed herself to the orcas.

By the time they were all on the beach cracking mussels Luce gave up trying to act cheerful. She let herself stare out at the deep blue clouds surging across the sky, the crimson rim of sunset. She could just make out the island where so many young men and women had died that day, a dim pinnacle breaking the red streaks of the clouds. There was the noise of chopped air now as helicopters began to converge on the spot; men would climb out onto the rocks, divers would search the wreckage, all unable to understand why none of the crew had made it to shore. Luce had never even spoken to the sailor with the dark curly hair, but somehow she missed him terribly. Catarina was quiet, too, with a look on her face that contained a mixture of drowsy satisfaction and hungry sadness; Luce wondered if she was dreaming of the man she'd kissed, and killed.

Luce couldn't just mourn for the curly-haired sailor in peace, though. She was surrounded by the other mermaids, who seemed tired but still giddy. Their chatter kept interrupting Luce's thoughts, and she realized they were talking about her.

"Did you *hear* that out there?" Samantha asked behind her. "I mean, how different Luce's singing is? It's like, 'Come here, little human; you're not so evil after all! No, really! I promise you're not evil!' You know what I mean?" Samantha's laugh sent a chill up Luce's back. "What a *joke*! But they fall for it like crazy . . ."

Luce felt a fierce impulse to spin around and smack Samantha as hard as she could. She wanted to scream at her, lunge for her throat. Instead she stared down through the water at the silver shimmer of her own long tail.

Catarina seemed to stir from her reverie. "Luce's song promises *forgiveness*," she agreed slowly. "Or—what's the word? Reconciliation. It's interesting. It never would have occurred to me to try to sing that way, but I have to admit it's effective. *I* certainly feel it when I hear her." Luce hadn't entirely grasped what it was that Catarina's song promised until she'd seen the ecstatic way the black-haired boy had kissed her, but now it seemed clear enough.

"Effective!" Samantha giggled. "You were way on the other side, Cat. You didn't see how berserk she made them. Luce had like twenty humans throwing themselves overboard before the ship even crashed! Like they were just dying to get to her!" Luce's hands were trembling, and her stomach seemed to be full of cold stones. Samantha laughed again. "It's amazing how stupid humans are! Believing that a mermaid could *forgive* them . . ."

But I do forgive them, Luce thought. I meant everything I sang. I forgive them no matter what they've done, and I wish they could forgive me. She remembered the choice she'd made out in the sea that day, to reject the enchanted numbness that had tried to steal into her heart. Samantha had obviously chosen differently. Of course it would be much easier that way.

"I thought Luce's singing was beautiful," Miriam said softly. "It made me remember all kinds of things . . ." Miriam hesitated, and Luce wondered if the things she'd remembered were from her human life. But what mermaid would admit to that? "Things from a long time ago," Miriam finally said, and from something lost and wistful in her voice Luce knew she'd guessed right.

"Who cares if it's beautiful?" It was Samantha's cold, calm, sneering voice again. "What matters is that it works! We never could have taken that ship down before we had Luce with us, right? It was just too big. We wouldn't even have tried!"

Luce turned around in surprise. "Catarina said you didn't need me, though! She said the rest of you would sink the ship whether I came with you or not!" She tried to meet Catarina's eyes, but the red-gold head swung away from her.

"Oh, no way!" Samantha trilled. "Cat, you seriously told her that? Why would you say that? You really don't want Luce to realize how good she is, do you?" Catarina wouldn't look at them. Her moon gray eyes were dreamily fixed on the horizon, but Luce knew she was only pretending not to hear . . .

Then Luce understood. Catarina had known all along that Luce wouldn't be able to resist the urge to sing, not once she was surrounded by the voices of the other mermaids and their wild, rising song called to hers. Catarina had deliberately tricked Luce into swimming out with her because she'd known she needed Luce's help. If only Luce had insisted on staying home in the cave, Catarina would have had to let the Coast Guard boat go on its way unmolested.

And maybe Catarina had reasons of her own for wanting to sink that particular ship so badly. Luce remembered the eager swishing of Catarina's tail when she'd come to the cave, the barely suppressed hunger in her voice. She'd seen the crew of beautiful young men.

"Luce? Are you sick?" Miriam touched her shoulder with her soft, icy hand. "You must be exhausted. You worked so hard today, and you're not used to it . . ." There was real sweetness in Miriam's voice, but Luce couldn't look at her. Would she really get *used* to murdering strangers? Luce's body doubled over as if she were about to vomit, and her trembling came in violent waves. "Cat! I think Luce is sick. Oh, she really wasn't strong enough yet to come out with us today! We should have let her rest for longer . . ."

"I'm okay," Luce whispered. "I just want to be alone for a while."

That got Catarina's attention. "Alone?" she asked, and her steely voice stroked Luce's skin. "Luce, are you upset about something? Because if you are we should talk about it." Her eyes flared at Luce, daring her to say it.

You lied to me, you tricked me into helping you kill all those people, and maybe you're the one who murdered—

Luce closed her eyes, trying to crush the thought before it went too far. Then she looked up into Catarina's searching moon gray stare.

"Don't you just feel like being alone sometimes, Cat?" Luce was amazed to hear how sharp and clear her voice had suddenly become. "It doesn't mean I'm upset. It just means I'm not in the mood—for a lot of talk." Samantha let out a short bark of laughter, but Luce didn't smile.

"There are a few little caves up the coast," Miriam offered; Luce thought maybe she wanted to get away, too. "Luce? Do you want me to show you? They're all kind of cramped, but one of them isn't too bad." Catarina was glaring, but Miriam made a point of ignoring her. "Come on. It's not too far . . ."

They drifted alongside the cliffs together, keeping their heads out of the water. One cave was open at the level of the sea, and the larval mermaids were already sleeping there, heaped up with their small arms wrapped around each other's waists. Luce and Miriam kept swimming on for another mile or so, then Miriam glanced back at her and dove. The entrance of the cave was so narrow that they couldn't even swim. Instead they had to wriggle through, pushing with their tails and using their hands to maneuver between the crags. The cave inside was as narrow as a tent, but it was deep and its beach was smooth, with round, small quartz pebbles. The roof was tall and fissured, opening onto a rag of dark blue sky.

Miriam twisted her body until she was halfway lying on the beach and stared up. There was just enough space for the two of them to lie comfortably side by side, and now that Miriam had brought Luce here she didn't seem to be in any hurry to leave. Her midnight-colored tail barely showed through the dark water, but Luce's gleamed with silver lights. "Do you mind if I stay here for a little bit?" Miriam finally asked. "It's just— everyone else gets so excited when we sink a ship. And some-times I feel like—like I don't want to *make* myself be happy about it. Does that sound crazy?" Luce sat up and looked down into Miriam's eyes. Their color was so deep and inky that it was impossible to guess what she was feeling.

"You don't need to act happy around me," Luce finally said. She wasn't sure if it was safe to tell Miriam how sad *she* felt about everything that had happened that day. She kept remem-bering the warm touch of dark curly hair, the glow in the young sailor's brown eyes. *More and truer love* . . . Luce knew she had the power now to force any human being who came within earshot to love her. But they'd only love her as long as she kept them enchanted, only as long as they were speeding toward death.

"I thought—maybe since you're metaskaza, or you just were, anyway—maybe you'd understand better than the others. Luce, I don't completely hate humans. Or at least I don't hate them enough. I mean, I understand why Catarina does, and I know she's right, but sometimes I can't help remembering . . ." It occurred to Luce that this might be another trick. Maybe Catarina had sent Miriam to find out how she really felt. "When I heard how you sang I thought maybe you remembered some good things about being human, too."

Luce lay back down on the pebbles and thought about this. She didn't want to say too much, but if Miriam was telling the truth about how she felt then Luce didn't want her to feel all alone either.

"I loved some of them," Luce finally said. "Before I changed, I mean. So I just— I don't totally care if humans are as evil as Catarina thinks or not." Luce stopped, feeling like she'd already admitted too much. From the corner of her eye she could see Miriam's dark shimmer swarming into those pictures that weren't quite pictures. Miriam *had* loved her mother, Luce realized, but then her mother ran away one night with a strange man and never came back. Miriam had waited alone for days in an empty house, waited until the food ran out, and then she'd swallowed the contents of a brown glass bottle from her mother's medicine cabinet, trying to die, and curled up in the bathtub.

"It's worse when you love them," Miriam whispered. "I think at first I wanted to kill all of them. Everyone. Because if there were no people left alive then I'd never have to love one of them again." She wouldn't look at Luce; her face was twisting. "But once I realized that was impossible . . . What's the point of killing any of them, Luce, when there are always so many left? And I've been in the water for so long now, and it's always the same. They listen to us, and they die, and then soon enough there's another boat . . ." Miriam sounded almost like she was talking to herself, and then Luce saw the gleam of a single tear.

Luce was surprised; it seemed like such a strange, pitiful reason for drowning people. But were her own reasons any better?

Were Catarina's?

Miriam sat up and gave Luce a sad smile. "I'm really glad

you're living with us now, Luce. I mean, I know you weren't singing for me today. It was all for those humans. But hearing you made me feel better, too. I don't feel quite as cold inside." Miriam looked away, as if saying it made her feel shy.

So, her fierce, powerful voice must not be completely evil, Luce thought. If it could comfort Miriam, even after all the long years she'd spent out in the sea, then maybe it would be okay for Luce to sing sometimes. Maybe, she thought, just maybe, she could even find a way to use her singing for good . . .

Miriam leaned in suddenly and kissed Luce on the cheek. Then she ducked down and squirmed out through the cave's narrow entrance. Luce stared up at the sky. Suddenly she wasn't sure she wanted to be alone after all. The world was so enormous, yawning like a hungry mouth. She could forget all that hunger and loneliness when her tribe surrounded her, their long tails swaying next to hers and their faces dreaming together on the beach.

In the end it was pride that kept Luce where she was. She didn't want Catarina to think she could get away with lying like that so easily.

* * *

That night Luce dreamed of her father. She was sitting on the bed in that cheap motel room outside Minneapolis, snow spinning in the window, while the sequin-covered woman dipped and leaped across the TV screen. Her father sat next to her, gazing into her eyes, a worried expression on his face.

Luce's voice poured out of her: too big for a small human girl, too big for the narrow mustard-colored room. She couldn't make her song stop, and she saw that her father wasn't enchanted by it in the way all the other humans had been. He winced, and Luce thought her voice was hurting him. It floated up into that high, trembling note and coiled just under the ceiling.

"You know you don't have to do this for me, Lucette," her father said. "You've made your point. You can stop now, all right?"

I never judged you, Luce wanted to say. *No matter what you did.* But her mouth was full of that pulsing, savage song; it took hold of her throat, her chest, and since she couldn't make the music stop she couldn't *say* anything. The piercing note broke and tumbled down an endless staircase.

"It's not that I'm judging you, baby doll," her father said as if he'd read her mind. His eyes were glazing from pain as Luce's song clashed like metal snakes inside his head, but he was doing his best not to let her see how terribly she was hurting him. "How could I? I just hate to think that you're doing things you might be sorry about later. And especially if you're doing them because of me somehow. You don't have to is all I'm saying. You can stop this right now."

But Luce couldn't stop. Her voice fell and fractured into aching chords and then her father couldn't stand it anymore. He grabbed his head, trying desperately to make the pain stop. And Luce saw that it wasn't snow in the window anymore, but tall lead-colored waves. The ocean knocked on the glass, asking to be let in . . .

No, Luce tried to tell the waves. *You can't come in. He'll drown!* But the song still controlled her voice, and she couldn't make her voice say the words. The waves crested and slammed at the window, and Luce saw the glass starting to bow from their weight.

The glass crunched and screamed with a sound like tearing metal, and Luce was lost in the dark sea. She looked around for her father, but she couldn't find him anywhere.

The scream of the breaking glass kept going, and then Luce realized that the scream was hers. She was flailing from side to side in the narrow cave, thrashing so hard that her body had rolled up out of the water and the top of her tail was exposed to the cold night air. It was the pain in her drying tail that had made her wake up. She was out of the water all the way to where her knees used to be, and for a second Luce just stayed where she was, feeling the burning claw through her.

It would be so easy to die, she thought. All she'd need to do would be to pull herself a little farther up the beach. So easy but also so terrible. She used her hands to slide herself back down into the sea, gasping as the pain gradually subsided.

If she could completely forget her human life, not miss any of it anymore, then being a mermaid would be so wonderful. She could be free and wild and beautiful forever; she could welcome the cold into her heart and not care how many people she killed. It would just be a game to her, the way it was for Samantha. A joke. She could laugh at the people she drowned for believing the forgiveness in her song was real, laugh at them for loving her. A trace of her father's warm voice still thrummed in her mind, a residue left over from her dream.

Luce decided then that she'd rather die. She would never let herself turn as cold as Samantha seemed to be, not even if she'd be happier that way, not even if what Miriam had said was right. "It's worse when you love them," Luce repeated to her-self, and the caramel-skinned boy smiled in her mind, his hair rippling in the green, shining water. Humans were grotesque a lot of the time, but—just once in a while—there was something about them that was marvelous, too. A sustained note of something that was greater and sweeter than any emotion . . .

There had to be some way she could stay a mermaid but still keep that note alive in her own song.

8

Quick Animals

Fifty miles inland, in a town called Henton, a woman paced the nighttime hallways of an ugly, flashy, oversized house. It had once been the mansion of a man who'd made a lot of money in the canning business, then he'd died and left his house to the county. They'd converted it into a home for orphaned and abandoned girls, the ones who were already too old when their parents died, so that nobody wanted to adopt them. The house was bigger than they really needed. Fourteen girls lived there, along with Mrs. Beebee Merkle, but the emptiness of the rooms made everyone nervous and all the girls slept in the three bedrooms that made up the house's east wing. Mrs. Merkle had her own apartment upstairs, but at night she had trouble sleeping and more trouble keeping still. She'd lie awake in a pile of knotted, sweaty sheets, convinced that animals she couldn't see were nipping at her feet with tiny fangs like crescent moons. She'd kick and throw off the covers, but the slithering animals were always too fast for her to catch sight of them, and when she couldn't stand the biting anymore she'd slide her feet into her grimy pink slippers with holes in the toes and pace through the unused rooms, turning on every light that still had a working bulb and rapping anxiously at the huge, dusty sofas and gutted home entertainment centers.

On nights when it got especially bad, she'd get out a hammer and saw and start ripping into the plaster. The animals that plagued her had to make their nest somewhere, after all. Sometimes she could just catch glimpses of them from the corners of her eyes: slippery, malignant weasel-like creatures with girlish heads, and Mrs. Merkle thought, a kind of dark shimmering around them.

This was a *very* bad night.

Beebee Merkle had begun tearing out a wall in what had once been a large formal dining room, making such a ruckus that all fourteen of her charges were wide awake. The twins, Jenna and Dana, who were the oldest, gathered all the younger girls together in their room. Girls in donated T-shirts and faded pajama bottoms sat huddled together on the floor, dirty comforters wrapped around their shoulders. Tufts of pale polyester filling leaked through the holes in the comforters, so that the girls seemed to have bits of cloud sticking to them. Some of the smaller girls were whimpering. Jenna tended to get impatient when the young ones cried, but Dana was cuddling them and doing her best to distract them with a story about a witch who kept turning kids into cats and rabbits because she liked watching them eat each other until the cats and rabbits wised up and formed a strategic alliance against the witch. Dana had just reached the part where the first brave rabbit accepted the cats' offer to join forces.

A drawn-out, musical crash shook the house, and Dana stopped her story and pulled the small girls closer. The girls all looked around at each other, realizing together that Beebee must have somehow managed to rip the huge brass and crystal chandelier out of the dining room ceiling. The crash turned into a relatively subdued tinkling as broken crystals slipped off the wide mahogany table and rained onto the floor.

"How much longer are we supposed to pretend that she's not completely out of her mind!" Jenna exclaimed in exasperation. "You sit there telling your stupid stories, but if we don't do something . . ." Dana hit her with a pillow to stop her from finishing the sentence, but not before nine-year-old Rachel, who was smart but constantly terrified, figured out what Jenna meant and started howling. Dana's dark brown hand stroked Rachel's soft pink cheek. Almost everyone in that part of Alaska was either very white-skinned or else Native American, and Jenna and Dana stood out: their mother had emigrated from India and their father was African American. They had thick ebony braids, huge dark eyes, and mouths like sad red flowers.

"What do you think she can do?" Dana said as strongly as she could. "We have her seriously outnumbered. Even if she tried something, we could throw a blanket over her head and tie her up. Okay, Rachel?" Rachel wouldn't stop crying, though. She knew as well as the others did that Beebee Merkle kept three guns in a locked drawer. Beebee liked to talk about them at dinner; sometimes she'd get hung up on a single sentence and keep repeating it over and over while the girls struggled to act normal and keep on swallowing their macaroni and cheese. "So the best thing we can do is stay together. See, Rachel, if we hear her coming Jenna and I will stand flat on either side of the door. You all throw the blanket, and we'll pull it down and get her splat on the floor, okay? So right now your job is to stay brave and be ready to help. Just like that little rabbit." Rachel tried to smile.

*　*　*

The chandelier ripped loose when Beebee jumped up from the table and got a choke hold around the brass flange at the top where the wires snaked into the ceiling. She'd just seen one of those half-weasel animals winding its way up until it vanished into the globby plaster above, and since that was clearly impossible Beebee decided it must still be hiding up on the flange where she couldn't see it. But she wasn't prepared for what happened next. At first the chandelier jolted and dropped a foot lower, still dangling from a few spark-spitting wires, and then as Beebee scrambled off the table the whole thing came smashing down. That didn't bother Beebee nearly as much as what came gushing out of the ripped mouth that had suddenly appeared in the middle of the ceiling, though. Hundred of lithe, horrible animals dribbled from the hole and then licked out across the ceiling and walls like black flames. The animals were eerily transLucent; Beebee could see the silver bamboo pattern of the wallpaper right through them, and the dark shimmering they emitted warped everything she saw like waves of intense heat.

By the time she'd recovered from the shock enough to pull herself up off the floor and straighten her bathrobe, the animals had all flickered out through the dining room door. Beebee followed them cautiously. There were far more of them than she'd ever imagined, and if she didn't use all the cunning she was capable of, they'd simply turn and devour her.

The weasels slicked soundlessly over the walls and floor of the long hallway. Occasionally one would glance back at Beebee and dab its long tongue in her direction, tasting the air, while it gazed at her with unpleasantly human eyes. It was hard to see the weasel-creatures very well, but their eyes were always glittering and definite and far too big for their pointed faces. Beebee couldn't help thinking that the weasels were wearing too much eye shadow; their eyelids gave off flashes of garish color, turquoise and lilac and even orange, contrasting disagreeably with their smoke-tinted fur.

The weasels sped up as they glided around a corner to the right; Beebee got the impression that they were trying to throw her off their track. That meant they must be afraid of her, which made Beebee grin to herself. Maybe she was finally going to uncover their secret lair. Then she'd be able to eradicate them, once and for all. She was just in time to see them fanning out in a dark corona around the kitchen door; they were so oily and tricky that they seeped right through the cracks and vanished.

Beebee padded quietly up to the kitchen door and eased it open. The hanging lamp was already shining; she'd left it on during an earlier stage of her explorations.

It looked empty, though Beebee had to admit to herself that the huge lime green and tan roses on the wallpaper might provide decent camouflage. Were they all hiding? Was this some kind of ambush? Beebee could still outsmart them, though. She murmured something out loud about how careless the girls were, always leaving the lights on, then flicked down the switch and backed away, shutting the door behind her. She stomped off loudly and then doubled softly back, hiding in a linen closet with the door left slightly ajar, and waited.

A single dim shape oozed out through the crack at the top of the door and cocked its little head from side to side, reconnoitering. Then it sucked back into the kitchen, wiggling like the tail end of slurped spaghetti, and to her astonishment Beebee could hear it jabbering softly to its companions. She'd never heard the weasels speak before.

They had the voices of little girls.

* * *

"She's quieting down," Dana said. "I bet she'll knock off and go to sleep soon. You guys should settle down and try to sleep, too, okay?" The room had two big double beds, enough room for eight of them if they squeezed, and they made nests out of heaped comforters for the smallest girls. Only Jenna couldn't relax. She stayed standing with her ear to the door, listening intently.

"She's still doing something," Jenna said after a while. "She's just trying to be sneakier, but I can still hear her shuffling around out there. You know what? Nobody's going to sleep yet. Not until she does."

"Jen, you're so paranoid!" Dana was exhausted herself; she didn't like hearing that she was expected to keep a bunch of crabby, frightened little girls awake for who knew how much longer. It was getting close to dawn. "Anyway, how's anyone going to know if she's asleep? She could just, whatever, stay up lurking in the kitchen."

"There's something wrong!" Jenna usually stayed fairly calm, so her anxiety sent waves of fear through the younger girls. Rachel had started crying again, along with Violet and Becka. "You are not going to tell me I'm paranoid when that psycho is out there plotting something. Don't you see, Dana? It's worse now that she's being quiet! When she's loud at least we know what she's doing . . ."

"You're scaring everyone for nothing." Dana was getting snappish; she was so tired her head felt like it might roll off. "Look, Jen, I'll go out scouting, okay? I'll find out what she's up to and report back. Then maybe you'll chill enough that we can get some rest."

Rachel started sobbing even louder at the idea of Dana going out there alone, and the others were upset, too. What if Beebee shot her? She was definitely crazy enough, and she would get away with it, too. She could just say she thought Dana was a burglar.

Hilary was eleven; she was homely and sulky, with stringy brown hair and a blob-shaped nose. She was wearing a T-shirt with a cartoon of a doe-eyed, thick-lashed beauty on the front, which only had the unfortunate effect of emphasizing how drab she was. Hilary tended to keep to herself and she hadn't said anything all night, so they were surprised when she looked up. "I'll go. Dana needs to stay here. In case her and Jenna have to do that blanket thing."

No one felt like arguing anymore, and after a moment of hesitation Hilary skimmed out of the room. She moved so softly that they couldn't hear her footsteps at all.

* * *

Beebee waited, keeping perfectly silent, until the last of the weasels slithered out of the kitchen. They crawled along the ceiling in a long, dark trail, and after a moment Beebee sidled out of her closet, staying as far back as she could without losing sight of them. Her heart was pounding with triumph. The weasels thought they'd lost her, and they were heading back to their lair. Beebee was minutes away from learning their secret hiding place. She was grinning so wide her cheeks hurt.

The weasels poured down another hallway and turned a corner. They were heading to the east wing, where the girls all slept.

Beebee's eyes went wide with sudden understanding.

She told herself to stay steady, stay crafty. She should make completely sure, of course, before she took any extreme measures.

It was incredible. There were hundreds of those weasel creatures living in the house. Maybe thousands. Each one of the girls must be made out of dozens of them! Cautiously Beebee tipped her head around the corner, just in time to see the last of the weasels melting through the cracks around the girls' bedrooms. Beebee waited another minute, trembling with excitement. Then the door opened again, and ugly little Hilary Deckard came sneaking out like a thief.

Beebee jerked her head back, but not before she'd seen something that made her gasp. Hilary had a kind of dark shimmering around her, a secretive sparkling. It looked exactly like the shimmer around the weasels.

Beebee was disgusted but not exactly surprised. She'd always known there was something very wrong with the girls she looked after, and now—well, now she knew what it was. They couldn't keep Beebee Merkle fooled forever! She tiptoed back the way she came, then took a sudden turn and ducked out through the front door. She was almost positive Hilary hadn't seen her.

Still, just in case, she thought she'd better work fast. Beebee ran to the garage. She'd need rags, gasoline. Enough to make sure that nothing would get out of the east wing alive.

She'd show them. Those awful slippery vermin would never torture her again. She'd make sure of *that*.

*   *   *

"I couldn't find her *anywhere*," Hilary said. Hilary was usually bland and distant, so they were all surprised to see her crying with frustration. "Jenna, I really tried, but it's like she's not even in the house anymore. What is she doing?"

"It's okay," Dana told her gently. "It was really brave of you to go." It didn't help, though. Hilary couldn't stop sobbing.

"I'm going to kill her myself!" Hilary said. She sounded hysterical. "I'm going to get one of her guns and put a bullet right through her brain! Oh, I'm so tired of her scaring everyone. We're always so frightened, and if she was dead we wouldn't have to be! Jenna's right, she's doing something horrible. I know she's doing something, right now!"

None of this helped the younger girls calm down. Dana was doing her best to soothe Hilary before everyone panicked, but Hilary was halfway out of her mind.

"Does anybody smell something weird?" Rachel asked timidly.

Hilary jumped up suddenly. Her eyes were wild and she was screaming at the top of her lungs. "We need to get out of here! We all need to get out now! She's trying to murder us!"

Jenna's gaze was fixed on the window, and suddenly everyone turned to see why she was staring. The blind was drawn, but it was glowing. It shone with a soft, yellowish, flickering light . . . The scream spread, jumping like flames from Hilary's throat to the throats of the other girls.

"Shut up!" Jenna yelled. "Shut up and stay calm! I'm going to get us out of here." Her face was so determined and fierce that most of the girls got quieter. "Everyone crawl on the floor so you don't breathe the smoke. I'll find a way out." They could all feel the heat throbbing through the bedroom wall now, and the glow in the window was as bright as molten iron. Dana had also jumped into action, filing the girls out into the hall on all fours, and Jenna thought of something. All the windows on the ground floor had iron bars over them, except for the row of high windows up over the sinks in the bathroom. If they stood on the sinks they might be able to pull themselves through before the flames outside became impassably tall. Maybe they'd get burned, throwing themselves across, but at least they'd live.

"To the bathroom!" Jenna shouted. "And—wait—Hilary, help me carry this dresser. We can use it to climb out." They could hear the fire roaring on all sides, and the heat came at them like a tide. Hilary and Jenna carried the tall dresser ahead of the line of crawling girls and slammed it against the wall under the windows. They were starting to cough, and their eyes were stinging. A haze of smoke blurred their vision. Jenna scrambled on top of the dresser, reaching to wrench the window open, while a crowd of desperate girls stared up at her from the tile floor.

Jenna's hand seized the latch, and she shrieked and pulled away. The metal was burning hot. For a second she was stunned from the pain, but then she jerked her T-shirt off over her head and wrapped it around her hand.

There was a tremendous crackling sound, the whoosh of a violent wind, the noise of something falling. Jenna was fighting to open the window, but it wouldn't move, and her face was tight with pain. She was higher than everyone else, right in the thickest smoke, and she started choking so hard she could barely hold on to the top of the dresser. There was a sound like an explosion, and the row of windows turned brilliant orange. Jenna gave a gasp and fell.

The girls were too shocked to cry. They looked around at each other, and at the storm of flames lashing at the windows. Fire licked up under the bathroom door. Dana pulled Jenna over to her and gazed down into her twin's blurry eyes. Maybe it was an effect of the overwhelming heat, but all of them began to see the clouds of dark shimmering that hung around each other's faces.

"Look at Hilary!" Rachel suddenly gasped. They all saw it. Hilary was wavering, shuddering, barely a girl anymore. And then Dana felt her own body shift, and knew that if she just let go of herself she would dissolve into a pool of brilliant liquid. She could tell from the amazed looks on her friends' faces that they were feeling the same thing. Hilary was just a puddle now, as bright as melted diamonds.

Dana suddenly knew what they had to do. She grabbed at the pool that was Hilary and found she could drag it along with her. It bounced and gleamed, and in the center of it Hilary's brown eyes winked like jewels. Hilary's clothes stayed behind on the floor, and Dana noticed that they were still dry. "The drains!" Dana said, and her voice was strong and almost happy. "Everyone in the showers! And whatever you do, don't fight it."

Two of the younger girls got Jenna's wrists and pulled her across the tiles. They were just in time, because their legs were staring to melt. Each girl became her own pool of living, shimmering liquid. The last thing to melt was their eyes, so they could watch each other shining and wobbling on the floor, then sliding one by one into the dark holes of the drains before the world vanished into a deep violet darkness. Still, even in the darkness, they were together, racing into something new and unimaginable. The darkness was absolute and fast-moving and silky, and it lasted for a very long time.

9

For Cigarettes

"Catarina said to get you." Kayley sounded embarrassed. Bright blue morning glowed through the fissure in the roof of the small cave where Luce had slept the night before. "There's something freaky going on— I mean, Catarina wants you to help."

"With another boat?" Luce didn't manage to keep the sarcasm out of her voice, and Kayley gave her a strange look. She almost seemed frightened, Luce thought.

"It's not that," Kayley said. She was acting like she didn't know how to explain. "We wouldn't ever do two boats that close together, anyway. It's something way weirder than that. I mean have you ever heard of more than one metaskaza showing up at a time?" Of course Luce was new and there were lots of things she hadn't heard of yet, but Kayley was so agitated that she'd forgotten that. "So I mean, how nuts is it that there are *fourteen* of them? They're all holding on to each other out in the middle of the sea, like just bobbing around, and they won't come back to the cave, and they're so totally freaked out that they'll barely even talk. They just stare at us like *we're* the crazy ones." Kayley gave a nervous laugh, and in spite of herself Luce began to picture the cluster of frightened new mermaids drifting around on the waves. "Catarina thought, since you were just metaskaza, too, maybe you could get them to listen? They aren't even really swimming, and the orcas could get them."

Luce was still angry at Catarina, but she realized that this was more important. "Where are they?"

Kayley looked relieved. "Sort of by the beach where we eat. But they're like half a mile from shore, and they're just drifting farther out. Luce, you've got to come *now*."

As they swam out, Luce was thinking it over. The new mermaids couldn't have come from very far away. For all she knew, some of them might be girls she'd gone to school with in Pittley. She didn't much like the idea of meeting anyone she'd known in her human life again; it would be so painful to be reminded of that time. On the other hand, she couldn't just leave them floating around on the sea.

When they found them they'd drifted out past the island where the Coast Guard boat had sunk, and the cliffs were just a gray scrawl against the horizon. The girls were holding one another so tightly that their bodies rose and fell in a kind of raft on top of the waves, and Luce couldn't see the girls in the middle at all. She didn't recognize any of the ones near the edge, though, so she was surprised to feel a pang of some dark emotion she couldn't identify at first. Then she realized what it was:

envy. These girls were frantic, bewildered, but they seemed to trust one another so completely; Luce wished desperately that she could trust Catarina that much. It was like they were all sisters. At least two of them really were sisters: there was a pair of dark-skinned twins with full, round mouths who, Luce thought, were every bit as beautiful as Catarina, though one of them looked angry and maybe a little mean. Kayley hung back, and the dark girl watched with obvious hostility as Luce swam over to her. Her sister looked nicer, but she was busy comforting a smaller girl, a weak-looking blonde.

"Hey," Luce said to the angry dark girl. She had such a strong look in her eyes that Luce was sure she was the leader. "Are you from one of the towns near here?" The girl seemed surprised, which Luce had expected. Catarina wouldn't have thought of asking them anything about their human lives, after all.

"Henton," the girl snapped warily. Luce had heard of it. It was inland and bigger than Pittley. Sometimes people from Pittley drove there to go shopping.

"I was living in Pittley," Luce told her, trying to stay casual. She couldn't let herself feel shy or awkward, not when so much was at stake. "I bet there's more to do in Henton." Then she couldn't suppress her curiosity: how had so many girls changed all at once? By looking out of the corner of her eyes, she could just catch glimpses of a fire, but the pictures merged and blurred together as she looked from one girl to the next. "Were all of you living together?" The girl seemed to take it as an insult.

"We were all in a home," the girl snapped, obviously expecting Luce to say something mean about it. "For orphans. We don't have parents."

"I don't either," Luce told her. The girl didn't soften much. "But now I'm living with some other girls. None of us have families anymore. I guess it's like a home. Except we don't have any grownups with us, so nobody tells us what to do . . ." Except Catarina, of course, but Luce decided to leave that out. The dark girl looked like she'd be attracted by the idea of not being bossed around by anyone. She clearly preferred to be in charge.

"In a house?" the girl asked, confused. Luce understood. It was so unbelievable to find yourself a mermaid that it could take a while to accept the truth, even when your tail was right there. And unless you really looked, the tails were hidden by the daylight flashing off the water's surface.

"It's a cave," Luce admitted. "But the thing is, it's safe. And it's not safe staying out here." The girl glowered at her. She'd already guessed where this was leading. Luce plunged ahead anyway. "You should come back with me. We'll help you find food, and you can all get some sleep." They looked tired, Luce thought, and some of the younger ones were whimpering. They were almost all looking at Luce now, even the ones in the middle squirming to see her, but they seemed content to let their leader do the talking, "Kayley still watched from a distance, her dark head disappearing sometimes behind the cresting waves."

The girl shook her head vehemently.

"That redheaded nutcase was saying the same thing. But we have a plan. We can float really well if we all stay together like this, so we're going to wait for a boat to come. They'll rescue us. We just have to keep calm."

Luce thought of telling the girl that they could easily swim to shore on their own in a few minutes if they felt like it, but she decided the girl wasn't ready to hear it. And it seemed like a bad idea to try explaining that being "rescued" would just kill all of them. She should keep things simple for now. "I'm Luce," she said. It seemed important to show she knew the girl was in charge, so she added, "Would you introduce me to your friends?"

The girl hesitated. "I think you should leave us alone. I already told your crazy redhead friend, we don't need any help." Then she said something that sent another pang of longing through Luce: "We know how to take care of each other really well."

"You're lucky," Luce said sincerely. There was a catch in her voice that attracted the nicer twin's attention, and she gave Luce a long look, then held out her hand.

"I'm Dana," she said. Luce smiled at her and swam over. "What, are you on some kind of crazy swim team or something?" Dana asked. "I noticed that about your friend, too, that she swims incredibly fast." They *really* hadn't accepted the truth, Luce realized. They didn't want to understand what was happening at all. Even if they saw their own tails, or Luce's, they'd probably convince themselves it was just a trick of the light. Luce grinned at Dana, trying to be playful.

"I bet you can beat me," Luce said. "Want to race?" Dana gave her sister a nervous look. The other twin was pursing her lips in disapproval.

"I've always *sucked* at sports," Dana said. "Everything except track. I can barely dog paddle." But she was smiling.

"I'll tell you a trick," Luce said. "It's *way* faster if you swim underwater. You lose a lot of power if you keep your head out." Dana looked skeptical, and Luce glanced around and spotted a silver log floating nearby. "How about just to that piece of drift-wood and back?"

Dana glanced at her sister, who was scowling but then obviously decided she didn't care.

"I will if you give me a head start," Dana announced. "I'm not whatever you are, training for the Olympics or something." Then, to Luce's delight, Dana took her advice and dove.

When she came up a few seconds later she was at least fifty yards past the hunk of driftwood, looking around in obvious astonishment, and a moment later Luce caught up to her.

"Isn't that fun?" Luce asked, but Dana seemed more upset than excited.

"How did I *do* that?" she asked, staring around. Her enormous dark eyes were wide with worry. "How did I *do* that? There's something really wrong with me . . ." Luce hated to upset her more, but she had to start explaining sometime.

"You're a lot stronger than you used to be," Luce said gently. "That is, you're a lot stronger as long as you stay in the water. But you can't go on land anymore, because the air will hurt you." Dana looked terrified. She was staring back and forth between Luce and her distant friends in disbelief, and the other girls had started shouting to them desperately. "Let's swim back. If you hold my hand I can make sure you don't just zoom past them. Okay?" Dana looked at her in alarm, but after a second she took Luce's hand, and the two of them dove together.

They came up right in front of the angry twin. She was beside herself with rage and anxiety.

"Don't you ever do that again!" she yelled at Dana. Then she turned to Luce. "You. Get away from my sister right now!"

Luce eddied back a little, keeping just out of reach in case the girl decided to punch her. "I can't just leave you here. You could get attacked by orcas."

"I told you to get away!" the girl shrieked. Then, because she couldn't hit Luce without letting go of her friends, she tried to kick her instead.

Her tail was gorgeous, caramel brown with green and golden iridescence shining on all its scales. It came at Luce like a whip, but Luce was too fast for her. She'd already swirled back out of the way.

"What *was* that?" Dana asked. "You saw that, right, Jenna? There was like a huge fish right there!" Jenna's eyes were round with shock.

"What did you do to me?" she asked Luce furiously. "And you did something messed up to Dana, too." Luce just waited out of reach, not saying anything. There was no point in trying to explain anymore. Jenna needed to accept it on her own. Then Jenna did something Luce hadn't expected. She glanced around, twisted her arms out of her friends' grasps, and dove. It looked like she was heading straight down, and Luce got ready to go after her if she didn't reappear soon.

Then something surged in the water just under Luce. It was the way orcas attacked their prey, coming at them from below and then erupting straight up out of the water with their jaws wide open around their victims. There was no time to escape. Luce's heart stopped, and she waited to feel the fangs closing in on her.

Jenna came up hard enough that she knocked Luce clear out of the water, and they landed in a confusion of thrashing tails and wild arms. Jenna was trying to get a lock on Luce's head, and Luce knew she couldn't let her. Kayley was still watching from a distance, and if Jenna managed to inflict any real damage then Kayley would certainly report Jenna for breaking the timahk. And if Jenna was banished the other new mermaids would definitely go with her. They'd all lose their chance at a safe haven. Luce was trying to twist her way free so she could dive out of Jenna's reach. Then Jenna's fist pulled back, and she hit Luce hard in the face. It sent Luce skidding sideways through the water. There was a pause while Jenna and Luce stared at each other. The ache throbbed in Luce's cheek.

"Jenna, stop!" It was Dana's voice calling.

"Make me!" Jenna yelled back, and in an instant Dana and Jenna were grappling with each other in a froth of bubbles while the younger girls cried out to them.

"It's like I keep telling you!" the fragile blond girl screamed. "We've all turned into mermaids! Jenna, why won't you listen to me?"

Jenna and Dana suddenly stopped fighting, and Luce hung back, ready to dive in case Jenna came at her again.

"That weird girl is a mermaid, too," the blonde kept on. Her voice was shrill and exasperated. "She has a tail! We all have tails! I'm not *crazy*!"

Dana stared from the blonde to Luce and back again, and Luce leaned back, stretching her body at full length on top of the waves so they couldn't just pretend her tail was a fish in the water with them.

"I'm not saying you're crazy, Rachel. It's just that everything we've been through is making you go temporarily out of your mind." Jenna said this as if she'd already been repeating it for hours. But it also sounded like she didn't completely believe it anymore. She was staring at Luce's long silvery tail, the broad curving fins at the bottom that moved as dexterously as fingers.

"Can't you see her?" Rachel screamed. She was starting to cry. "Her top half is a girl, and her bottom half is a fish! That's totally a mermaid!"

"It's true," Luce said. "You're not crazy at all, Rachel, I promise. And there are a lot more of us living in a cave near here. If Jenna will just stop freaking out I could take you back there."

Jenna let out her breath in a long hiss.

"Jen?" Dana said. "I think we should go with her. Everyone's exhausted. We can look for a boat again after we get some sleep. Okay?"

"How do you psychos think we're supposed to get there!" Jenna exclaimed. "Like half of us don't even know how to swim!"

Luce smiled. Finally they were starting to come to their senses.

"You can all swim incredibly well, actually," Luce told her. "Just try it."

* * *

Kayley had reached the cave ahead of them, and Catarina was already seething with anger by the time Luce broke through the smooth sheltered water there with fourteen new mermaids behind her.

"I'm not sure they're welcome here after all," Catarina snapped. "At least—which one was it who hit Luce, Kayley?" A sudden, queasy silence fell over the girls floating around Luce.

"I can't tell them apart," Kayley said. "One of the black girls. I think the one with more green in her tail? First she like tackled Luce, and then she just went and punched her in the face! Look, Cat. You can totally see it! Luce's cheek is really swollen. That *bitch* . . ."

"Whichever one is responsible, then," Catarina announced. "The rest can stay if they feel like it. But the one that broke the timahk has to leave." Her voice was rasping and utterly cold. Luce couldn't believe how hypocritical Catarina was being.

"No one hit me," Luce said. But there was still the bruise on her face; she had to explain it somehow. "Not on purpose, anyway. We were just playing and Jenna—she's not used to her tail yet, and she smacked me by accident."

Kayley was shocked. "You're *lying!* Luce, how can you lie about that? I was watching the whole time, and she hit you on purpose. Hard. And it wasn't with her tail either, so don't try to say that it was."

"You were pretty far away from us, Kayley," Luce told her softly. She felt bad about lying, but she couldn't stand the thought of the new mermaids lost out in the middle of the sea, exhausted and hungry. They would be such easy prey for orcas or sharks; they might drift on and on until they lost their strength and drowned, or they might try to leave the water. Wasn't every girl there lost enough as it was? "I know you *think* you saw her hit me, but it's really not true. You just couldn't see what was happening that well."

Catarina was looking from Luce to Kayley and back, trying to decide which of them to believe. Meanwhile the new mermaids were starting to recover from their shock.

"If we're not wanted here," Jenna said calmly, "we'll all leave right now."

"You *are* wanted here!" Luce shot back, and she was surprised by how fierce her voice sounded. Almost as if she thought she was the queen. She glanced at Catarina and tried to keep the intensity out of her tone. "You're wanted here; it's just that there's been a misunderstanding. There's a rule that no mermaid can ever hurt another," and here Luce desperately hoped that Jenna would swallow her pride and play along, "and Kayley's made a mistake. She thinks you broke the rule and hit me deliberately."

Jenna and Dana looked at each other, both of them understanding at once.

"Luce," Catarina hissed. She was using her quietest, deadliest voice. "Luce, do you realize how much is at stake here? If even one mermaid who's broken the timahk stays with us, the whole *tribe* is dishonored." Luce looked straight into Catarina's level gray eyes, wondering how Catarina could be so shameless when she'd broken the timahk herself, and loving her anyway. Even her hypocrisy had something ferocious in it; it was like a beautiful scar. "It's not something you can ever lie about. Not even to protect your best friend." They stared at each other. Catarina's eyes shone with their stony, moon-colored light. "You know I love you, Luce. You're like my little sister. But if it came to that—if I saw you break the timahk—I'd drive you out myself."

Luce knew it was true, but she didn't care. She'd lie a thousand times to protect Catarina if she had to, and she'd lie to protect Jenna, too.

"I do understand, Cat." Luce's voice was still passionate, but it was much more controlled now. "Jenna slapped me, but it was an accident. She didn't dishonor us."

The new mermaids were stunned, but at least no one contradicted her. Luce's heart was pounding. She'd done something tremendously reckless, but she also knew she'd had to.

* * *

When Luce had first changed it hadn't been easy, but she soon realized that adjusting was much harder for some people than it was for her. Some of the new mermaids were overjoyed, glad to be free finally of the paranoid woman who'd made their lives hell, and who almost killed all of them. But others were in shock, weeping uncontrollably and staring around at the cave in dismay. Luce hadn't missed human things like televisions and stuffed animals at all, but some of the new girls were horribly upset to realize that they'd be spending the rest of their lives in the cold sea, living on seaweed and mussels and sleeping on a pebble beach.

Without even talking about it Luce and Dana became a kind of team; Dana soothed the crying girls, stroking their hair and promising that everything would be okay, and Luce answered questions and explained how it had been for her since her own change. Luce could hardly believe that she'd been human less than a week ago. It felt like she'd been in the water for years.

Jenna was still sulky and glared over at Dana and Luce sometimes, but she seemed to understand that they'd been lucky to find shelter. Jenna was keeping quiet, and though Luce hadn't known her long, she already realized that it was out of character.

When no one was near them Dana leaned close and whispered in Luce's ear. "Thanks. You really stuck your neck out for us, right?"

"I had to," Luce whispered back. "I wasn't kidding; it's not safe out there. I couldn't take the chance that something bad would happen to all of you."

Dana smiled and twisted one of her long black braids. Her tail flicked up: caramel brown, like her sister's, except that the shimmer on her scales was ruby and copper colored rather than green-gold. "Jenna will come around," she said. "You'll see. It always takes her a while to like new people, but once she likes you she's a really great friend."

Their conversation was interrupted by a loud scream. One of the new mermaids, a twelve-year-old named Violet, who was especially upset at not being human anymore, had found a dark, out-of-the-way corner and then hauled herself onto the beach. Now her tail was drying, and she was writhing horribly from the pain, thrashing farther back from the water in her agony. Luce and Dana had to squeeze through a stunned circle of mermaids who were watching Violet shriek and flail at the stones. Luce saw the problem at once. Violet was far enough up the beach that it would be impossible to reach her without her rescuers leaving the water themselves. The pain would be too shocking for the new mermaids, but she and Catarina . . .

"Cat!" Luce called, looking wildly around for the blaze of fiery hair. She couldn't see her anywhere.

"She left the cave," Miriam said. "She said it was too noisy in here, with all these metaskazas. I think she's still kind of mad about you sticking up for them so hard. I don't know if she totally believed you." Luce looked at Violet, who was going into convulsions, her tail sending showers of pebbles into the air. They clearly didn't have much time.

"Miriam," Luce said, "I know it'll really hurt, but . . ." Miriam understood at once, and without another word she and Luce threw themselves up onto the beach.

It was terribly hard to move now that she was out of the water. The stones dug into her stomach as she elbowed her way awkwardly along. Her tail, which was so strong and graceful in the water, became a horrible burden as soon as she was on land. It dragged heavily behind her and wriggled uncontrollably, as if it had its own independent ideas about what Luce should do, and leaving the water absolutely wasn't one of them. Luce could see that Miriam was having trouble, too, and meanwhile Violet kept throwing herself around. Every time another convulsion took hold of Violet she seemed to end up a few inches farther back—and each of those inches was like miles to Luce. Cold wind blew across her back, across her exposed tail.

Then the pain started in earnest. Luce felt like she was swimming through fire but swimming so slowly that everything except the pain just kept getting farther away from her. Violet couldn't even scream anymore. Now she was panting loudly, her hands reaching out in wild spasms.

Luce gave a final desperate heave and grasped Violet by the wrist. She looked around for Miriam. Her friend wasn't there, and Luce's tail started to shake and beat at the stones. She couldn't stop it, and then she heard herself screaming.

"Luce!" The voice was blurry and strange. "Luce! You have to roll! Roll back to the water!"

All Luce could understand was the pain, though. Roll? The word didn't make any sense. She was lost in a sea of icy flames.

"Luce! Let go of her! You have to save yourself. Now roll!"

Somehow Luce understood this time, and she rolled down the beach with all her strength. But she didn't let go of Violet, jerking her arm as she went, and Violet's body lurched in a confused mess until she was lying halfway across Luce's middle.

"Just one more time! We've almost got you!" Luce let out a long, trembling gasp and threw her tail in a heavy arc toward the sea. The momentum flipped her body over and over, and then dozens of hands seized her and Violet and the salt water lapped across her burning scales.

Catarina grasped Luce's face hard in both hands and stared at her. Luce was still swaying from the pain, barely in control of her movements. But oh, the water, the cool, smooth living sea!

Then, to her amazement, Catarina burst into frantic tears and threw her arms around Luce's neck.

"Jen?" Luce barely heard Dana's voice. "Don't you dare give that girl a hard time ever again. Why wasn't it one of us out there saving Violet? She's our responsibility."

Miriam couldn't stop crying either.

"Luce?" Miriam whispered. "Luce, I'm so sorry; it just hurt so *much*. I tried but I couldn't keep going." Luce tried to smile at her, then gave up and buried her face in Catarina's hair.

"You know you're a lot more trouble than you're worth." Samantha was sniping at the new mermaids. "All I can say is you'd better have some awesome singers to make up for all the problems you're causing."

Dimly Luce was afraid there would be another fight. But nobody besides Samantha seemed to be in the mood for an argument.

* * *

By evening all the drama was over. None of the new mermaids felt like complaining now that they'd seen Violet come so close to dying, and even Kayley seemed to be getting past her anger at Luce. Some of the girls who had been most upset at changing were starting to discover just how much fun swimming was now, too. It was a beautiful spring evening; the air was fresh and soft, and the sky was a dome of pure gold. The water in front of the beach where they ate was full of laughing, splashing figures. Jenna was practicing her leaps. It was amazing how high she could go. And after a while two baby seals appeared and started playing with them, shyly at first but then coming closer. The younger metaskazas were overjoyed, stroking the seals' sleek fur and spinning in circles with them. For some reason watching them play only made Luce sad; it reminded her of something, but she didn't know what at first. Then the image came into focus: she was a tiny girl, spinning with a dark-haired woman on a lawn . . .

Luce grasped for a way to distract herself and realized there was something that she didn't understand. She and Dana were sitting on the sofa-shaped rock twenty yards from shore.

"Dana?" Luce said. "So when you all changed, you were still in Henton, right?"

"We were in that group home with crazy Beebee Merkle," Dana agreed. "She tried to murder us." Luce was bewildered by this. Henton, after all, was a good distance inland.

"So when I changed," Luce said, "I was on a cliff high over the sea. I still don't know how I survived, but somehow I fell over the edge without it killing me." Dana looked at her curiously. "But, I mean, the sea was right there. That part is easy to understand. But I can't see how all of you made it to the water."

"Oh, boy, that's the *weirdest* part!" Dana agreed. "I'm afraid to try to tell you, even. You'll think we're a bunch of loop-de-loops."

"I won't think anything bad," Luce promised. "I just don't get it, and I'm trying to figure everything out. I'm still new, too, even if they don't call me metaskaza anymore." *Not since I helped sink that ship,* Luce thought, but she didn't say it. Dana was so nice that Luce was worried she'd react badly when she learned about that part of being a mermaid.

"Okay," Dana said a little edgily. "Okay, you're not going to believe this. But it was like we all turned into puddles, except we were still alive. I mean, we could still think and everything." Luce's eyes went wide. She remembered how strange she'd felt when her own transformation started. It *had* felt like turning into liquid there on the grass. And maybe that could explain why the fall off the cliff didn't kill her. "So—okay, you really won't think this is nuts? The whole place was surrounded by fire, and there were these bars on the windows. We couldn't get out." She gave Luce another doubtful look, but then she went ahead and said it. "We escaped through the drains."

"*Through the drains?*" Luce was amazed. "Like, you stayed in one piece even though you were liquid, and you were able to squish down that much?"

"I mean, I guess so," Dana said. Now she was smiling; it was kind of funny, actually. "We definitely watched each other go down the drains, though. In these watery blobs. And then it was really dark and, like, we were moving super, super fast. For a really long time, too. And the next thing I knew I was bobbing around in the sea, and Rachel was grabbing my arm. I realized if we all linked arms we'd be safer, and we could help each other float with our heads above water." Dana gave an odd, rueful smile. "I was, like, surprised and impressed that we could all float so well. And I knew my legs felt wrong, but I didn't want to look. I told myself I was just numb from how cold the water was."

Luce grinned. "I didn't believe it at first either."

Dana was curious about this. "So how did you find out?"

Luce suddenly felt embarrassed. She didn't want Dana to hear the story of how she'd sunk that first boat by accident, and her stomach turned over as she realized that someone would definitely tell Dana the whole thing sooner or later.

Luckily Catarina chose that moment to swim over to them. She had a slightly tense look on her face, though. Luce took advantage of Catarina's arrival to change the subject. She told Catarina what Dana had said about all the metaskazas changing into blobs of liquid and racing to the sea through drains.

Catarina seemed sad and a little distracted.

"It can definitely happen like that," Catarina agreed. "I mean, if the metaskaza—the change—if it comes over you while you're inland, then you need to travel to the sea any way you can: through drains or a river if you're close to one. I don't know what happens if some poor metaskaza is stuck out in a desert!" Catarina seemed to be thinking of something far away, though. Her hair spread out around them, catching the golden sunset light so brilliantly that it looked as if the waves had caught fire. "You don't take your new form until you reach salt water. I came to the sea through a drain myself. So did Miriam." Luce was surprised; it was the most Catarina had ever said about her past.

"So, where are you from originally?" Dana asked.

Of course Dana didn't know yet how touchy Catarina could be about questions. Luce could see Catarina hesitating, and she half expected that Catarina would tell Dana off for being too nosy.

"Anadyr," Catarina admitted after a minute. "It's a town in Russia." That explained Catarina's odd, delicate accent, Luce thought, but the accent was so subtle that Catarina had obviously been speaking English for a very long time.

Dana was impressed. "Wow. So you actually swam across the Bering Sea? Were you alone? That must have been intense. What *happened?*"

Luce was already startled to hear Catarina tell them so much, but when Catarina spoke again Luce could hardly believe what she was hearing.

"Do you think I'm beautiful, Dana?" Catarina asked. Her voice was icy and very formal, and there was still that faraway look in her eyes.

Luce was relieved to discover that Dana had the sensitivity to take the question seriously.

"I think you're completely gorgeous."

Catarina barely glanced over at Dana, nodded, and then looked off again.

"Thank you." Catarina's accent was suddenly thicker; her voice took on an exotic lilt. "Do you think I'm beautiful enough to be worth more than ten cartons of cigarettes? I believe they were Marlboros. Black market. Not so easy to get then. And three bottles of vodka, let's not forget that . . ."

Luce was amazed to see that Dana's eyes were brimming with tears. Dana clearly understood more of what Catarina was talking about than Luce did.

"I think you're worth much, much more than that, Catarina," Dana said firmly, and a tear spilled down her cheek. "Whether you're beautiful or not. You're worth too much for anybody to ever put a price on you."

Catarina couldn't even look at them anymore. She dove away. Luce and Dana were both silent for a minute, and Dana splashed water on her face.

"Dana?" Luce was almost afraid to ask. "Dana, I don't understand. What did all of that mean?" Dana couldn't answer at first, but when she turned to look at Luce again her huge dark eyes were wide with pity.

"Oh, Luce." Dana was quiet again for a minute. "It means Catarina's parents *sold* her. For cigarettes!" Luce was confused.

"Why? Do you mean as a slave?" Dana gave Luce a long look, and suddenly Luce wasn't sure she wanted to understand. She felt very young compared to Dana, though Dana was only a year and a half older than her.

Luce felt something sucking at her fins, and flicked her tail wildly away before she saw what it was: just one of those poor little larvae. It shrank back with a wounded look on its doughy face.

"Why do you think?" Dana hissed. "Why does somebody *buy* a beautiful girl?"

10

Voice Training

It was an unusually warm spring but often rainy, and they all spent a lot of time lolling around in the cave. They were used to being wet, of course, but fresh water felt different on their skins than salt water did. It was tolerable but somehow slimy and unpleasant. Luce knew it was odd to think of clear water as "dirty," but that was still the word that occurred to her whenever the rain slid around her face. They all tried to swim underwater as much as possible whenever they went outside.

Luce slept in the cave with her friends, but during the day she sometimes slipped away to spend time alone in the narrow cave Miriam had showed her. She had a project of her own that she didn't want anyone else to know about, at least not yet. She was determined to learn to control her singing; more than that, to *change* it. She had a persistent fantasy that, if she could just discover another kind of magic her singing could accomplish, something besides enchanting humans, maybe she could get Catarina excited about it. It wouldn't be fair, after all, to expect her fellow mermaids to quit singing; the feeling of that music racing through them was simply too magnificent, and Luce knew that no one who'd felt it could ever give it up. Her voice, she thought, was her truest self. But if they could sing in a new way, a different way, then maybe the others wouldn't *want* to kill people anymore. Everything else about being a mermaid was so purely wonderful, after all. There was just that one problem. Why shouldn't she at least try to solve it?

If she let her voice go where it wanted it always turned into the same thrilling song, the death song: a single sweet, high note sustained for an impossibly long time then an endless fall . . . But Luce's song had brought Miriam comfort, and because of that Luce decided that her voice couldn't be completely evil. It was just a matter of understanding it. Luce knew her voice contained enormous power, and she was excited by the prospect that it might be capable of more than luring humans to their deaths. She had to admit to herself, though, that she had no idea what form that other magic might take. There was nothing to do except try experimenting.

Rain spattered down through the crack in the cave's roof, so Luce was sitting squeezed against the stony wall, leaning against the rocks with her tail trailing out into the water. She let her voice rise into that high, aching note. But then she held it right there, pinning it like a butterfly and refusing to let it tumble down the scale. She could feel that her voice was angry with her, trying to fight free of her control, and she stopped singing.

"You're *mine*," Luce told her voice sternly. "You're mine, and you're going to do exactly what I tell you!" She let the note rise again.

This time, instead of tumbling, it soared even higher, fluttered, wheeled around in space. Luce was thrilled. Finally she was singing a new song! And the emotion in the song was different, too. Instead of filling her with soft, warm longing for everything she'd lost, it was full of quick, dizzy magic, a leaping celebration.

Humans would certainly be enchanted by this song, Luce thought, but she was almost sure it wouldn't make them want to die. It just wasn't that kind of feeling, and Luce laughed out loud. The new song faltered and disappeared.

When Luce tried again, the death song came back, and it was even more beautiful, even fiercer with tenderness and hunger, than ever before. Luce was ready to cry from sheer frustration, and suddenly she was tempted to give up. She'd almost discovered a new song, but then she'd immediately lost it again. She swam disconsolately back to the main cave.

Luce drifted in the smooth green water near the cave's floor, watching the blue medusas pulsing their way along. It seemed like the cave was empty, even though the rain was still splattering down outside. The others must have gone out to get something to eat, and Luce rolled deep underwater, glad that no one was there to notice her depression.

Then she heard something, and realized she wasn't alone. A single high, piercing note sustained for a terribly long time and then an endless fall . . . Except the voice singing was thin and tinny, and the notes didn't fall in quite the right away. Luce was bewildered, and then she understood. It was Samantha. Samantha was doing her best to copy Luce's song!

Luce had never liked Samantha much, but now that she heard her own song thinned and mangled this way she actively detested her. Samantha made the song seem so feeble, so worthless! The emotion in it was ridiculous. It didn't promise forgiveness anymore; it didn't promise that everything lost would be restored. Instead, at best, it gave you the kind of feeling you might get from a stranger asking to take your picture or maybe from seeing yourself in the background on TV. You would be flattered, and the weaker kinds of humans might be enchanted for a while, but the feeling definitely wasn't worth *dying* for! Luce let out a single, hard laugh of pure contempt. The song above stopped abruptly, with a kind of gagging sound.

Luce's contempt turned into embarrassment. It was pointlessly cruel to humiliate Samantha for her singing when everyone already knew Luce was so much better than her, the second-best singer in the tribe. Luce slipped carefully back out through the entrance, hoping Samantha hadn't realized who had laughed at her.

* * *

Luce found all of them at what she thought of now as the dining beach. The rain had finally stopped, and Catarina was talking closely with Jenna, which, Luce realized, was happening more and more often. Luce had the sudden miserable thought that she was too young for Catarina really to consider her a friend. Catarina had simply been through too much; she might feel protective of Luce, she might regard her with a slightly condescending affection, but she couldn't possibly think of her as an equal. It was only Luce's singing that had made Catarina respect her at all.

Luce was even more hurt when she realized that Catarina was talking about her first tribe, one that lived on the Russian coast. She had never mentioned a word about it to Luce.

"The queen was Marina," Catarina was saying. "She was crazy, but so brave . . . She'd take on any kind of ship. Things I would never dream of trying now . . . Once we made two container ships crash into each other in a storm, far out at sea, and some of the humans managed to escape in lifeboats. We were all up all night hunting down the survivors. It was madness!" Even though Catarina's words were critical, her eyes were shining from the memory. "One man—I don't know how he managed to resist her. Marina was a singer like no one I've ever heard; her voice could swallow a ship whole. But he held out, so three of us shot up from beneath his lifeboat and capsized it. Marina pulled him under herself." Luce couldn't help feeling dismayed by the story, but Jenna was laughing. No wonder those two had become such good friends, Luce thought bitterly. Jenna shared Catarina's ferocity, her rage at humans. Luce had been surprised to discover that even Dana was excited by the thought of sinking ships; she agreed that humans deserved it. After all, they'd left fourteen orphans alone with a homicidal lunatic, and no one had done the smallest thing to protect them. Dana was eager to try singing to a ship as soon as possible, but Catarina insisted that they had to wait a while longer. Too many ships sinking soon after one another might make the humans suspicious.

"What happened to her?" Luce asked hesitantly. "To

Marina?" Catarina suddenly turned somber and stared down, and Jenna glared at Luce.

"She wasn't talking to you," Jenna snarled. "And you should know not to go around asking questions like that! Like, do you ever think that *maybe* there are some things Cat doesn't want to be reminded of?"

Luce's face turned hot, and her only comfort was the thought that Jenna couldn't sing at all. The two new mermaids who showed signs of real talent were Dana and the fragile, skittish little blond girl, Rachel, the one who had insisted on the first day that she wasn't crazy. Secretly Luce thought that Rachel *was* a little crazy. She would wake up screaming in the night, and she imagined monsters lurking everywhere they went. But her craziness gave her singing a disturbed, haunting, feverish quality different from anything Luce had ever heard before. Luce thought it might make people want to die simply by making them too terrified to remain alive.

Samantha popped up through the water, shot one furtive look at Luce, and then turned her face away, her lips compressed with resentment. Luce swam off on her own, feeling almost as lonely as she had when she was still human.

She didn't want to be shut up in a cave, not when she was already so sad. Instead she decided to explore farther up the coast. She still hadn't been very far from her home cave, and as long as she stayed next to the cliffs she probably wouldn't have any trouble with orcas. She swam for half an hour, finding a few more small hidden caves with entrances on the water—too far away to be convenient, though—and eventually the cliffs dipped away, wide rocky beaches spread out along the sea, and in the distance Luce could glimpse the docks and bright fishing boats of a small village. She curled into a crevice between boulders; it was risky to come too close to a human settlement, and she'd have to be very careful not to be seen.

Anchored in the water outside the village Luce noticed an immense, shiny white yacht, and even from this distance she could see the gleam of what looked like a chrome tiller. The water made voices carry much farther than they would on land, and Luce could hear a booming man having some sort of tantrum. It sounded like he was screaming at his cook; Luce could just make out the words, "A very inferior sauce . . . What do I *pay* you for?"

Ugh, Luce found herself thinking, *humans*. Still, she was re-lieved that the yacht was keeping a safe distance from the mer-maids' cave.

By the time Luce strayed home, around twilight, she was somehow more determined than ever to master her singing. It was the only thing she had ever had that made her special, after all. She started spending more time alone, grappling with the music that lived in her, and as time went by controlling it got just a little easier.

The days were lengthening rapidly now, and the nights were starting to dwindle. Their darkness had softened from the black of winter into the color of deepest twilight.

* * *

A week after Luce saw the yacht she was in the main cave with Rachel, Dana, and a few other mermaids she didn't know very well. Dana was encouraging Rachel to practice singing.

"Everyone says you're going to be really good, Rachel, but you have to keep working on it. Okay?" Rachel looked terrified, as usual, but Luce knew she worshiped Dana and wouldn't want to disappoint her. Rachel opened her mouth. At once an enormous, devastating sound leaped out of it, metallic and savage, spinning with dark chords. Rachel threw herself backward with a splash as if she thought her own voice was an attacking lion, and then cowered and gasped. She reached to shove up her glasses, forgetting that her eyes had been perfect since her change and she didn't wear them anymore. Luce couldn't help smiling at Rachel's reaction. She'd almost felt that way herself sometimes.

"Oh, Dana." Rachel was sobbing. "I can't! I can't stand it! I can feel it; it wants to take me over . . . Like it's going to eat me up, from the inside . . ."

"I've had that problem, too," Luce said gently. "I've been working on getting more of a hold on it. You want me to show you, Rachel?" Rachel looked over through her tears, shaking her head in alarm, but Dana was interested.

"I want to see if Rachel doesn't," Dana said. " 'Cause my voice gets away from me, too. I've been wondering how you guys all deal." Luce smiled, and saw that Rachel was still peering curiously.

"Just try and hold one note," Luce suggested. "Like, it'll put up a fight, but just hold it steady for as long as you can . . ." Dana tried, and at first her voice jumped away. Her song was so different from Rachel's, lulling and warm, like being sung to sleep by the perfect mother. After a few tries Dana managed to keep her voice in one long, constant hum.

"Wow, is that hard!" Dana said at last, breaking off the note with a gasp. They hadn't moved at all, but she was out of breath from the sheer effort it had taken her to maintain control. "It is like having some kind of weird animal inside you, isn't it?"

"That's because it's magic," Rachel whimpered, but she couldn't keep the curiosity out of her eyes as she added, "Dana, I don't *like* it."

"I'm going to try that again," Dana said after a moment. "See, Rachel, I bet it's going to be a lot more fun if it doesn't feel, I don't know, like the song is just pushing you around." Then Dana added something unexpected. "I'm so sick of being told what to do! Jenna just keeps getting bossier, now that she's, like, second in command here." She didn't seem to be aware of how her words affected Luce. For a second Luce found herself fantasizing about sinking another boat, a bigger one, even a container ship; everyone would see who was *really* second in command then! Then the implications of the fantasy sank in, and Luce felt sick with shame. How could she be so exhilarated at the idea of killing people?

"I'll try this time, too," Rachel said. Luce was surprised, and relieved to have something to distract her from the awful thoughts that had just been crowding her mind. "Luce, how do I do it? I mean, you say to hold it. But it's way too big to hold. Like it's going to *maul* me . . ."

Luce let out a very small low note then smiled at Rachel. "Just try to copy me, okay? I'll sing one note, really softly, and when you feel ready you can join in. Okay?"

Luce's new method made it easier for both Rachel and Dana to keep a handle on their voices. After an hour she was leading them in a run of a few notes, the beginning of a new little song she'd been practicing alone, and Rachel's terror seemed to be leaving her. Other mermaids swam in now and then, watched for a while in disbelief, and then dove out again. Luce didn't pay much attention. She was too absorbed now, in coaxing Dana and Rachel carefully through the opening notes of Rachel's own ferocious song; it took all of Luce's concentration to keep the song from overwhelming all three of them.

"You see, Cat!" The voice was Samantha's, and it was almost spitting with vindictive glee. "I told you what she's doing! Luce is teaching them *singing!*"

Luce was confused, but she was even more annoyed. There was nothing in the timahk about not teaching singing, after all. But when she met Catarina's icy gray stare Luce could see she was upset. It didn't seem fair, and Luce braced herself to listen to a burst of irrational rage. Then she noticed something else. Catarina was furious, yes. But she was also doing her best to pretend not to be.

"What do I care?" Catarina snarled, and her rage was directed not at Luce but at Samantha. "It would be fantastic, of course, if Luce could actually succeed in teaching them anything. But all she's doing is wasting her own time, and Dana's . . ."

"She's taught me a lot!" Rachel objected in her shrill, panicky, mouselike speaking voice. "She's taught me a lot already! I'm not as scared to sing now. Luce, you're not going to stop teaching me, are you?" Samantha's face fell, and Luce felt unexpectedly warm inside.

"Really, Rachel?" Catarina asked coldly. "I suppose there could be some kind of *psychological* benefit." Catarina managed to say this in a tone that suggested Rachel wouldn't need singing lessons if she weren't half crazy, and Rachel's face crumpled in humiliation. Dana was looking around at everyone, and from something sly in Dana's face Luce knew she guessed all the hidden reasons Samantha and Catarina had for acting so unfriendly. Luce appreciated again just how sensitive Dana was and how clever at figuring out people's secret emotions.

"Luce is a really good teacher, Cat," Dana said levelly. "Maybe it's a talent of hers you haven't had a chance to see before. But now you know, it would make sense to take advantage of it, right?" Catarina stared blankly into Dana's warm, round eyes. Dana's look was innocent, but Luce thought she could detect a trace of suppressed amusement. "Like, maybe Luce should start teaching *everybody*, right? That way you'd have a lot more help. Next time you decide to tackle a boat, I mean. Hasn't it been long enough since the last one that we could try it soon? Without making people pay too much attention?"

"I'll think about it," Catarina snapped, and then all of Luce's happiness left her in a rush. She hadn't let herself think it through, but Dana's words forced her to recognize the truth. If she taught the other mermaids how to sing better, she'd just be helping Catarina kill more people. Once she finally discovered some new magic it might be different but now!

Luce turned away abruptly without even saying goodbye to Dana and Rachel and dove.

"What's got into *her* now?" Samantha sneered behind her. "I swear, Luce just gets more neurotic all the time."

There was *one* mermaid, Luce thought angrily, that she definitely wouldn't help in improving her singing. She swam off fast, lashing the water with quick, circling strokes of her tail until she shot out of the tunnel and dashed off through the waves, not coming up until she was a mile out. She was too upset to pay attention to where she was going, and she almost knocked her head against something white and glossy. She felt a jolt of alarm at not being able to reach air before she realized what was in her way: just a boat. She could easily slip up around the side and breathe where no one on board would be able to see her. She skimmed along the curved white underside and came up in the waves that lapped against the shiny hull. Wind wrapped her face like a scarf of cold silk.

The boat wasn't moving. Luce knew, of course, that the people on board had no way to know how dangerous it was to anchor here. How were they supposed to guess that a mermaids' cave was just a few minutes' swim away? Even so, Luce felt a stab of disdain; humans could be so careless, so *stupid*.

"Kitten?" a man's voice said. It was so close that Luce jumped, but then she realized it was coming through the ship's glossy side. "Kitten, it's really exciting to see all the wildlife here. I'm sure you'd enjoy yourself if you'd just try coming out on deck. Just for a teeny little while?" The voice was distorted by the ship, reverberating strangely in Luce's ears, but after a second she was sure she recognized it. It was the booming man she'd heard yelling at his cook. But now he was simpering, pleading . . .

Whoever he'd called kitten didn't answer. Luce could hear a thump, probably someone throwing themselves face downward on a bed to sulk.

These were disgusting people, Luce thought. What did she care if Catarina killed them? Then she remembered the cook, the crew. She knew a man like that wouldn't do any of the actual work on his own yacht.

She wanted to see more. But where could she hide out in the open ocean? She couldn't allow any of these people to catch sight of her. She stared around and spotted a small motorboat that had been left tethered to the yacht at the end of a long rope. Luce dipped underwater and came up on the far side of the motorboat so she could peek up over its edge and watch while she decided what to do. She had the vague idea that she should somehow try to sneak a note to the crew, warning them to get away from here immediately. But it was a ridiculous plan, and she knew it. How could she possibly get her hands on a pen and paper?

A middle-aged woman with a white bandana tied over her head was standing out on the deck. A girl about Luce's age in a dark blue hoodie and jeans was standing with her, her head tipped over while the woman carefully brushed her long brown hair. They were both giggling about something.

"So, okay, so you know how she never reads anything?" The girl was shaking with impish laughter as she told the story, and the woman smiled down at her with such tenderness that Luce almost choked from envy. "So I told her that in the Narnia books Peter turns out to be a vampire, and she actually believed me! And then I said he eats Lucy at the end of *Prince Caspian*, and she believed that, too, so I just kept on making up crazier stuff . . ." Even the woman was laughing now, though she kept trying to stifle her giggles and pretend to disapprove.

"Oh, Tessa! Can't you be more careful? You know if she ever realizes you've been fooling her all this time she'll probably get me fired? I don't think she has much of a sense of humor, unless somebody hurts themselves . . . Now straighten up and I'll do your braids."

"She's not going to figure anything out!" Tessa said confi-
dently. "I mean, she'd have actually to read the books to realize
I was lying to her, right? Even in school she just pays other kids
to do her work for her. And she actually brags about it!" Tessa
went off into another peal of laughter. "I just pretend to be really
impressed. Like I say, 'Oh, I wish I were rich like *you* . . . Oh,
wow, there was a pony at your birthday party? I'm so sad my
mom is *only* a cook and not an idiotic, noisome, sadistic banker
like your daddy!' And she falls for it!"

"You don't actually use those words, though, do you?" But
Tessa's mother was still beaming, stroking Tessa's hair as she
worked it into braids.

"Okay, I wouldn't say *idiotic* . . ." Tessa admitted. "Even she
probably knows what that is. She asked me what I meant, and I
told her 'sadistic' meant he was incredibly smart at business, and
'noisome' meant, like, he has really, really good taste in clothes
and stuff." Her mother bent and kissed her on the cheek.

"You feral beast," her mother said softly. "How am I supposed to finish my dissertation if I have to keep putting it aside
to look for work? But honestly, that little sociopath is asking for
it. Just try to be a touch more discreet from now on, all right?"

Suddenly Luce couldn't see them anymore. Instead she saw
herself leaning on the railing, laughing so hard it hurt, while a
dark-haired woman much younger and prettier than Tessa's
mother smiled beside her. A warm arm squeezed her shoulder,
and Luce closed her eyes to feel soft fingers tousling her hair. Of
course, Luce told herself, of course Alyssa Gray was every bit as
playful and loving as the woman beaming at Tessa. Of course
Alyssa had come back to lift her lost daughter out of the sea and

hold her close . . . Luce was so distracted by the daydream that she didn't realize, at first, that Tessa was talking again.

"Oh my God! Mom, there's a girl out there!" Luce looked up from the gray jagged waves in shock—and met Tessa's hazel eyes. She had a long, straight nose, a funny crooked mouth, and her full cheeks were flushed from the wind. "Hey, you! Come over here, we'll pull you up. You can hold on to the rope there . . ." Luce ducked under the motorboat. How could she have been so reckless?

"Tessa, where?"

"She was just holding the side of the boat out there. A girl with short dark hair. She didn't seem scared or anything. She looked right at me and vanished. Mom, I swear . . ."

"Well . . ." The woman hesitated for only a second. "If there's any chance you're right, we have to get help right away. You say she was holding on to the boat back there? Oh, why did she have to let go? She must be delirious from hypothermia . . ." Luce heard the thumping as Tessa's mother ran off down the deck, calling "Ethan? Ethan, Tess says she saw a girl in the water." Luce knew she needed to get away, but for some reason she couldn't explain she lingered where she was in the shadows under the small bobbing boat. Tessa didn't go anywhere either.

"Hey. You can stop hiding, okay? I know you're still out there. Why don't you come on board and hang out with me for a while? You can borrow my clothes, and I'll make you some cocoa."

Luce wished she could. They could talk about books, tell each other crazy stories. Luce felt convinced she and Tessa would be best friends if only it wasn't against the timahk for them even to say hello.

Unless . . . But there was no way, of course. No chance at all. Her mother was so kind that it was obvious Tessa could never become a mermaid.

Tessa was actually *happy*. And she was clearly very much loved.

Then Luce heard footsteps pounding along the deck, and forced herself to dive deep and fast, far down into the cool gray water, where she didn't even have to feel her own tears.

She needed to find some way to warn them, and she thought of trying to get Tessa's attention and telling her that the yacht had to speed away as fast as it possibly could. But even though Luce knew perfectly well that at least two of the mermaids in her tribe had already broken the timahk, she still didn't want to break it herself.

11

Tessa

It rained hard that evening and on into the night. Luce was grateful for the awful weather; as long as the mermaids lounged around inside the cave they wouldn't notice the yacht. Surely it would sail off soon?

Once everyone was asleep Luce slipped out, taking a sharp rock with her just in case the yacht was still there. She had the idea that she could scratch a message on one of the seats of that trailing motorboat, making the letters big enough that anyone who looked out from the yacht's deck would notice. She swam slowly, trying to think up a warning that the crew would take seriously. She had the queasy feeling that Tessa might sometimes play practical jokes.

Even though she was swimming well below the surface of the water Luce saw the yacht before she was anywhere close to it. A huge blob of glowing light wavered in the water ahead of her; the yacht was blazing with lamps in every window and large floodlights that shone down on the deck even in the pounding rain. There was a ruckus of drunken voices shaking up the quiet evening, and the thump of ugly music drowned out the soft rhythm of cresting water.

Luce was beside herself with rage. Why did they have to make such a clamor? Did these people *want* to die? At least the motorboat was still where she'd seen it last, swinging around with the rising waves. The currents were so strong tonight that swimming through them forced Luce into a kind of dancing motion, her body constantly adjusting to counteract the heavy push and pull. She was worried. She'd have to hold the boat with one hand while reaching far enough in with the other to gouge the paint on the seats, without either tipping it over or pulling her tail out for too long. She circled the little boat for a moment, wondering how to proceed, while the water popped all around her with the impact of the rain. No matter what she did, it was going to be tricky. At last she took hold of the side and peered in. Two inches of grayish rainwater slopped around the bottom, and there was a pile of old tarps Luce hadn't noticed earlier. She'd decided to keep the message simple: GO AWAY NOW. She bent in as far as she could without putting too much of her weight on the side and began scratching the G. It was harder than she'd hoped, especially with the boat bucking around so hard. She was digging in with the rock, trying to ignore the slippery, repulsive sensation of fresh water pouring down her face, when something moved, and the tarps shuffled over . . .

Luce lurched backward, but the hand was already tight on her wrist, and Tessa's face was wild and determined. If Luce yanked any harder, she'd just pull Tessa in with her.

"I knew you'd be back!" Tessa whispered fiercely. Ribbons of rain-drenched hair striped her face, one cheek lit up by the shine from the boat. They pitched dizzily together with the manic gesturing of the waves. "Do you know how bad you upset my mom? She thinks you drowned because we didn't help you fast enough. She's still crying about it."

Luce didn't answer. Her thoughts were in chaos: this definitely seemed like contact with humans, but on the other hand she hadn't actually *said* anything, and she hadn't touched Tessa on purpose either. A second human hand was gripping Luce's arm now, and Tessa gave such a vicious tug that she almost over-balanced the boat.

"I think you owe my mom an *apology*," Tessa snapped. "You're going to come on board and tell her you're fine. Okay? Why don't you say anything?"

If Tessa was still talking about Luce coming on board, then she must not have seen Luce's tail . . . That was a relief. But she had no idea how to make Tessa let go without drowning her, and for a second Luce felt tempted to do exactly that. In just a few minutes the problem would be completely gone. Tessa was squeezing her arm so hard it ached, and the throbbing bass from the yacht made her head hurt.

"Seriously," Tessa insisted. "Seriously. Why are you acting like this? What's your problem? I thought we could be friends but not when you're being so selfish!"

"*Shut up!*" Luce exploded. She was crying now, and she

couldn't control herself any longer. "Just shut up! If I was that selfish I'd kill you right now. It would be *easy*."

Tessa looked shocked, but she didn't let go of Luce's wrist. Luce didn't know whether to be impressed by her courage or infuriated with her stupidity.

"You're the one who's being selfish!" Luce added. "You're making me break about fifty laws when I'm only here to warn you. At least you and your mom, if you can't get anyone else to listen. Just steal this boat and get away!" Tessa was so surprised that her grip relaxed, and with a wrench Luce was free again, floating far enough from the boat that Tessa couldn't grab her.

"What are you *talking* about?" Tessa squealed in exasperation. "What are you, anyway?"

"That's a really rude question," Luce snapped. The brilliant light from the yacht made the raindrops look like tiny bursting stars all over the black water. She was still half out of her mind with fury, both at Tessa and at herself. "What, you think everybody's supposed to be *human*?"

For half a second longer they stared at each other, the only sounds the harsh thudding music, the slap of waves and the sigh of heavy rain. Then Luce dove. It would have been easy enough just to slice straight down, keeping her body hidden, but from some mixture of defiance and heartache Luce deliberately let her tail flick above the surface. No one would believe Tessa if she said she'd seen a *mermaid*, Luce knew. Not even her mother. Luce felt a little gleeful at the thought of Tessa trying to convince anyone of *that*.

And besides, it was too late anyway; she'd already ruined everything. Somehow the other mermaids would find out what she'd done and banish her, and even if they didn't Luce wasn't sure she could live with the shame. The honorable thing would be to go ahead and expel herself from the tribe. Swim away tonight. She wouldn't necessarily die. After all, Catarina had somehow survived a journey all the way from Russia!

Had Catarina been caught breaking the timahk by her first tribe? Luce realized she'd never heard any explanation of why Catarina had left the Russian coast. Suddenly Luce imagined that was it: Catarina'd been seen kissing some drowning human boy and cast out, and she'd swum across the Bering Sea in disgrace.

All at once Luce was overcome by exhaustion. Maybe, she thought, maybe it would be okay to sleep in her own little cave away from everyone, just for tonight. She could decide what to do in the morning.

She curled up against the cave wall to keep out of the rain that slashed down through the crack in the roof and sang herself to sleep. A new song, a dreamy song, made of sweet, spreading chords. It would have taken half a dozen great human singers all working together to try to copy it, Luce knew, and even then they couldn't have come close.

* * *

Luce woke to brilliant sun striping the dimness of her cave. The water covering her was dotted and streaked with luminous green where the light hit it, and for a minute Luce lolled happily. She loved swimming on sunny days, watching the beams of golden light parting around her outspread fingers as if she were running her hands through long shining hair.

Then she remembered the night before and sat up abruptly. The other mermaids would be out enjoying the sunshine, and they'd catch sight of that yacht in no time. Luce could only hope that the yacht had moved on, or at least that Tessa had persuaded her mother to run off. But how would that sound? *"That girl came back, but she's actually a mermaid, and she said we should get away . . ."*

And then there was the other problem: Luce had spoken to a human. She thought about the plan she'd made the night before of traveling down the coast alone and shivered. It wasn't sharks and fishing nets that scared her as much as the idea of being so utterly lonely. How could she give up the only family, the only home she had anywhere in the world? Even if she lived, no one besides this tribe and her father had ever wanted her, and she couldn't imagine that anybody else ever would.

But had she *really* broken the timahk? Luce told herself that she hadn't planned to speak to Tessa, after all. Tessa had grabbed her and held her by force. There must be some kind of exception for cases where mermaids were taken captive by humans against their will, even if Catarina hadn't mentioned it. And how was Luce supposed to make Tessa let go of her if she didn't say anything? Luce deliberately suppressed the thought of the other way she could have forced Tessa to release her arm, but for a second the image pushed its way into her mind: Tessa's enchanted face, her eyes wide in dark gray water, silver bubbles leaking through her lips . . .

Luce reminded herself of something else: Catarina had said that any human who heard the mermaids *singing* had to die. But Tessa hadn't heard one note from Luce! That might be a big enough loophole in the timahk; it seemed possible now that Luce hadn't done anything quite bad enough to deserve expulsion after all.

Luce still felt a little sick, but she decided to head back to the dining beach. She took a slightly out-of-the-way route and spotted the white yacht still sitting there. She didn't see the motorboat anywhere, though, and her heart quickened with hope. Maybe Tessa and her mother had escaped in the night; maybe they were safe, talking and laughing in a diner somewhere over strawberry-topped waffles and coffee . . . Luce's relief was suddenly mixed with an ugly stab of envy.

* * *

"There you are!" Catarina called. "Luce, I wish you wouldn't go sneaking off like that. I get worried that something might happen to you." They were all at the dining beach, as Luce had expected, nibbling their way through a lazy breakfast and soaking up the sun. It felt delicious after all the rain and darkness of the past several days. Well, almost all of them were there; Luce realized that Violet and Samantha were missing. Maybe they were still asleep?

"I'm fine," Luce said. "I'm really careful when I go out alone, Cat. I stay right next to the cliffs." It was a lie, but Catarina wasn't paying much attention. She was too busy stretching her long body out on top of the water, rolling slowly over and over to sun herself on every side. Her bronze tail flashed, and the broad fins at the end rippled sensuously. Luce remembered her conversation with Dana: Catarina's parents had actually sold her. But had Catarina changed as soon as that happened? Or had it taken something even worse?

Luce was distracted from her dark mood by a sudden splash of silver-blond curly hair, which was followed a second later by Violet's sleek brown head. Samantha was twittering with excitement.

"Oh, Cat, you're not going to believe this! Some doofus humans have just parked their yacht right near here!" Samantha laughed shrilly. "Even for humans it's got to be the dumbest thing I've ever seen!"

Luce felt embarrassed when she remembered that she'd thought something similar. She didn't like having anything in common with Samantha, who just seemed to become more childish all the time. Catarina rolled over and let her body tip upright; she didn't seem to be in any hurry, though.

"Oh," Catarina said slowly. Luce was surprised to notice that she seemed bored by the news; she was even flicking her golden tail in irritation. "I noticed that, too. We'll have to be careful to keep out of sight until they leave." Samantha looked horribly disappointed.

"Aren't we going to sink them, Cat? I mean the retards are just *sitting* there!"

"Oh, Samantha, use your head for once," Catarina snapped. "How many people can there be on a yacht like that? Maybe fifteen? Twenty, at the very most. Pathetic. And if we take them down we'll have to wait for weeks before we do the next one, probably let all kinds of bigger ships go by . . ." Luce had the feeling that if Catarina had noticed any handsome young men on that yacht she wouldn't be taking such a dismissive tone. Catarina shook her head, sending ripples through her fiery hair. "It's a waste of our time, especially with all these new singers. No, we'll wait for something better."

Luce looked away so that no one would notice the relief on her face. She didn't need to worry anymore that Tessa might still be on the yacht.

"But there's a *girl* on the boat," Samantha pleaded, and Luce jumped. "Cat, she looked like a metaskaza."

Luce was confused; she'd only heard the word used for new mermaids. What did it mean to call a human being that? She was appalled to see Catarina brightening suddenly at this, as if it changed everything.

"Really? Are you sure? Violet, did she look like a metaskaza to you?" Violet was obviously just as bewildered as Luce was by this; she was glancing around in alarm, hoping somebody would explain before she made a fool of herself. Luce decided she didn't care if she sounded stupid. If Samantha was talking about Tessa, Luce had to know what she meant.

"What does that even mean, Cat? I mean, calling a *human* metaskaza?" Luce tried to assume the same lazy, disdainful tone Catarina had used, to suggest that Samantha was just being silly. Samantha pouted.

"Oh," Catarina said, smiling over at Luce. "Oh, I still forget sometimes . . . Luce, when a human girl is almost ready to change, she starts to have that . . ." Catarina shook herself and waved her hand at something just over their heads. "That *indication*, just the way we do. You can see it. Humans can't but we can." Luce realized she was talking about the dark shimmering that clung around the mermaids, but it made her feel only more confused. She definitely hadn't seen anything like that around Tessa! Or had she?

"Well, I mean, I saw that girl, too," Luce said as casually as she could. It felt dangerous to admit so much, but she plunged ahead. "I noticed her on my way over here, and I didn't see any of that kind of sparkling around her."

"She *totally* had it!" Samantha yelled. "I saw it! Cat, don't listen to her! Luce just has some kind of messed-up problem with being a mermaid. I sometimes think she *likes* humans . . ." Samantha turned quiet right away when she saw the scowl on Catarina's face, the angry swishing of her tail.

"Have you ever heard Luce *sing*, Samantha?" Catarina asked; her tone was heavy, almost menacing. "Oh, that's right, you have. You heard her sing so well that twenty men hurled themselves straight down into the ocean." Luce listened to this with a tumult of emotions; it hurt to be reminded of what she'd done to those men, but at the same she was grateful to hear Catarina defending her. "Maybe you should think of that before you make these . . . these senseless accusations."

"But maybe Luce just didn't notice it?" Violet put in shyly. "Because I think I saw some kind of—indication?—that, like, weird kind of sparkling in the air around her, too. Not that— I mean, I'm sure Luce is telling the truth." Violet had been nervous around Luce ever since the time when Luce had crawled on shore to save her life.

"Well . . ." Catarina said. "The girl could be wavering. Sometimes the indication—it goes in and out, like a light blinking. But if there's a metaskaza on the boat we can't just leave her there! Trapped with those . . ." Catarina shook her head like she could barely stand to say the word. Luce's heart was pounding now; she hoped no one could hear it. "We simply have to help her change. Save her from those *humans*."

"But if . . ." Luce tried to think it through, fast. "But if that girl is wavering like you say . . ." Catarina and the others were staring at her too hard, and she struggled to clear her thoughts. Tessa's life was at stake. "Does that mean if we get her . . . at the wrong moment, when the indication isn't there . . . she'll just drown?" A distinct look of relief flashed on Catarina's lovely face.

"Oh, Luce! Now I understand why you're looking so worried!" She smiled brilliantly and stretched out on the waves again. "No, if that girl is on the edge of changing into one of us I can help her. It's difficult. Very difficult. But I've done it before. And when you think that our only alternative is to leave that poor metaskaza with humans who are doing who knows what disgusting things to her, Luce, you can see we have to try."

Luce understood Catarina's point of view. But she still had trouble believing that Tessa was unhappy enough to become a mermaid, and even if she did she'd be heartbroken at her mother's death. And then Luce stopped thinking about that, overcome by fascination with what Catarina had just said: *help* someone change?

"How do you do it?" Luce asked. She still didn't want all the people on that yacht to die, but she couldn't help feeling tempted, just a bit, by the prospect of Tessa joining the tribe.

"I told you, Luce. It isn't easy. You need to leave this to me." Luce felt more impatient than she ever had with Catarina's habit of avoiding questions.

"Of course I'll leave it to you! I just want to know how. What do you have to do?" Catarina gave her a strange, almost angry look.

"What do you imagine, Luce? That someday I won't be around anymore"—Luce's stomach tightened as she thought of what those words might imply—"and you'll have to do it without me?" Catarina's tail was thrashing up foam now, and Samantha grinned maliciously. Luce ignored her, and spoke as calmly as she could.

"No, Cat. But think about it. What if someday there was a ship with *two* metaskazas? It's possible, right? Wouldn't it be good if I was able to help?" Catarina considered this, and her tail's swirling slowed.

"Two? I suppose it could happen. I hadn't thought of that." She gave Luce another strained, sad stare. "You're certainly the only other singer here who might be able to pull it off. Dana's not bad at all, and Miriam, even if she doesn't have much confidence . . . But I wouldn't want to see them try *that*. They'd hurt themselves for nothing, and the girl would just drown."

Of course, Luce thought. Catarina was so touchy about it that she should have guessed. The method for changing human girls into mermaids involved singing.

"Oh, it's just a singing thing!" Samantha squealed. "Wow, I thought you meant something a lot harder than that!" Luce bit her lip at the irony of Samantha, of all people, calling singing *easy*, and Catarina glowered.

"Do you remember how you felt when you changed, Samantha?" Catarina hissed, and Luce watched Samantha's giddy face collapse into dismay. "Go on. Try to really remember. Feel it again, just the way you did when you were lying beside that road with all your bones broken, watching your mother drive away and leave you to die. Like you were no better than garbage." Luce was shocked at how cruel Catarina was being. Samantha's behavior was obnoxious, but did she really deserve this? "Now tell me how *easy* it would be to go back into that feeling, as deeply as you could, and sing it! Knowing that if you couldn't

bear the pain and stopped, even for an instant, the metaskaza
would drown . . ."

Samantha looked as stunned as Luce felt. Her green eyes
were goggling and her mouth hung open. Luce shivered as she
thought about attempting the kind of singing Catarina had just
described: reliving that horrible night on the cliff and somehow
making her song contain all that suffering. She was relieved now
that Catarina didn't want her to try it.

"Oh, Catarina," Luce whispered. "You've done that before?
It must be"—words failed her, and she gazed into Catarina's
moon gray eyes. Catarina stared back at her, and Luce saw a
dark, violent grief in Catarina's face. Luce imagined that she
must have looked that way at the moment when she'd first felt
her body melting into brilliant liquid, threatening to flow away.
"That's an incredibly courageous thing to do, Cat," Luce said
softly. "I don't know if I could be brave enough." Catarina visi-
bly shook herself, and then Luce seemed to wake from a trance:
she could see the warm golden sunlight streaming down all
around them again, flecks of sun flashing on the waves.

"It's the only way," Catarina said. Her voice was calm and
hard now. "You have to *sing* the metaskaza into that feeling and
hold her there until she changes. And the only way to do that is
to feel it yourself. It's terrible, yes, but it's only temporary, and
then when you think that if you don't do it you could be leaving the poor metaskaza with men like your uncle, Luce, or even
worse . . ." Catarina was starting to get that faraway look again,
the way she did when she was remembering her past. "When
you think of it that way you really have no choice."

They were quiet for a minute. Catarina was gazing off across
the sea and Samantha looked like she was about to be sick. Luce

watched both of them, and couldn't stop herself from remembering that night on the cliffs. Even in the brilliant sunlight she could still feel the sharp grass cutting her face, the icy wind rushing over her back. Then Catarina slid a hand through her gleaming hair and smiled at them, though her cheerfulness looked a bit forced.

"We can't go after the yacht while it's anchored, though. Samantha, do you want to keep a lookout? Come back and tell me as soon as the yacht starts to move, and we'll take it down. We'll get that metaskaza out of there."

Luce wondered if Catarina could be right. Was it possible that Tessa needed them to rescue her? If somebody was doing horrible things to Tessa, Luce was sure it couldn't be her mother. The love between them had been so apparent, so immediate and vital.

But even if Tessa was fine where she was, Luce had already done everything she could to warn her. There was nothing to do now except wait.

The air was warm and sweet, the sea glowed green with sunshine. Even the last lingering blobs of sea ice were completely melted. But Luce couldn't keep from shivering.

* * *

Samantha was back an hour later.

"Cat, they're just starting to move now! Really slow! Oh, and I saw the girl again"—and here she shot Luce a nasty look—"and she was definitely sparkling like crazy. Maybe Luce is still so new she's just *clueless* about this stuff."

Luce knew she couldn't bear to sing that yacht into the rocks, but she couldn't say that. On the other hand, she had much stronger control of her voice now, and she knew she could listen to the other mermaids without just breaking into song herself.

"Hey, Cat?" Luce said. "I've been thinking. Since it's such a small boat? Maybe the two of us should kind of hang back and just watch, so Rachel and Dana can get some practice. And then you can concentrate on the metaskaza."

Luce suddenly had a new worry. If Tessa changed would she tell everyone that she'd already met Luce?

Catarina gazed tensely at Luce; maybe Luce had said the wrong thing?

"That might be a good idea," Catarina said at last. "If we're there, we can jump in if Rachel and Dana get into trouble. Doing a boat that small is pretty boring, anyway. Okay." By now a circle of excited mermaids pressed in around them, waiting for orders. "We're going to let the new girls practice this time. Dana, do you want to take the lead?" Dana looked anxious at the idea but also thrilled.

"Sure, Cat. As long as you and Luce are there if I need help?" Luce wasn't happy with what they were doing, but she couldn't help admiring Dana's nerve; it was brave to try leading her first time out. Soon Catarina and Dana had moved off to the side, discussing the route Dana should take. Catarina thought it was still too soon to go back to the rock where the Coast Guard boat went down, and they were debating alternatives. They eventually decided on some particularly high, steep cliffs several miles back in the direction of Pittley. It would mean a fairly long chase and a lot of singing, but Catarina insisted they had to use a new location as a precaution against the humans noticing a pattern.

They spread out, racing along underwater in a V like flying geese, and in just a few minutes the yacht was surrounded. Dana darted out of sight and pulled ahead of the rest of them while Rachel took up the position Luce had been in with the last boat, right in the center of the wake.

Luce swam off to the side, sad and worried. She had to stay underwater most of the time to avoid being seen by anyone on the yacht—a round, silver-haired man with a squashed red face was wandering around, glaring critically at the deck—but as often as she dared she peeked above the water line, scanning for Tessa. She didn't see her anywhere. She pushed farther ahead and spotted, sprawled on deck chairs, three practically identical middle-aged women with stiff, frosted blond hair and what looked like expensive sunglasses. One was painting her toenails.

"Of *course* I didn't want to come someplace so cold and depressing," the toenail painter whined to the other two; Luce wondered if this was the person she'd heard being addressed as "kitten." "But Harris—you know he has these delusions that he's some sort of amateur marine biologist, and he said he wouldn't replace my Jaguar if I didn't come along. I don't think he knows the difference between a seal and a whale!" Then Luce heard the first curling line of song and watched the bottle of polish slip from the woman's hand and clatter onto the deck.

It was immediately obvious to Luce that Dana was nowhere near as gifted a singer as Catarina—but then, who was? The notes jumped in much too fast, without the coaxing subtlety of Catarina's song. The people on board weren't instantly enchanted in the way the Coast Guard sailors had been. They had time to be nonplussed, to gape at one another with disoriented expressions. Luce was a little surprised that Catarina could re-strain herself from just taking over. After a minute, though, Dana seemed to become more confident, and the song smoothed out and warmed the air. One of the women Luce was watching suddenly stood up from her chair, then threw herself down on the deck again and embraced the complaining woman's knees, showering them with adoring kisses. No one seemed to think this was un-usual behavior. Their eyes were wide, glazed, unfocused from so much bliss.

Luce dove down and shot across to the other side of the yacht, in case Tessa and her mother were over there somewhere. The yacht was speeding up now as the pilot strove to reach the source of that wonderful sound.

A few more people came out on deck, their mouths lax and round with wonder. They all seemed to be grizzled old sailors, probably hired from the local towns; Luce wasn't surprised that Catarina hadn't been able to work up much enthusiasm.

The yacht was going so fast now that Luce gave up on swim-ming with her head above water and just ripped along below the surface. She heard the eerie, volatile thrum of Rachel's song join-ing Dana's velvet tones and then other voices she recognized: Kayley and Violet, followed by Samantha's tinny soprano. She and Catarina were the only ones keeping quiet, Luce thought. It was overkill, far more enchantment than they needed to drive such a small boat to its doom, but she knew no one cared. They were all caught in the exaltation of their own voices, mad with the joy of power. She felt a rush of compassion for all the girls singing now: after all, they'd spent their human lives being so utterly helpless; how could they fail to be delighted by their ability to dominate anyone who heard them? When Luce shot above the water for another glimpse, the men she could see all looked drugged.

Ten minutes passed, the yacht driving so hard its engine squealed and then began to smoke. Up ahead the cliffs stuck out in a hard jag, and Luce knew it must be the spot Catarina had chosen. Luce could see smoke pouring out of another place near her, too, maybe from the kitchen. It looked like something had caught fire in the yacht's center, but no one moved to go put it out. Luce braced herself for the crash.

There was a grinding, earsplitting crunch, a shudder, and the first body pitched into the water. Luce could tell from the limp way it flopped overboard that it was already dead from the blow, and when it hit the water she saw to her horror that it was wearing a white bandana blotched crimson with blood . . .

How could we? Luce thought numbly. *How could we?* The yacht was still driving forward, its hull splitting wide like a skull hit with an axe, and human bodies tumbled from inside. All Luce wanted was to get away.

Then she thought of Tessa. Catarina must have her by now. Luce began to swim dizzily between hunks of debris, expecting to hear Catarina's voice swell with the wrenching song that would change Tessa forever. A second later it came faintly from far ahead: unmistakably Catarina's exquisite voice, but transfigured into a sound so cold and painful that Luce's chest was crossed by lines of cutting ache. Luce recoiled, and bumped into a warm, flailing body.

It was Tessa, submerged with her eyes closed, her lips oddly pinched. Her brown braids pitched rhythmically with the movements of the water. And Catarina was nowhere near them.

There was only one thing Luce could do. She caught Tessa in her arms, and willed herself as hard as she could into that icy night on the cliffs, into the broken heart of a girl whose uncle had almost raped her, whose mother was long dead, whose father was lost at sea. She felt the pain and darkness beating within her, until the whole cold ocean seemed to be trapped in her heart. And when the ache grew so fierce that she didn't know how she could stand it for another moment, she sang.

It was a terrible, beautiful song, different from anything Luce had ever heard before or would ever want to hear again. The whole sea seemed frantic with grief. Tessa opened her lids and gazed at Luce. Her hazel eyes shone like blood and shattered crystals. And then, to Luce's infinite relief, a cloud of dark shimmering winked around Tessa's head. Luce's song reached into the girl in her arms, bringing back all Tessa's secrets, and in the sparkling Luce saw the beginning of a story: a man screaming at her mother, slamming the door, the sound of a car starting . . . An ugly divorce . . .

It wasn't all that bad, really. Not by mermaid standards. But it was all Luce had to work with. Her song gathered up the angry screams of Tessa's parents and twisted them into bitter music. The screams became another strand of music, weaving through the dark melodic cries of the girl lost on a cliff above the sea.

Tessa squeezed her lips closer, and Luce watched a soft, watery trembling blur the lines of Tessa's body. She was changing! Luce felt ice cold and weak from the pain of her own song, but she knew she had to keep on, just a little longer.

Tessa suddenly thrashed wildly in Luce's arms, and a look of determination tightened her face. Another thrash and her body was solid again, kicking a pair of strong human legs. She glared at Luce, and then an awful realization almost made Luce choke.

Tessa was *fighting* the change. She was struggling against Luce's enchantment with all the strength she had left. Luce looked around and realized they'd been sinking deeper and deeper into the sea as she sang. There was less sun down here, and spiny creatures propelled themselves through the deepening green on all sides.

"No," Tessa said. Luce couldn't hear her speak over the singing that still throbbed up from her chest, but the movement of Tessa's lips was all too clear. A rush of bubbles escaped, and Luce moved to pull Tessa closer, to blow her own air into Tessa's lungs the way she'd seen Catarina do with the young sailor. Tessa raised one hand and shoved Luce back. The dark shimmering around her was completely gone.

"No," Tessa said again, more bubbles gushing out with every word. "I won't let you." Luce was still singing, but the song was much quieter, losing force, and she could hear what Tessa said with the last trace of air in her chest. "I want to die *human*."

12

Anais

Luce barely knew what happened next. She swam uncertainly, still holding Tessa's heavy, unmoving body and feeling its warmth ebb away. It was only when she reached the surface that she really understood she was cradling a corpse, and abruptly let go. Her tail began to lash from rage. Why hadn't Tessa let Luce save her? She had been so *close* . . .

From somewhere around a bend in the cliffs, Luce could hear a song that seemed to be made of metal claws, slashing knives, bright rivulets of mercury. Without thinking, she swam toward it. Even sinking into the cutting grief of Catarina's song was better than being alone with the image of Tessa's face.

The song stopped dead, and Luce could hear Samantha screaming hysterically. "Oh, Catarina, please let her have more air! Just one more try! I can tell, she's about to change, she's about to . . ."

"Samantha, I can't keep *on* like this! I'm exhausted. We're going to have to let her drown." It was Catarina speaking, but Luce was still too stricken to make sense of the words. What did it matter?

"Catarina, please!" Samantha was sobbing, and Luce felt a dull surprise. She hadn't known Samantha could care so deeply about anything besides herself. "She's not human, Cat, even if she does still have legs! She's really one of us! Please, please don't let her die."

Oh, Luce thought vaguely. The metaskaza Samantha was so obsessed with hadn't been Tessa at all, then. There'd been a second girl on board that yacht. That made sense. It was meaningless, stupid, but it made sense. She heard Catarina release a deep sigh, and the cruel song started again. Luce turned the corner and saw a crowd of mermaids with faces contorted from pain, their hands pressed over their ears. They parted to let Luce through, and she saw Catarina and Samantha. On the water between them there was a face, tilted back so that each wave splashed over it. The face was surrounded by a cloud of golden hair, and it was so beautiful Luce could hardly believe it belonged to a human being. Dark sparkling surrounded the girl's closed eyes, and a liquid wobbling took over her limbs in sudden fits . . . She was right on the verge of changing, Luce could see, but Catarina looked so tired that she seemed like she might faint. The song broke off again, and Catarina gasped. The golden-haired girl's body reverted to a distinct human form.

"Drown her," Catarina snarled. "If she hasn't changed by *now* . . ."

Samantha stared around, tears streaming down her swollen face—and spotted Luce.

"Oh, Luce! Oh, please! You've got to help Catarina! I know if the two of you sing together . . . Luce, I know I've been mean to you sometimes, but *please* help!"

Catarina stared wearily up at Luce. Luce was stunned. Now, when she was so utterly sick and empty, she was supposed to do for this girl what she hadn't been able to do for Tessa?

But how could she just stand by while the girl was drowned?

"Only if you hold her *under* this time, Samantha." Catarina moaned. Samantha started to stammer some objection, but Catarina glowered until she fell silent. "I'll only try again if you hold the girl underwater while we sing. It's her last chance."

There's been enough death, Luce thought. *Enough death to last until the world rolls away and leaves the sun forever.* Sick as she felt, she nodded at Samantha and drew a deep breath.

In the next moment the circle of mermaids around them broke—mermaids were diving under the water and racing away, desperate to escape from the nightmare music Luce and Catarina made together. Only Samantha stayed, the human girl's immersed golden head cradled in her shaking hands. Luce felt so drained that she didn't think she could sing well at all. She was astonished to hear the alien power of her voice. She was singing her own grief but also Tessa's death and Miriam's longing as she wandered the rooms of her silent house waiting for the mother who never came back again . . . Luce even sang Samantha's broken bones. For a moment she even wondered if she should make an effort *not* to sing so well—would Catarina think Luce was trying to outdo her?—but the song had her tight in its grip, in its living darkness. Even as they sang together, Luce noticed

Catarina suddenly looking up at her, her eyes wide with pained comprehension. But the song itself was a laceration, a deep wound; surely that was reason enough for Catarina to stare that way.

The face in Samantha's hands trembled, turned into transparent jelly, then vanished, leaving only a pair of blue human eyes. A wave rocked the girl's clothes away. Luce was too consumed by the terrors of her song to feel even faintly surprised, but she could hear Samantha shriek. Then the wavering came back, the water frothed . . .

And the golden-haired girl reappeared. She was even more beautiful than before, and her brilliant azure eyes opened and gazed up at them dreamily through a veil of rippling waves. Her tail was the same sweet, hazy blue as her eyes, her skin was like porcelain, and her golden tresses swished through the shining water. Even in that first moment something about her made Luce uncomfortable. She looked like something off the prow of an old sailing ship, like somebody's fantasy of a mermaid or like a plastic mermaid doll. The iridescence on her sky blue tail was actually *pink*.

Luce and Catarina both stopped singing and watched her. Now that it was quiet the other mermaids started gliding back toward them. Samantha was sobbing with relief.

The blue-tailed metaskaza caught Samantha's shoulder and pulled herself upright, water streaming from her luxuriant hair. Most of the tribe was floating close by now, but no one spoke. Catarina's lids were half closed and she was leaning heavily on Jenna's shoulder. The sky blue eyes gazed carefully at each of them; again Luce felt the same cold unease.

"You killed my *daddy!*" the metaskaza said, and burst into tears.

* * *

It took everyone a moment to recover from the jolt produced by these words. What could they possibly say? Luce was particularly disturbed; her first impulse was to cry out that they'd killed her father, too; that they had to *stop* . . . Then Luce had the sickening realization that, even as the new mermaid howled melodramatically, she was sneaking glimpses through her fingers, watching how they all reacted. Were her tears even real?

"But we—but you—oh, you need to understand, we had to *save* you from him!" Samantha was stammering. Catarina was still too depleted to react at all, and the new mermaid seemed to decide that Samantha must be in charge. She threw her graceful hands around Samantha's throat, though she didn't seem to be making any real effort to squeeze.

"YOU—KILLED—MY—DADDY! It was *you*, wasn't it? Wasn't it?" Samantha was wide-eyed, sputtering garbled attempts at excuses. The new mermaid watched her for a moment with fury that Luce was suddenly perfectly sure was faked. "Admit it!"

"I had to!" Samantha wailed. "I couldn't help it!"

The metaskaza's wails stopped as suddenly as they had started, and her stunning face suddenly composed itself into a sly, halfway smile.

"Well," said the metaskaza shrilly, "I guess it's a good thing I don't care!" And she let out a high, tinkling laugh.

Luce felt like she might vomit. Catarina stared up from Jenna's shoulder, her mouth open, and a look of what Luce hoped was aversion in her eyes. Samantha was also gaping, but her expression was very different, a blend of astonishment and fervent admiration. Jenna and Kayley seemed to be impressed as well. Mermaids might be used to killing, but even for them it was breathtaking to hear someone be so callous about the death of her own family.

The metaskaza seemed to be bored of laughing now. She was inspecting her own tail as if she were trying to calculate how much it had cost.

"*Mermaids!*" she said. "Now, that's going to blow Sasha Jennings's mind when I get back to school!"

This was Catarina's cue, of course, and she tried to launch into an explanation of the situation, that from now on the girl would be living with the tribe. But she was still exhausted, and she sounded strangely feeble. The metaskaza barely listened for a few moments before waving Catarina's explanation away.

"These things don't come off? That's a *serious* drag. Oh, no, you mean I'm *stuck* here?" She looked around at them with obvious distaste; no one but Luce seemed to realize they were all being insulted. "Can't you take me back to Miami?"

No one even tried to answer this. Luce was starting to feel desperately sorry that they hadn't drowned this girl. Was it really too late?

"What's your name?" Samantha asked nervously. The metaskaza looked sharply at her, and seemed to note her expression of rapt adoration with approval.

"Anais," the metaskaza said, flipping back her golden locks. She pronounced it "ann-eye-EEESS."

"I'm Samantha . . ." It came out in a murmur, and Anais fixed her azure eyes on the other blonde's face, assessing something. Luce thought she was deciding how useful Samantha might be.

"Yes?" Anais's voice was suddenly much sweeter. "Well, Samantha, could you please have these . . ." She cocked her head at the watching mermaids. "Your followers, I mean. Could you please have them take me back to Miami?"

"*Catarina's* our queen," Luce snapped before Samantha had time to respond. Anais appeared to notice her for the first time, and she didn't look at all impressed. "Miami's farther than we normally go, but we'd be happy to point you in the right direction." Luce gestured vaguely southward, hoping urgently that Anais would simply swim off before anyone mentioned orcas.

"Luce!" Catarina had snapped out of her stupor to glare reproachfully at Luce; she calmed herself before she spoke again, at least. "I don't think that would be the best idea, do you? Let's show her to the cave . . ."

This was too much for Anais; she let out a sudden whinny of derisive laughter. "Oh, you can't be *serious!*" The mermaids stared at her, and while Luce felt nothing but the purest loathing she could see that some of the others were suddenly self-conscious, even ashamed. "I mean, you guys don't seriously live in a cave! Wow, not even our servants are *that* poor."

"Anais?" Luce said. She was trying to be a bit more careful now, since no one else seemed to share her profound dislike of this brassy girl. "You don't have any servants. Not anymore."

Anais faked bursting into tears again, and Samantha rushed to comfort her.

* * *

All evening Luce waited in vain for someone to tell Anais that mermaids simply didn't talk much about their human lives; it was bad manners. Luce floated on her back in the dim waters of the cave, gazing up at the handful of stars she could see through the holes in the roof and the soft green glow of the luminous crystals, thinking of Tessa. If she swam off to her own little cave, Luce knew, she wouldn't be able to stop crying, and so she turned in drowsy circles here instead. Everyone else was listening raptly to Anais as she prattled on about her father's huge mansion back in Miami, her shopping trips to New York, all the amazing things her cell phone could do. Why didn't anyone tell her to shut up?

"Oh, I love those jeans, too!" Samantha exclaimed eagerly. "I think I had about eight pairs."

Luce put a hand over her mouth to stifle the cough of sick laughter she could feel coming. Of course, Luce didn't know anything about Samantha's human life, apart from what her mother had done to her. But it didn't take a genius to figure out that almost everyone in the tribe had grown up in one of the nearby towns; they were the daughters of fishermen, cannery workers, maybe truck drivers. Their jeans almost certainly had been the cheapest available, and they'd worn hand-me-down sweaters and jackets with the sleeves too short. Luce had a sudden wistful memory of the silvery down jacket her father had given her when they moved up to Alaska.

But the great thing about being a mermaid, Luce thought bitterly, was that none of that stuff mattered. What counted was who you were and how well you could sing . . . And suddenly Luce understood why Samantha was so excited by Anais's bragging. Samantha couldn't fake her singing, after all, but she *could* pretend she'd grown up rich. How would anyone know if it was a lie?

Anais had launched into a feverish description of her sixteenth birthday party. "We had like two hundred people come, and of course it was all catered. Four huge pink cakes! It was on our lawn, and there were hundreds of lanterns everywhere, like this fairyland, and they hired this awesome band! Such hot guys. The keyboard player was just adorable. And at ten these, like, Chinese acrobats came out and performed. This girl could juggle a table with her *feet!* But really, I thought that part was kind of dumb. Like, who really cares about stupid tricks like that? Like trained animals or something."

Luce started to think of heading back to her own cave. Crying by herself would be better than listening to this.

"Oh, *yeah*," Anais trilled. "I keep forgetting to ask you. Where are all the guys?"

In spite of herself, Luce started paying more attention. She'd wondered about this too, and might have asked if she hadn't been afraid of upsetting Catarina. She'd had a feeling this might be another of those subjects Cat found hard to discuss.

"Oh," Catarina said, and Luce was glad to hear that her tone was slightly curt, if still weary. "Boys can't be mermaids. There aren't any."

Anais was so surprised she shut up for a second, though Luce thought grimly that the quiet probably wouldn't last for long.

"But, I mean . . ." It was Violet's shy, hesitant voice speaking now. "I mean, boys get hit and stuff, too. Like *horrible* things happen to them sometimes. My brother—"

"Yes," Catarina agreed shortly. "Humans don't just stop with their daughters."

"So—I mean—that sparkling, what you called the *indication* . . ." Violet seemed so intimidated that her voice was slipping into silence, and Luce could barely make out what she was saying. "I mean, have you ever seen the indication around a boy? If you did, then couldn't you change him, Cat?"

Luce glanced over at Catarina; she couldn't help feeling worried about her. The beautiful red-gold head was leaning back against an outcropping of rock. Her skin looked deathly white, and her eyelids kept sinking. She was so drained by the effort it had taken to change Anais that it was as if she were just emerging from a long and severe illness. Luce was more than a little unwell, too. Her head felt airy, feverish.

"I've seen it," Catarina said, and there was such sadness in her voice that everyone went silent. Even Anais seemed to be listening intently. Luce was suddenly positive that Catarina had tried to change at least one human boy into a merman, and that she had failed. "I've seen it but only a few times. But they just drowned, Violet. I don't know why, but they can't be like us. No one can help them . . ."

"Maybe you just didn't try hard enough," Anais complained. "It's going to be pretty boring if we don't get some guys here soon." Luce was more disgusted than ever. How could Anais accuse Catarina of not really trying when it was only Catarina's excruciating efforts that had saved Anais's rotten life?

Luce was glad to see that Catarina was finally getting angry. It brought some color back to her cheeks, some of the fire back to her voice.

"Queen *Marina* couldn't do it, Anais," Catarina snarled. "And she was far and away the greatest singer I've ever heard. She almost *killed* herself trying to change the boy she I—" Suddenly Catarina seemed to realize she'd said too much. The silence in the cave became so overpowering that only Anais had the gall to violate it.

"The boy she *what*, Cat?" Anais's voice was sickly sweet but venomous at the same time. "You mean, the boy she *loved*?" Anais seemed to be considering this. Catarina glared, refusing to answer. "But, wow, think about it. I mean, how would your Queen Marina have had *time* to fall in love with a boy unless she was breaking that—what do you call it? Those silly *rules* you were telling me about."

Only Samantha and Jenna laughed at this, and even they sounded a bit too shrill. Everyone else seemed shocked. When Samantha stopped tittering, the quiet lasted for a disturbingly long time.

"If you think the timahk is so silly, Anais," Catarina finally said in a silky, deadly, regal voice, "then by all means. Try breaking it."

* * *

Anais was finally quiet, and the mermaids went back to talking about other things, especially the singing Dana and Rachel had done. Luce was still drifting on her back at a distance from the beach, but now and then she glanced over at Anais—who seemed to realize she'd miscalculated. She looked sulky, but her blue eyes were hard and focused on her own hands, as if she were concentrating on working something out. Luce had the idea that the next time Anais spoke she'd be taking a very different tone.

Luce kept peering sideways at the shimmering around Anais. What was it that had brought her here, especially if her human life was so ridiculously perfect that she couldn't stop bragging about it? But somehow Luce couldn't get the sparkling to cohere into images. At most she could see rare, blurry winks of what seemed like perfectly ordinary events: Anais sitting in a hairdresser's, Anais on the phone to someone . . . Luce was perplexed. How could getting a haircut be so heartbreaking that it would turn you into a mermaid? It made no sense.

And most of the time Luce couldn't even manage to see that much. It worried her. If anything, the dark glimmering was even thicker around Anais than it was around the other mermaids, but it was *empty*. It was like a vacant house. It didn't seem to hold a story.

Luce felt a powerful urge to be alone and think, even if that meant remembering Tessa's death. She swished over to the beach to tell Catarina she was going back to her own small cave, half expecting an argument.

Catarina just nodded, though. "You must need some peace after everything today, Luce." She stopped and gazed at Luce searchingly; there was something tense in her expression. "You shouldn't have had to go through that. I should have managed it alone, or else . . ." Catarina barely glanced at Anais.

"It's okay, Cat," Luce said; she suddenly felt nervous. "You couldn't help it." She wanted to ask Catarina why the indication sparkling around Anais was so different, so void, but it seemed like a bad idea to bring that up where someone else might hear. She settled for glancing as pointedly as she could at Anais, hoping that would encourage Catarina to look for herself. "Maybe she wasn't quite ready?" Luce suggested in a low voice. "And that's why changing her was so hard?" Catarina didn't seem interested in pursuing the question, though. Instead her gaze was so intently focused on Luce that they might have been all alone in the cave.

"Luce . . ." Catarina seemed to be searching for words, but she was so exhausted that her eyes began to scan the rocky walls helplessly, looking for something that wasn't there. "Luce, the way you sang today . . ." Luce didn't know what it was in Catarina's tone that made her feel so shy all of a sudden.

"I was just . . . trying to help you, Cat. I mean, of course you didn't actually *need* my help . . ." Luce noticed how dishonest this sounded; they both knew perfectly well that Catarina couldn't have managed Anais's transformation without her. Luce scrambled to make it sound more convincing. "It seemed like you were getting so tired out." Catarina shook her head slowly and a wounded look came into in her eyes.

"Oh." Her gaze flitted restlessly around the cave; she might have been tracking a vision that winked through the dark corners above them. Then abruptly she was completely fixed on Luce again, actually glaring, her gray eyes much too bright. "That's not what I *mean*, Luce. I think you know that! Do you think I can't see when you're lying to me?" Now Catarina was definitely angry; her voice was somewhere between a hiss and a growl. "*Why* do you want to control me, Luce? Is it so satisfying for you to force me to remember these things? If you can't be loved you can at least have power? But Luce, really, that's a terrible choice to make . . ."

Luce felt even more alarmed than hurt by this; Catarina's gaze was wandering dizzily again, and her voice flared up in sudden fits and then collapsed back into a weakened murmur. The only explanation Luce could think up for Catarina's aggression was that she was still half deranged from the terrible singing they'd done that day. Had changing Anais damaged her irreparably?

"Cat!" Luce stared into those blankly shining gray eyes, and her words came out jumbled and urgent. "You're still feeling sick from all that or you wouldn't . . . You'd know I would never want to do anything that could hurt you! Or *control* you."

They watched each other for a while. Only moments before Catarina had actually seemed to hate her, but now she reached out and caressed Luce's hair with slow, airy strokes. The hardness in her face was replaced by longing; her mouth was pursed. This inexplicable tenderness disturbed Luce as much as her rage had; either way, Catarina seemed more than a touch unbalanced.

"Of course." Catarina shook herself and smiled; Luce still thought she looked unwell, though. "Of course you wouldn't, Luce. Forgive me. I'm not . . ." She gave another quick twisting movement, and squeezed her eyes closed for an instant. "I'm not myself. Samantha kept begging me to go on singing for much too long, and the strain of it . . ."

"It's okay." Luce could barely get the words out; the awful things Catarina had said to her were still swirling through her mind. Could they be true? "I don't mind, Cat. Just as long as you're okay, and you don't still think—"

"Oh!" Catarina seemed to start up out of a reverie. "No, Luce. I was being terribly unfair. You *do* forgive me?" She was still stroking Luce's head, and her hand lingered lightly against Luce's cheek. Luce thought for a second.

"I mean, I don't want to *say* I forgive you, Cat. Because I wasn't mad. I just got worried, like maybe you were seriously hurt by—by what we did today."

Catarina's smile was suddenly as warm and vibrant as it had ever been; Luce found herself beaming in response.

"Oh, my strange little Luce . . ." The smile sharpened into a lopsided grin, odd on Catarina's magnificent face. "Say it anyway."

Luce was almost too discomfited to say the words, but she forced them out. "Then I forgive you, Cat. Except I *really* wasn't angry."

"I was being unfair." Catarina's tone had turned thoughtful, dreamy. "It's not like you've been working to learn how to sing that way. It just came out spontaneously, out of who you really are. A gift . . ."

Luce looked down, hoping Catarina didn't notice the heat rising in her cheeks.

"Go get some rest, Luce. You pushed yourself too hard today, too . . ."

Anais started chattering again as Luce swam off. Luce could hear her lavishing compliments on Catarina and asking how she got her hair to be so shiny.

*   *   *

That night Luce dreamed about her father again.

She was swimming alone in a lead gray ocean, over high, chaotic waves. There was no land in sight, and even the sky was so low, so flat and dark that it didn't seem to be a sky at all but rather a sheet of tarnished metal just a few feet above her head. She'd been swimming for a long, long time; she needed to find someplace to rest . . .

Up ahead was a square of yellow light. Luce swam toward it, and found herself staring through a picture window with the curtains drawn back on either side. On the far side of the glass was a cheap motel room with mustard-colored walls. She recognized it at once, even before she noticed the girl propped on her elbows on the bed watching a dance contest on TV, the tall curly-haired man pacing and talking on his cell phone. Luce felt disoriented, annoyed. What was she doing out in the water? She belonged in that warm room, but there was no door. Nothing but the window, isolated like a ship on the sea, water slapping at its front. Luce rose and fell with the waves, her face inches from the glass.

Then the girl on the bed shifted, rolling onto her side so that Luce could see more of her face, and Luce's stomach lurched with a horrible realization. The girl wasn't her. Someone else had taken her place! She watched as the girl knocked one long brown braid out of the way, revealing her hazel eyes and her funny, crooked, half-smiling mouth . . . Luce knocked frantically on the glass, but Tessa ignored her.

Her father snapped his phone shut. Even through the glass Luce could hear it perfectly. He looked upset, but as Luce watched he meticulously pulled his face into a smile, then sat down next to Tessa and started ruffling her hair.

"That was Luce," her father explained as he threw down his phone. "She just can't understand why I've had to replace her."

Tessa sighed sympathetically and sat up, throwing her arms around his neck.

"It's none of Luce's business!" Tessa exclaimed. "You tried and tried to persuade her to stop being so—so *destructive,* and she just wouldn't listen. She couldn't expect you to wait around forever, could she?"

Luce screamed at them and banged on the glass, but they didn't seem able to hear her. At least they were pretending not to hear. Her heart felt like it was about to split in her chest, and she could hardly breathe. The waves supporting her pitched faster, and the room in front of her veered and lunged in her eyes.

"It's not even the destructiveness that gets me the worst," her father said. "Maybe I could've lived with that. But she won't stop being *self*-destructive either. It's like she doesn't respect herself at all anymore, and I just can't stand to see it. Killing her own friends!" He gave Tessa a rueful smile. "But at least I have you instead, baby doll. And once your mother gets here we'll be a real family again. Settle down someplace, and get you going to school as a regular thing . . ."

Luce's head was above the water line as she jarred up and down on the smoke-colored waves, but that didn't help. She was still suffocating, clawing the bright window with both hands. It wasn't real air around her here, and she would only breathe again inside that room . . .

A woman in a white bandana and a black sequined dress walked out of the shadows, and Luce felt a surge of hope when she saw how young and lovely her face was. It must be her own mother not Tessa's! She'd be furious with her father, tell him once and for all that Luce was completely irreplaceable, then somehow gather Luce in her arms and pull her into warmth and safety. Luce waited anxiously to hear what she would say.

Instead of speaking the woman caught her father's chin, leaned in, and started kissing him ravenously, pushing him back onto the bed and straddling him while Tessa watched. And then Luce realized why the woman was wearing that bandana. It was to hide her fiery red-gold hair. Even Catarina, then . . . Everyone had betrayed her . . .

The waves rocked at her shoulders. They were waiting. Luce was the *real* queen of the mermaids, and the waves would obey her commands. At one word from her the glass would shatter, and all of the people in that room would drown. She could hear herself shriek the order, telling the waves to *kill* . . .

There was a terrible sound, and then a different darkness was around her, and a narrow, rocky space. It was a long time before Luce was able to understand that she was awake in her small cave, that it had all been a dream. And it was even longer before she could stop sobbing.

13

The Mirror

Over the next several days Luce started having more trouble being around the other mermaids. When she heard them talking cheerfully about anything, but especially about sinking ships, she had to fight down tears. And Anais chattered so much that hanging around the main cave or the dining beach meant being constantly bombarded by her hard, chirpy voice, her descriptions of diamond necklaces and pop stars. Being reminded of human things only made Luce feel sad. It didn't help that Catarina hadn't recovered from the frailty that had afflicted her ever since they'd changed Anais; she was moody and remote and didn't talk much.

Luce felt happiest alone in her own small cave, singing quietly to herself or making up the songs she would have sung for Tessa if only she had lived. She could lead her voice through soft, flowing formations as complex and airy as clouds, make it spread like feathers, divide it so that she was singing several interwoven melodies at once. Her voice was usually willing to obey her now, as if it also enjoyed the unexpected new songs Luce was inventing. Once in a while it still grabbed hold of her and dragged her into the death song, but that was happening less often now, and Luce had learned to be patient when it did. She'd let the death song exhaust itself then lure her voice back into spirals like rising smoke, pleats of folded silk. Conjuring new sounds became a kind of game for her: she'd spread her voice out, shake it, make it into falling leaves or crackling ice . . . She had the feeling that she simply must be getting closer to discovering the new and hidden power she'd been looking for; sometimes she could almost feel it, just waiting around the next curl of her song. She could just catch glimpses of it, and it had its own secret shimmering, not as dark as the shimmering around her body: something surprising, eloquent, blue-white and blue-gold.

Luce was lying on her back with her eyes closed, twirling her fins, as she tried a new experiment. She spread her voice out in a single deep note as flat as a sheet of paper, then let it start to curl in on itself, wrapping into a slow aching chord at the edges. Something wet nudged at Luce's shoulder, and she opened her eyes enough to peer through the fringe of her lashes, still singing. It was probably just a larva; sometimes her singing attracted them, and this cave was easy for them to crawl into.

It wasn't a larva at all. Instead a stiff, pointed wave was standing next to her, moving in small fidgety, eager leaps as if it couldn't wait for her to notice it. Luce stopped singing in surprise, and the enthusiastic little wave collapsed with a splash.

For a while Luce just stared down at the gently lapping water where the wave had been. It seemed as if the wave had actually been responding to her voice, but of course that was impossible.

At least she *hoped* it was impossible. It reminded her far too much of the hideous nightmare where she'd commanded the waves to murder her father. Luce didn't want the ocean to start obeying her, not after that dream, and she told herself that the freakish little wave must have been some sort of aberrant result of water currents. That had to be it. Her voice might be magical, but there was no way it could control something that wasn't even alive! Whatever the new magic was that she was looking for, it simply couldn't be *this*.

Luce repeated these thoughts over and over until she half believed them. Even so, she didn't try bending her voice in quite that way again, and the solitary cave suddenly seemed too narrow, its dim walls pressing in on her. Before too long she couldn't stand her isolation anymore, and squirmed out through the narrow passage into the widening green-gold sea. Luce wasn't keeping track of the days, but she guessed it must be early June, and while the water would still be bitterly cold for a human it felt luxuriously warm to her.

She drifted toward the dining beach, thinking the whole time of turning and swimming back the other way. She stopped often, lingering to observe orange starfish whose long, tangled limbs were dense with bright spikes, then a yellow warty animal like a rotten banana that crept across a mass of barnacles. She wished she'd taken the time while she was still human to learn the names of the creatures she lived with now.

As she came around the angled cliff that opened onto the dining beach she could already hear Anais holding court. A cluster of larvae clung to one another, drawn forward by the sounds of laughter and nosing cautiously forward; Luce swam past them and into Anais's chirpy voice. "Yeah, I wasn't sure exactly where the yacht went down, but Samantha remembered. I don't get what you guys were thinking just *leaving* all that stuff. Like who wouldn't think that was the whole point? I mean, here's this, like, really classy yacht for once instead of all the crappy fishing boats and whatever that these losers up here sail around in. And you didn't even look to see what was in it!" She laughed; the sound of it was raspy, grating. "I mean, yeah, Jenna says, like, the TVs and things wouldn't work after they'd been underwater. She talked me out of bringing one back. But that one friend of my mom's had some great clothes . . ."

As always when she heard Anais's voice Luce felt as if she'd swallowed some slime-covered, rusty lump of metal; it distracted her from paying much attention to what Anais was actually saying, so when she came around the corner it took her a moment to understand what was in front of her. Almost everyone was lounging around in a row at the edge of the beach: the dreamlike, nuanced colors of their tails gleaming through the shallow silver water, their beautiful faces framed by the pale sand behind them and then the steep gray of the stones. But there were other, more jarring colors intruding on the image in front of Luce: Samantha, Anais, and Jenna were all wearing brightly patterned bikini tops under filmy chiffon wraps in shocking shades of lime green, turquoise, magenta. Complicated diamond earrings swung against their necks and gold watches flashed on their wrists; Samantha was wearing a pair of huge sunglasses with baby pink frames, pouting in an exaggerated way and staring into something round and white, then passing it on to Jenna. They were laughing, posing. Jenna was busy applying lip gloss, but it seemed like salt water had seeped into the tube. It was too runny and kept dribbling in a candy pink tentacle down her chin.

A *mirror*, Luce realized, and in the same moment she felt a stab of inexplicable anxiety at the idea of seeing what her own face looked like now. She hadn't had a glimpse of herself since she'd changed.

"So, the thing is, there's still a bunch of stuff none of us really liked, if anybody wants to go back for it. Of course it's only fair I got all the best things, since it was my daddy's yacht!"

It was just Anais being stupid, Luce thought. What would a mermaid want with a lot of human leftovers? She felt a kind of sick amusement at the thought of Anais trying to lug a television back through the waves. Vapid as Anais could be, hadn't she realized that the cave didn't exactly have electric outlets? Luce waited for someone to tell Anais how clueless she was being.

Instead there was a patter of excited voices, and after a moment Luce realized that half a dozen mermaids were planning an expedition back to the site of the yacht's wreck so they could search for plunder.

"Want to come, Luce?" Dana called out as she swam up next to her. "Check out what's left on the yacht? You know what would look great on you, would be if we could get some kind of sparkly barrettes for your hair. Get you styling *harder*." Luce was staring around for Catarina when Dana popped the mirror right in front of her face. Reflexively she jerked back, but it was already too late.

The face in the mirror was recognizably her own, Luce realized; she had the same long, charcoal brown eyes and very pale olive skin as ever, even if now that skin gave off a faint greenish radiance. She still had slightly sharp, slightly foxlike features and a broad, smooth forehead under spiky dark hair; her lips were still unusually red. But Luce had never thought of herself as particularly pretty, and the face hovering in front of her was uncomfortably, aggressively beautiful. The sight of her own face was like needles stabbing at her eyes, and Luce found herself thinking that the girl in the mirror had beauty in the same way that someone might have a consuming disease.

She couldn't have explained why, but Luce knew her inhuman beauty had the color of endless loneliness. She lowered her eyes and wondered if her darkly splendid face had seemed horrifying to Tessa. Maybe *that* was why Tessa had preferred death to becoming what Luce was now?

"I bet you just can't believe how *hot* you are now, can you?" Dana laughed. "I was always pretty hot and everything, but I was seriously blown away when I saw myself. Scoring the mirror was a *great* idea." It was out of character, Luce thought, for Dana to be so oblivious to what someone was feeling, but in this case Luce was grateful that Dana didn't just see through her. Her feelings now were too awful and too private to ever share with anyone.

"It's incredible," Luce said; that much was true, at least. "I mean, I wondered sometimes if I was gorgeous now in the way you all are." Dana smiled sweetly. She seemed gloriously happy, delighted by the soft, swirling breeze and by the newly discovered power of her own face; Dana's happiness made Luce only more aware of her own aching restlessness.

"You *totally* are."

Luce shook her head. "You're still a lot prettier than I am."

"Don't be so sure." Luce was sure that Dana was just saying it to be nice; Dana's clear, dark face had a haunting glamour that even Luce's transfigured appearance couldn't approach. "You have those amazing eyes. And such great lashes. Maybe we could find you, I don't know"—she laughed, too brightly—"some, like, waterproof mascara? You're coming with us, right?"

Luce looked for Catarina again, but she wasn't on the beach. She couldn't help thinking that Catarina would put a stop to this. It wasn't exactly against the timahk, maybe, but it still seemed wrong. The clinging larvae had paddled closer now; they massed together like seaweed, except with a scattering of sorrowful human eyes. As they approached the beach a couple of the braver ones began to break away from the group, and Luce noticed that a lot of them were staring at Anais.

"I don't really want any human stuff," Luce finally said; Dana just looked uncomprehending. "I mean, isn't that kind of weird for a mermaid? If we want to be like them, then why do we go around killing them?" Luce knew instantly that she'd said too much. Dana was obviously offended.

"God, Luce. Don't you think you're maybe being too uptight about this? We're just having *fun* for once." Dana's tone suddenly shifted; the flippant irritation was gone, and she spoke in a sudden rush of wistful sorrow. "I mean, whatever, we all have to deal with . . . with all the things we're never going to have now. Like, I really wanted to go to college and be a pediatrician. I'll never get to do any of that. And Rachel . . . she just had this one necklace from her mom, and she lost it when we changed. So just because *you* don't miss human things, Luce . . .

I mean, it's easy to go around *saying* we shouldn't want anything that might, kind of, make up for all that . . ."

Luce wasn't sure how to answer this, and stared off with her cheeks burning. Maybe Dana was right; if owning a few human objects helped the mermaids ease the ache they all felt, then why shouldn't they collect whatever they could find? After all, she could comfort herself with her singing, but that wouldn't work for everyone. She wondered if she should apologize, but Dana wasn't looking at her anymore, and she couldn't bring herself to try to break through the awkward silence that had come between them.

She noticed that one fairly large bluish larva had gone nuzzling up to Anais's satiny cobalt tail, watching the brilliant scales with obvious fascination. Anais was busy chattering and seemed not to see it. As Luce watched, the larva reached out and barely touched Anais's fins, and when Anais didn't react the larva grew bolder, and closed its small lips softly on the waving, pink-shimmered tail.

Still Anais didn't seem to register what was happening for a second. Then she let out a wrenching shriek and flung her tail up in an enormous cascade of water. The bluish larva jerked back and splashed down on its side, waving its stubby arms in fright. It seemed too disoriented to swim away and only gabbled, a bubble of saliva swelling on its pink lips. Everyone cracked up laughing, even Luce.

Everyone except for Anais, that is.

"That is SO not funny! That disgusting thing was actually tonguing me! Oh God, that was just so *gross* . . ." Anais raised her tail threateningly above the larva, which cowered below her, too afraid to move away. "I should bash its nasty little head in."

Do it, Luce thought eagerly. *Do it, and then we can finally get rid of you.* Then Luce saw the helpless terror on the larva's face and felt deeply ashamed of her wish to see it injured.

Samantha threw herself across the expanse of water separating her from Anais, and caught the blue tail in her arms before it could strike. Anais tried to twist free, and rocked sloppily over into deeper water so that she and Samantha landed in a wet heap. Samantha's pink sunglasses were knocked off one ear and hung at an absurd angle across her face, and Luce could hear the raspy sound of ripping chiffon. The larva finally had the sense to flop back a few feet, but then it stopped and gawked again. It seemed mesmerized by Anais, by her bland golden perfection.

"Samantha! Why are you trying to stop me from killing that thing? Eeew, we should really kill all of them. If I just had our housekeeper here I'd make her do it. Clean this place *up*." Anais sat up, and abruptly seemed to realize that every mermaid there was staring at her in stunned quiet.

"Anais! I've told you! The timahk! If you hurt that larva Cat will throw you out on your own!" Samantha wailed. She was still clinging to Anais's tail, sprawled across it and pinning it to the seabed. To talk she had to torque her upper body back and crane her neck, barely holding her mouth above water.

"Jeez," Anais said. "It's not like Catarina's even here. She wouldn't have to know about it, would she?" But there was a dubious look on her face as she glanced around at the circle of mermaids watching her. Samantha finally let go of the sky blue tail and pulled herself upright, straightening her sunglasses.

"You can't hurt larvae, ever," Kayley finally said. She sounded nervous, and the words clearly cost her tremendous effort. "Maybe there are a few mermaids here who would lie to Catarina about something really important like that, but most of us wouldn't even dream of it." Luce knew Kayley meant it as a dig at her; she clearly hadn't recovered from her resentment of the time Luce had lied to protect Jenna. Jenna shot Luce a long, contorted, almost hostile look.

Luce found herself wondering what she was doing with them. Had her idea that she belonged here never been more than a fantasy?

"So you're saying you'd tattle on me, Kayley?" Anais asked disdainfully. "You would never break one of Catarina's big bad rules, would you?"

"They're not just *Catarina's* rules," Luce objected, but her sudden discomfort made her voice shrink almost to nothing, and no one seemed to hear her.

There was a long, disturbing pause; Luce was acutely aware of the silvery diamond patterns flowing across the surface of the water.

"Want to head back to the yacht?" Dana asked uncomfortably. "I'd like to look around." No one answered.

"Who says Catarina gets to be queen, anyway?" Anais snapped after a moment. "Like, how do you guys *decide* that?" Luce was grateful to see that even Samantha seemed piqued by this. Luce couldn't understand how even Anais could ask that question; Catarina was so savage, so strong and elegant. Who could compare to her?

"Catarina is our best singer! Definitely. You haven't really heard her yet, Anais—like, you were sort of half unconscious when she was singing to you before—but she's just—she has the most gorgeous voice! And the things she can do with it . . ." Samantha had begun with enthusiasm but then trailed off enviously and looked away. Anais gazed around at everyone.

"So *what*? Like, just being the best singer makes you queen automatically? Shouldn't it be, I don't know, something that makes sense? Like, whoever was oldest when they changed?" Kayley shot her another look; they all knew that Anais was almost seventeen, three months older than Catarina had been at her transformation. Luce grimaced at the lack of subtlety. But Kayley's courage seemed to have exhausted itself. A glance shot around the group, passing from one girl to the next before Miriam finally looked up, and Luce suddenly realized that Miriam almost never talked anymore.

"Of course it has to be the best singer who's queen! That's how it is with all the mermaids in the world. You can recognize the one who has the right to be queen by her song."

Anais glared around and seemed to realize that no one disagreed with this. "Okay. You guys say that's how it is; I guess it must be." She tipped her golden head and mulled this over. "So, who's *second* best here?"

"Luce." Miriam said it instantly, as if it were simply unquestionable. "She's amazing, too. Almost as great as Cat is, really." Luce could see Anais recoil with a look of mingled surprise and irritation, then flick a contemptuous glance in her direction. "You don't know that, Anais? Luce was the one who helped Catarina change you. If it wasn't for her you would have died." There was a cold edge to Miriam's voice now.

"Ooooh!" Anais said. "Then I guess I owe her a huge thank-you." Luce had never heard anyone sound less sincere. "Luce, I want to thank you very much for being so brave and wonderful and saving my pitiful little life!" She didn't even bother to meet Luce's eyes as she said it, and the stab of queasy alarm Luce had felt the first time she met Anais came back in her stomach.

Luce wasn't about to answer. She didn't see any reason to play along with one of Anais's games.

"Luce! What's your problem? You could at least tell Anais 'you're welcome'!" Samantha sniped. So she was back to being Anais's sycophant, Luce thought bitterly. "She said 'thank you', like, totally nicely! Don't you think her feelings will be hurt if you just blow her off?"

Luce gaped at Samantha for a second. Did she really believe a single word she was saying?

"I don't think it's possible to hurt Anais's feelings," Luce announced flatly. "I don't think she has any." Several of the girls gasped and Anais crumpled up her face; Luce knew there was going to be another fit of fake sobbing. Even if Luce had belonged here at first, she thought, maybe she didn't anymore; there was no way she could belong in a place where anyone took Anais seriously, admired her, much less let her boss them around. At the same time this was the first place where anyone had ever accepted her, where it had almost seemed she might finally have a home; why did Anais have to ruin everything? She knew, too, that nothing was waiting for her in her own small cave except loneliness, and the fear of what her voice might be able to accomplish.

Anais started whimpering, pointing at Luce with a trembling finger while she sank her face against Samantha's shoulder.

The murmuring got louder, and Luce saw Jenna scowling at her, her forehead crimped from anger, her knuckles pale in her brown hands. Luce decided to get away before anyone could insist that she apologize. She spun out into the open sea, rolling her body over and over to try to shake the anger she felt at everyone. How could they possibly fall for Anais? She was so horribly, transparently phony, so obviously out to take over control of the tribe if she could. Why else was she so interested in what it took to become queen?

Something long and bright yellow rocked in a sloppy, haphazard way on the surface a short way ahead, but the quick rippling distorted it so much that Luce wasn't sure what it was. A large school of fat, bluish fish suddenly stirred the water in front of her, making it hard to see much besides quick winks of color. Still, she was glad to have something distract her from the seething aversion that made her keep thinking about Anais. She swirled up to get a look at the yellow thing: it turned out to be an empty single-seat kayak, tossed on the waves. It was still right side up, though, and Luce noticed a bottle of water and a bag lunch tucked at the bottom, along with a single gray man's sneaker. Whoever had been paddling it hadn't capsized, then. A neon orange life jacket was floating a few yards away, and Luce had the disturbing sense that the kayaker had stripped off the life jacket deliberately before diving overboard. She knew immediately that there'd been something in the water he'd wanted more than life itself, something with cream-colored shoulders surrounded by drifting rays of red-gold hair, something with a voice like living flames. He'd sunk down held in the arms of the most perfect beauty he'd ever seen, breathing the bubbles she fed him from her lips, until he didn't breathe anymore . . .

It was *much* too close to the dining beach, Luce thought. Someone could have heard, someone could have swum out to see what was happening. How could Catarina take a risk like that? Impulsively Luce grabbed the kayak and started towing it away. It would be better if none of the other mermaids saw it; that way no one would ask questions. As she swam on dragging the kayak behind her she found herself roiling with anger. It was bad enough that Catarina had just murdered someone, but did she really have to be so stupid about it? Was she *trying* to get caught? Luce tugged the kayak a full two miles from shore before shoving it away. The awful image of Catarina surrounded by a pack of indignant mermaids kept recurring in Luce's mind: Catarina banished and swimming off into gray emptiness while Luce watched helplessly.

By the time she got back to her small cave Luce was in such a foul mood that she didn't even bother to control her own singing. She didn't care if the death song came back, how high and wildly it rose, or where it carried her. She even wanted it. She let her voice stretch out in free, feverish expansion, waiting for that heart-piercing note at the top of the stairs. She waited, but her voice was somewhere lower, smoother. It was the first time she'd deliberately allowed it to do whatever it wanted, and to her amazement it ignored the death song completely. Instead it glossed itself outward, rolled up at the corners . . .

And a feather-shaped wave appeared directly in a beam of brilliant sun: a frond of water, golden green, with a star in its heart. It pranced and waved at Luce as if it were overjoyed to see her, then as her voice tightened in on itself it gave a little gleaming leap and raced at her. Luce tried to make her voice stop but its hold was too strong, and the tiny, shining wave rose taller and straighter, bobbing a little at the tip. It swayed and waited for Luce's voice to tell it what to do.

It was real, then. The wave was at her command. It was exactly, exactly like her horrible dream. She must have a secret desire—one she couldn't even consciously acknowledge—to hurt the people she loved most. She must be just as cruel as Anais, or maybe even worse. Anais had laughed when her father died, but even so, she probably didn't have dreams about murdering him herself!

Luce held her tail out of the water long past the point where the pain throttled her song. She kept it up, her fins contracting frantically in the cool air, until a scream ripped out of her throat.

It took an hour of lying there, promising herself that she would never, ever allow that particular song to escape from her again, before Luce had the courage to try singing at all. Her voice seemed much more docile now, and by the time she'd spun through a long series of airy, haunting trills Luce began to feel better. There was evil in her voice, and cruelty, but she told herself that as long as she kept practicing she'd eventually learn to control it; she'd make it into something beautiful and even innocent. She'd change what it meant to be a mermaid, and they could all live at peace . . .

By the time she left her little cave she was exhausted from so much concentrating, and ravenously hungry. Her thoughts were so completely taken up with the prospect of dinner that she wasn't paying much attention as she wriggled through the cave's skinny entrance, still humming softly. There was a sudden heave in the water and a splash as if something like a seal had just dove off the rocks right next to her, but when Luce looked toward the disturbance the thing that had made it was already gone.

14

Happy Birthday

Over the next few days Luce kept mostly to herself, but she still noticed that the warmer weather seemed to be bringing more boats into their territory: small cruise ships crossed through the waters not far from their cave, their decks crowded with tourists who leaned eagerly over the railings to gaze at seals and whales, and now and then there was a glossy private yacht like the one that had brought Anais. Those boats were all safe for now, though, Luce thought; Anais's yacht had sunk not long after the Coast Guard boat, and she knew Catarina would want to hold off for a while, maybe even for a few weeks, so that the number of shipwrecks in their area wouldn't become too outrageous. Luce thought that it must already seem a bit suspicious to the humans, and she wondered sometimes if anyone on land had recognized a pattern. She couldn't escape the disquieting sense that some sort of danger was approaching, and she'd finally made up her mind to try and get Catarina on her own and confide her worries about Anais.

It made her nervous, though. Catarina had become so unpredictable, so moody; she either adored Luce or scowled at her, both for no apparent reason. What if she just got angry? Luce swam slowly back to the main cave, stopping often to drift along submerged, with her face turned up to watch the broken, writhing filaments of sunlight weaving through the water. She was dreading the conversation with Catarina so much that when she finally slipped through the tunnel into the main cave she lingered at the bottom for a while, reluctant to sweep up and show herself.

After a minute she realized that there were just a few mermaids in the cave. From her vantage deep in the cave's pool she could see the tips of three tails flicking lazily, their colors dimmed and wavering in the shady green water. One of them definitely flashed red-gold, though, and Luce thought she could make out the very pale, pearly green of Samantha's tail, too. She wasn't sure who the third mermaid was until she heard Anais's brash, piercing voice. The water barely muted it at all.

"You know, I'm just dying to hear you really sing, Cat. Everyone keeps telling me how fantastic you are. Like, I keep asking them to compare you to some, you know, some famous human singer I've heard, but they say it's impossible. They say it's just too incredible to even describe that way!"

It took a moment for Catarina to answer, and when she did her voice was weary and smoldering, as if her thoughts had been lost in some other world. "I don't think you can compare any mermaid's singing to a human's, Anais . . . Even a mermaid who we'd barely count as a singer is better than *any* of them." There was another lull; Catarina seemed to be having trouble focusing. "Haven't you tried singing yourself yet?"

"Oh, I've just tried a little bit with Samantha," Anais chirped. "I'm too shy to sing in front of you and Luce, when everybody keeps saying how great you both are." Luce knew that had to be a lie. She couldn't imagine Anais having the sensitivity to feel *shy* about anything.

"Hey, I have an idea!" It was Samantha's voice now, and even through the dulling and distortion of the water Luce thought it had a very strange sound. It was too hard and bright and tinny, as if Samantha were rehearsing lines from a play. "Luce has been giving singing lessons to Dana and Rachel, right? Why don't you ask her to help Anais, too?" Luce squirmed with discomfort at the idea, even as she wondered what could have possibly prompted Samantha to suggest such a thing. She must have noticed that Luce and Anais couldn't stand each other.

"Oh, Samantha, you know Luce doesn't like me." Anais had the same peculiar sound now, and Luce began wondering if she and Samantha had composed this scene together in advance. "I don't know why. I really try as hard as I can to be nice to her, but she always acts like she hates me! The only reason I can think of is that she knows I've heard her practicing singing by herself all the time, like maybe she doesn't want anybody to know about that. But *why* would she want to keep that such a big secret?" The water around Luce felt colder and darker; there was the sensation of something squeezing her, a giant clammy fist.

"Luce is always practicing?" Catarina was paying more attention now, but her voice turned flat and metallic, the way it got when she was trying not to let anyone know she was upset.

"See how *weird* Luce is?" Samantha shrieked abruptly, with a sudden spasm of her pearly tail. "Like, you're practically her best friend, right, Cat? And she doesn't even tell *you* what she's doing. That's totally why she's always going off alone. Yeah, she just sits in her cave and sings to herself all day long. I've heard her, too. I mean, I can't imagine why she feels like she needs to practice so *much*. Miriam thinks she's already just as amazing as you are." That wasn't what Miriam said at all, Luce wanted to object; she'd only said that Luce was *almost* as good. Why was Samantha lying about that?

"Does *Miriam* think so?" Catarina wasn't hiding her bitterness anymore. Her voice cut like razors through dead skin. "I haven't heard anyone express the opinion that Luce's singing is equal to mine, but maybe if she's been working so hard on improving she's better now than I realize." There was a glacial silence, but Luce could see Anais's blue tail rippling from suppressed excitement. When Catarina spoke again her voice was thick with calculation. "She *was* remarkably good when we changed you, Anais. I admit I was surprised when I heard her. She was *too* good, and there was something in the sound of it . . . like listening to things I'd forgotten, like hearing my own life whispered to me . . ." Catarina's voice trailed off dreamily, and Luce remembered all the bewildering accusations Catarina had fired at her that evening and how unhinged she'd seemed. Catarina's tail gave a little flip as she broke from her abstraction, and when she spoke again she sounded harsh and deadly. "I suppose now I know why she was able to do that." Luce suddenly had a sickening sense of what was coming next.

"But why on earth?" Anais asked with such fake, cloying innocence that Luce's nails dug into her palms. "I don't get it at all. I don't understand why Luce wants to work so hard on her singing instead of hanging out with everyone, and I *certainly* can't understand why she'd want to hide it from you, Catarina! I just assumed she must have told *you* even if she's been keeping it a secret from everyone else."

Samantha and Anais had definitely rehearsed this, Luce thought. And they'd been spying on her! Were they trying to get her expelled from the tribe? She wanted to rush to Catarina, but the thought of how terribly hurt Catarina must be kept her frozen where she was.

"Oh, Anais, you can be so naïve sometimes!" It was Samantha again, trilling almost gleefully. Wouldn't Catarina realize that this was all a show they were putting on for her? "Isn't it obvious? There's only one reason Luce could have for trying to become a *better* singer than Catarina!" Luce saw the wave start up in Catarina's tail; it began slowly, then ended in a convulsive whiplash. But how could Cat possibly believe them? "Isn't that seriously messed up, though? I mean, after you saved her life and everything? You'd think she'd have more loyalty than to go around scheming to squeeze you out as queen!"

"I'd like to see her try!" Catarina's voice was rough but too shrill and wild to seem really confident; Luce had a sudden apprehension that something in Catarina's heart was truly and irrevocably broken. "I suppose Luce thinks she's the new Marina, and that I'm just a kind of pretender, always getting in her way . . . And there *is* something about her voice that—that pulls me back . . ." Cat was starting to drift again, her words ascending into an ethereal, mournful lilt, a drowsy half-song. Luce had the sudden fear that Anais and Samantha might start to think Cat was going insane; a desperate impulse to somehow intervene and protect Catarina surged through her, but she didn't see what she could do to help.

Luce began sliding very carefully back toward the tunnel. She couldn't try to talk to Catarina now, not if Cat really thought that Luce was plotting against her . . .

Once she was outside Luce noticed how wondrously beautiful the light patterns were that skimmed across the surface of the sea. It was deep green with lozenges of shining sky blue, running streaks of silver, a crosshatching of milky white where the water reflected a patch of clouds. But, Luce thought suddenly, the sea would be just as beautiful somewhere else. How could this still be her home if Catarina believed Luce was betraying her? Hadn't she always showed Cat that she was loyal?

It had been a terrible mistake, Luce realized, not to tell Catarina herself about her singing practice. If only Catarina weren't always so ridiculously touchy about everything to do with singing, and if she hadn't seemed half crazed after they'd sung Anais into her new form, then it would have been so much easier . . . but maybe it had been cowardly not to at least try to talk to her about it.

And then, Anais and Samantha must be planning something awful, Luce thought. That much was clear now. And they'd made sure that Catarina wouldn't listen if Luce tried to warn her.

Luce floated for an hour, thinking of swimming south alone, but then she changed her mind. She had to be ready to fight on Catarina's side if serious trouble came. Catarina had saved her life more than once, after all, and the least Luce could do in return was stick by her, even if Catarina didn't trust her at all anymore. Still, it took all Luce's determination to swim to the dining beach that evening and eat with the others, then go back to spend the night in the main cave. She hadn't come above water and looked around the cave in days, so she was startled to see the jags of rock festooned with Anais's trophies: leather belts and sunhats hung from protruding spikes of stone, and the beach was littered with makeup kits, dishes, ornate cut-crystal lamps, and even, Luce saw with a jolt, a few paperback novels that had probably belonged to Tessa. She picked up a copy of *Jane Eyre*, but it had been underwater for too long: its pages were lumped together, stiff with salt, and only crumbled when Luce tried to peel them gently apart.

She kept glancing over at Catarina all evening, but the red-gold head stayed stubbornly averted. Even when Luce deliberately swam to a spot only a few feet away Catarina didn't look at her once, and Luce saw Anais smirk and nudge Samantha.

Luce was too worried now to go off alone and practice singing. It would only confirm Catarina's suspicions if Luce spent time away in her small cave, and Luce forced herself to stay with the group, chatting and splashing as if nothing were the matter. When Dana and Rachel asked her for another lesson Luce cringed and then reluctantly agreed, looking at Catarina the whole time. Catarina still wouldn't meet her eyes, and Luce constantly had to fight down tears.

Three days after that awful overheard conversation, Luce woke up in the greenish dimness of the main cave, convinced she'd heard something. It was so early that the few bands of sunlight crossing the darkness were apricot-colored and angled near the ceiling; near dawn, then, but dawn came so quickly now that it might have been only two or three in the morning.

Everyone else was asleep, their lovely faces lined up along the shore while the water lapped across their chests like a living blanket. Miriam seemed to be having a nightmare; she whimpered and flailed, one pale hand raised to ward off something only she could see. Had that been the sound that woke Luce?

No. She heard it again: a distant voice that pulsed through the water and then echoed lightly inside the cave until all the air was brushed with ecstatic sound. Luce looked around and realized Catarina's fiery head was missing from the row of sleeping faces. Was Catarina singing to someone out there in the sea? Luce listened for a while to the voice that merged and fluxed inside the constant ringing of the waves. Catarina's singing was so luxurious, so strange and sweet that Luce still couldn't believe the incredible compliment Miriam had given her. Could it possibly be true that Luce's own singing was almost that wonderful? Luce shook her head as she considered the idea. And how could Catarina be insecure about it when the music that emerged from her was so beautiful that it seemed to come from a place far beyond Earth? Luce had the unwelcome thought that, if Catarina weren't queen, if she weren't so determined to protect her tribe, there'd be nothing to stop her from descending into furious self-destruction.

The music flowed through Luce's mind until her thoughts seemed to bend and sway in time with it. She saw moving amber lights caught in a pale blue web, and a boy with dark curly hair reached out his hand and waved to her through water that shattered into blobs and then reformed like mercury . . .

When she woke again the sun was high in the sky and the other mermaids were flashing away one by one to go to breakfast. Luce couldn't shake the feeling that Catarina hadn't come home at all, and the warm crashing water outside the cave seemed veined with frightening possibilities. Worry made her careless, and she slipped up for breath too close to a huge, sleek yacht sailing along at a somnolent pace under a sky so blue it graded into throbbing violet at its meridian. There were at least a dozen people leaning on the railings with their hair streaking out along the breeze, and Luce dove again as fast as she could. She was almost sure no one had seen her, but even so, she thought it showed that they all needed to be more careful, at least until the summer passed.

* * *

As she'd expected, Catarina wasn't at the dining beach, but the other mermaids were all there, and they seemed oddly excited. Luce broke through the water into air that trembled with eager voices, and she heard Anais saying, "Well, we can't just wait *all* day for Catarina to get back, can we? It's not like they're just going to sit around forever . . ."

Luce was confused. Who was she talking about? Luce looked around at the bright, blazingly lovely faces, all gathered in a circle near the shore. Only Miriam was keeping her distance from the others; she was lying prone some twenty feet away with her face buried in her folded arms, her jet black hair in rivulets along her faintly blue-shining back. Luce couldn't tell if she was asleep.

"Let's at least see what Luce thinks, now that she's here," Dana answered; her tone was a disquieting combination of nervous and exuberant. "Maybe she can decide if that boat is too big or not. I mean, if we don't have Cat with us . . ."

"It is *so* not too big," Anais griped, shoving back her white, rhinestone-studded sunglasses, and Luce realized they were talking about the yacht she'd swum so close to minutes before. But even Anais couldn't be crazy enough to sink it without Catarina's approval, could she? "If you don't want to be helpful, Dana, then I'll just do it with whoever feels like coming with me. I can't see why you want to ask *Luce* about anything." Dana's warm, wide-eyed face squeezed into a grimace, and she glanced from Anais to Luce and back again.

"I know Luce has sometimes been—not super fair to you, Anais—" Dana began, but Anais cut her off. Her voice was higher and more ragged than Luce had ever heard it; it thrummed with a kind of hysteria.

"Jenna, *you* want to sink that bitch, don't you? And Rachel, you're definitely going to come after I gave you that great ruby bracelet, right? And Violet . . . there's no way you'd be so goody-goody that you'd just let that awesome boat get away, would you?" Violet and Rachel clung to each other, their eyes shifting around as if they didn't know where to look, but their tails were stirring fervently under the water. They were intimidated by Anais, Luce thought, but they were also dying to go with her. Luce understood. Even the thought of going after that ship made her crave the bliss of singing, too; her mouth actually started watering, although she knew perfectly well she wouldn't permit herself to succumb to the desire. Besides, the idea was so insane that for a few moments Luce was completely speechless, lost in calculation. It was too soon after Anais's yacht, for one thing, and then the boat she'd seen had seemed very crowded; it was probably ferrying at least two hundred tourists, maybe more. A boat that size would be child's play for Catarina, of course, but if they didn't have her *or* Luce with them, wouldn't there be a strong possibility of human survivors?

"I'm not going to help with any boat unless Catarina says it's okay," Luce announced angrily. "Dana, you *really* shouldn't either. It's completely crazy. You'll attract way too much attention, and you'll wind up breaking the timahk . . ." Luce hoped Anais would see reason, but it occurred to her that if Anais did refuse to listen, there might be some positive aspects.

"There's a woman on deck wearing a Dolce and Gabbana dress!" Anais snapped. "This season's! I bet those people have all kinds of great stuff! Maybe Luce is stupid enough to let a chance like that go by, but I'm not. I'm sinking it."

"Without me, *or* Catarina, *or* Dana?" Luce asked; she couldn't keep the sarcasm out of her voice. The idea of sinking a ship in order to rob the passengers' corpses struck her as the most repellent thing she'd ever heard, a sick distortion of what being a mermaid was all about, but she didn't expect anyone there to agree with her. She'd have better luck persuading them if she stuck to the practical issues. "Who's going to lead the ship in? You're just going to screw up completely."

"Dana's going to lead!" Jenna snapped. "You think she's going to listen to *you*? Just 'cause you've given her, what, a few lame singing lessons? Dana did it before; she can totally do it again . . ." Everyone was staring at Dana now, who was twisting her long golden necklace around one slim brown finger, biting her full lower lip. Luce knew she must feel terrible being put in the middle this way, but there didn't seem to be any alternative. Her stomach tightened as she waited to hear what Dana would say.

Anais opened her mouth, and Luce glowered at her, expecting another burst of shrill bullying. But instead a note came out, spun out long and smooth like a glowing silk ribbon wrapping up the air. Then it rose higher, leaped and twirled. Everyone was gaping at her, and Luce felt her own face fall in dismay. She'd secretly assumed that Anais would be a terrible singer; how could you sing well unless you had a real heart, real emotions? But now it was obvious that, even if Anais's singing was steely and somehow brutal in spite of its beauty, it was also powerful, fierce, and wonderfully controlled. Luce hated to let it affect her, but she couldn't completely prevent the enchantment from infusing her mind, and she felt its promise. It filled her with shapeless dreams of power, with a cold urge to dominate and possess everything she saw . . .

Anais broke off with a nasty laugh, and Luce shook the remnants of that awful magic from her mind. She stared around at the others. Was it possible they'd consider Anais as good a singer as she was? For a full minute everyone was silent, dazed by the emotions Anais had sent coursing through them.

"Wow!" Jenna said at last. "Well, it looks like we know who's leading now! Dana can take the position Rachel had last time, at the back." Anais smirked while Samantha broke out in gleeful tittering, shaking her pale curls; Dana only nodded blearily. "Luce is just going to have to suck it up; she can't get her own way for once." Luce couldn't understand why Jenna seemed to hate her so much all of a sudden, but she was still too stunned by the force of Anais's singing to think of anything she could say in reply. There were the splash and froth of quickly spiraling tails, and streaks of bubbles silvered the water as the mermaids dipped quickly away.

Dana was one of the last to go; she angled an apologetic smile at Luce. "Don't worry, okay? I won't let them get too crazy.

Catarina won't have any reason to be pissed off with us, I promise." Then she was gone, too, with a crimson and coppery blink of scales. Only Miriam was left, still sprawled against the shore, not even moving when a big bluish larva, maybe the one Anais had wanted to kill, ambled over and began slurping on the corner of one midnight-colored fin. She had to be asleep, Luce thought, if she was tolerating that sad little creature chewing on her.

"Luce?" Miriam suddenly pushed herself up on her elbows, and twisted around to gaze back toward the patch of water where Luce floated limp and shocked, her tail brushing loosely against the pebbles on the seafloor. Luce swam over and stretched out beside her; Miriam's dark eyes were troubled. "I know she doesn't deserve any help from you, but shouldn't you go with them? Just to make sure they don't break the timahk?" Luce couldn't believe her ears.

"Why would I care if they do?" Luce snapped. She had the impression she was saying too much, but now that her feelings were starting to seep out it was hard to stop them. "I hope Anais *does* break it. Cat will throw her out, and then . . ." *Then everything will be okay again,* Luce thought. *Then Cat will trust me and be my friend again, and we'll all learn to sing in ways where nobody has to die because of it. I'll finally have a real home.* But she didn't let herself say those parts out loud. They could hear the stirring vibration of the mermaids' song now, echoing from far across the water.

"But, I mean, Luce, don't you see what she's doing?" Miriam seemed horribly depressed, Luce realized. The words dragged out of her. "Even if she blows it and there are human survivors, who's going to throw her out? You and Catarina won't be able to do it alone, not if everyone else . . ." Luce suddenly understood what Miriam was saying. Of course, Luce thought; she'd been so focused on Anais that she'd overlooked the obvious. Anais had made sure that almost everyone in the tribe was complicit in what she was doing. They'd all be equally guilty, and they'd almost surely turn on Catarina before they'd help her expel their de facto leader. "But, Luce, if anyone gets away from them, the humans will definitely come after us. And it's not just our tribe either. If people start to really understand we're out here, soon they'll be hunting mermaids all over the world. You see? I'm not asking you to like it. I don't either. But you *have* to help her."

Luce understood the reasoning, but the idea of going out and singing those people to their deaths just because Anais had said so was more than she could stand. "I'm not going," Luce said; she felt reckless, almost desperate. "I'm not killing anyone, not ever again. That's not why I sing." It was out before she could stop herself; still, it was a relief to finally say it out loud. But Catarina already thought she was a traitor, Luce realized with a rush of vertigo; what would she think if Miriam reported that Luce was such a human lover that she'd rather let a bunch of strange humans escape than help her fellow mermaids? Miriam's blue-black gaze was fixed on Luce's face; it was calm, cold, and sad. There was a long silence as they gazed at each other.

"Maybe the humans *should* hunt us down," Miriam said at last, and Luce recoiled. It was eerie how dull and emotionless Miriam's voice was now. "Maybe mermaids and humans don't belong on the same planet. It would be a lot easier to slaughter all of us than all of them. They have us so outnumbered . . ." Luce couldn't tell if Miriam was serious; was she just trying to shock Luce into swimming out? "I just don't like to think about, you know, you and Rachel . . . I dream about it some-times, Luce. Men with guns, and machines in their ears so they can't hear us, and blood everywhere . . . But maybe it's better that way . . ."

Luce wondered if Miriam was right. Was it really impos-sible that humans and mermaids would ever be able to live without fighting?

"I just . . ." Luce didn't know how to say it. "I feel like . . . like maybe we could figure out another way? I know they do all kinds of terrible things . . ." *But so do we,* Luce thought. A bizarre, unwelcome idea occurred to her: that mermaids were really just as *human,* just as brutal and destructive, as the humans themselves.

Miriam gave her a slow, bitter smile. "They're *still* hurt-ing you, aren't they?" Luce didn't know what she was talking about. "The humans you loved, I mean. They're still killing you inside. You can't get over it. Isn't that true? Or is it really just *one* human?"

Luce was overwhelmed by heartache. She felt as hurt and bewildered as if Miriam had suddenly stabbed her in the gut. "That's none of your business!"

"You'd rather see them kill all of us than help kill them!" Miriam didn't seem so depressed anymore; instead her face was frozen in a mask of unfeeling savagery, her voice dead. "It's your decision. But the only reason you'd make that choice is if you still secretly love one of them. Luce, I'm not *stupid* . . ." Luce didn't want Miriam to see her cry. She turned and dove through water that shivered with the high, sweet death songs of the other mermaids. If they were heading out to that rocky island, then the yacht must be very close to crashing now.

She rolled violently over and over in the green waves, her eyes wide open while streams of shining bubbles lashed across her vision. Foamy crests rose and fell just above her face, then the green shade of the depths rotated past, then the daylight again. It occurred to Luce that it was possible Miriam hadn't meant to be cruel, that maybe she was overreacting, but those thoughts didn't do anything to calm the ferocious emotions that gushed through her heart. Her dream had been right: *everyone* was turning on her, and she'd been crazy to trust any of them. Was she even lonelier now than she'd been as a human girl?

She knew, of course, that she had to stay away from her small cave, at least until she'd proved to Catarina that she was faithful to her—that she didn't want any other queen, not even if that queen was her, not even if she didn't agree with every single thing about how Cat ran the tribe . . . But Catarina was still away, and if Luce went to the main cave she'd have to face Anais and Jenna much too soon, see them giddy with celebration over the downed ship. What would it hurt to steal a few hours alone, just this once?

* * *

"Luce!" The voice was Catarina's, and Luce pulled herself up from a well of darkness in her mind into the blue glow of her cave. Had she fallen asleep? "Luce, I'd like to talk to you if you could spare the time." Luce winced at the brittleness and formality of Catarina's voice.

"I've never—tried not to talk to you!" The words tumbled out awkwardly, and Luce pulled herself through the lingering blur of sleep to see Catarina watching her critically, her shining head propped on her hand as she lay at Luce's side. It was exactly the way she'd been positioned when Luce first saw her, and for a second the pain of that memory blindsided Luce. How had everything gone so wrong?

"You do know they sank a ship today." Catarina's voice was flat. Luce felt a tentative hopefulness at these unexpected words; maybe she was upset with Anais and not Luce; maybe she was even here to ask for Luce's help?

"I know they did," Luce said. She was still ashamed to think of how the others had acted, rushing out without even asking Catarina's permission. "Cat, I really tried to stop them . . ."

"You tried to stop them, Luce?" The voice was still bitter, but now there was a trace of stony amusement, a faint sneer. "So, I suppose you thought that was your decision to make? That everyone should simply obey you? Since the queen they have now is so obviously unworthy to rule?"

Luce's mouth fell open with shock; she wanted to make so many different objections to this that for a second she was completely flummoxed. "No! Cat! What I meant was that they shouldn't do anything like that unless they asked you first!" Catarina gave her a horrible smile, and Luce had the sinking sense that, no matter what she said, Catarina would just take it as a lie.

"I heard, of course, that that was what you *told* everyone. That you picked a fight with Anais about it. A perfect excuse, wasn't it, not to go out and sing with them? Otherwise everyone would have insisted that you had a responsibility to help. I suppose you were so blinded by your selfish concerns that you didn't even consider the risk of human survivors?" Luce was too taken aback to react to this. "But now that I think about it, you didn't actually want to sing to Anais's yacht either. You tried to hide it, but I knew! And when you realized that you couldn't prevent the rest of us from taking it on, you had a lovely excuse ready not to sing then, too, didn't you? 'Oh, we should let Dana and Rachel get some practice!'" Catarina cooed the last sentence with mock helpfulness, in a squeaky parody of Luce's voice. "It's funny, isn't it, how you keep finding these—these pretexts not to really sing? I don't count these ridiculous *lessons* you've been giving, just singing one or two notes at a time . . ."

As hurt as Luce was, she wasn't sure what Catarina was getting at. Did she suspect that Luce didn't want to participate in killing humans? It was true, of course, that Luce had been looking for ways to avoid luring any more humans to die. Luce braced herself. She couldn't hide her real feelings from Catarina forever; she'd have to face her anger sometime . . .

"I don't want to kill anyone again." Luce tried to say it as gently as possible. She didn't want Catarina to feel judged, and she waited for a blast of invective. Catarina would definitely give her another lecture on how evil humans were, how they didn't deserve any mercy.

To her surprise, Catarina laughed. The laugh was dull, sick, clanking, like something forged from iron. "I'd say that's hardly up to your usual standard, Luce. Your excuses are usually much cleverer than that. When I think of how you've had me fooled . . . And now the best you can come up with is some childish prattle about not wanting to hurt *humans*?" Catarina's voice had been rising as she spoke; by the last word it was almost a shriek.

"It's not an excuse!" Luce sputtered; she was getting angry now, and Catarina obviously wasn't listening to her.

"You haven't broken the timahk, Luce. Not as far as I know. I can't rightfully expel you." Catarina's tone was calm again, in that sickening dull way. "Why don't you simply tell me the truth? Tell me, Luce. I did save your life, you know. I've earned some— at least—some consideration from you. Tell me to my face that you're careful to do your real singing where none of us can hear you because you don't want anyone to realize what you're up to until you're positive you're good enough to beat me!"

"I never wanted to beat you!" Luce was shouting, but even as she said it doubt twisted inside her. It was true that she'd never wanted to take over as queen, but was it also true that she didn't want to sing as wonderfully—or even better—than Catarina did? "Cat, it's true I've been singing sometimes—by myself—but it wasn't anything to do with, with trying to hurt you!" *I still love you,* Luce thought. *You should trust me.*

"I don't suppose you want to hurt me purely for entertainment, Luce. And it's not as if I can't understand why—why you might feel such an overwhelming urge to gain power. Oh, we've all been thrown away!" Catarina laughed, but it sounded worse than a howl. "What can ever make up for that? I can see how, with your gifts, the temptation might be overwhelming. But, Luce, all your deceit . . . when you must know how I've *cared* for you . . ."

"I'm *sorry,* Cat. I just—I didn't want to tell you I was practicing until I figured some things out—but it's not about what you think, about trying to take over! I don't want anybody but you to be queen."

Catarina snorted. "I can see you've given a great deal of thought to the implications, though. If you did manage to surpass me. And you're perfectly correct, of course. *If you could do it*, you would have the right to depose me, take my place. But that might be more difficult than you realize. What makes you so sure you've heard my best singing?"

Luce couldn't suppress the sense that Catarina was only bluffing, and all at once she was so angry that a terrible impulse seized hold of her. If Catarina was so convinced of her disloyalty anyway, why shouldn't Luce go ahead and insist that they take turns singing in front of everyone? Catarina was obviously terrified that Luce would outdo her, and suddenly Luce began to believe that maybe she would. After all, even the waves obeyed Luce's voice!

Luce shuddered and closed her eyes. *Don't do it!* she told herself. *Lucette, stop it right now!* But her voice was already sliding out of her, spreading out like a sky made of music, but a sky that curled into running clouds at its edges. Then the curling rose higher, vaster; it raced and lunged, and in the darkness of her sealed eyes Luce heard Catarina give a brief, startled scream. A wave taller than she was had come at her call—Luce knew that even without seeing it—and it was flying toward them in a sheet of upright silver . . .

Cool water like an icy palm smacked Luce's face and shattered around her shoulders. Her mouth stung with the sharp taste of salt, and as the music faded Luce opened her eyes to see Catarina gaping at her, seawater still trickling down her cheeks. All the tense strength in that lovely face had collapsed. Catarina's gray eyes were wide and frightened, and her mouth hung weakly open.

"I don't *want* to be queen, Cat," Luce started to say. Catarina recoiled from her, though in the narrow cave there wasn't really anywhere she could go. "I'm just trying to learn—how to do things besides kill people!" Catarina shook her head in disbelief, still gaping, and Luce began to understand the enormity of what she'd just done. For a minute they stared at each other in silence.

"I knew it the first time I heard you," Catarina murmured at last, and even in the dusk of the cave Luce saw the tears brimming in her eyes. "I knew I should let you drown. I considered it, believe me. I had every right to simply leave you there to die. I almost didn't go after you, and I wouldn't have except . . ." Catarina stopped, staring wide-eyed as if she were seeing unspeakable visions. "You'll be the queen of a tribe that hates you, Luce, don't forget that!"

"Catarina!" Luce cried, but it was already too late. All she could see of her friend was the trail of bubbles foaming in her wake, and after a moment's hesitation Luce dove after her. Catarina wouldn't simply run away from the tribe, would she? There was no trace of Catarina once Luce reached the open sea, and she darted at random through rising swells of gray water, searching for the blaze of bright hair that must be out there somewhere. The water echoed with whale song; it entered Luce's mind and made her dizzy. It wasn't until she'd swum in confusion for an hour and the pallid dusk closed in on her that Luce had to accept it was pointless to keep looking. It seemed unlikely that Catarina would have gone back to the main cave when she was so upset, but Luce thought she might as well check there, just in case.

Even underwater Luce heard the babble of cheerful voices, and then, to her amazement, Catarina's harsh laughter. A wave of silence flowed through the dim cave as soon as Luce's head broke the surface, and immediately Luce met Catarina's bleak gray stare. Then Catarina deliberately looked away with ornately faked casualness and began chatting brightly to Jenna. Anais, though, kept her blue starry eyes fixed on Luce's face. She was lying stretched out parallel to the shore wearing a long, bloodred dress, probably the same one she'd been coveting earlier; as distressed as Luce was, she still found herself thinking how ridiculous the dress looked with a tail sticking out at the bottom.

"Oh, Luce, there you are!" It was Dana, already swimming over to her with something gleaming in her raised hand; she was talking much too fast. Luce wondered what they'd all been saying about her. "Boy, I was worried you weren't going to get over being pissed off about that yacht! But see, it was totally fine. Catarina wasn't mad at us at all, and there were no survivors, and oh, you would have been so proud to hear me and Rachel! I've been telling everyone we only sang that well because of you, and it's true. We missed you tons, but I brought you back a present. I really hope you like it . . ." The pale thing was a necklace, Luce realized: a long strand of creamy pearls. Luce tried to smile as Dana slipped it over her head.

Anais was still staring at her; she almost leered as the pearls skimmed down around Luce's chest. An image of Dana lifting the pearls from a drowned woman's neck flashed through Luce's mind.

"That was really sweet of you, Dana," Luce said, but she didn't manage to keep her agitation out of her voice. Anais's smirk tightened.

Catarina was looking at her again, too. Luce's heart froze for a second as she saw those gray eyes blazing from the shadows.

"Happy *birthday*, Luce," Catarina hissed. Her tone was so sardonic that Samantha started tittering.

Luce just stared at her former friend, and tears flooded into her eyes as she finally grasped the words. Of course; it was still her fourteenth birthday; it always would be.

Still her fourteenth birthday, and yet she'd ruined everything.

15

Responsibility

"Challenge me," Catarina snarled in her ear. She'd swum up behind Luce, deep underwater, as they sped toward the dining beach. Even though Catarina had done the same thing repeatedly for a week now, Luce's chest still seized up with fear at the sound of that hissing voice. She forced herself to be strong.

"No." Her voice warped and bubbled in the water, but the word was definite enough.

"Challenge me, Luce. In front of everyone. You have the right." Luce tried to spin around to face Catarina, but the older mermaid was too fast, always slipping back so skillfully that Luce couldn't look in her eyes. For a minute they just swirled in place, forming a kind of mermaid whirlpool, before Luce gave up trying. No one could swim as well as Catarina.

"I keep telling you, Cat! I don't want to!" Her voice sounded more weary than angry now. She'd already tried yelling, and it hadn't stopped Catarina from gliding up behind her whenever she was at a safe distance from the others, someplace where no one else would hear, and hissing in her ear. Goading her . . .

"The best singer is the rightful queen, Luce. And even Queen *Marina* couldn't conjure the waves the way you can. She told me she'd heard stories about it, but she'd never succeeded in doing it herself. Marina! If you'd heard her, you'd understand what this means." It sounded like praise, but Catarina's tone as she said it was so cruel that Luce felt nauseous. "Challenge me. I insist. What kind of coward *are* you?"

Suddenly Luce realized that Catarina had pivoted around in front of her. The gray eyes were so close that Luce reared back with the sense that she'd almost collided with a terrible mirror, one much worse than the makeup mirror the mermaids were always passing around these days. The water lifted Catarina's hair behind her so that it pitched in a wall of liquid fire, and webs of sunlight scrolled across her milky skin.

"You can't *force* me to sing, Cat," Luce said; she was surprised by how calm she sounded. It seemed impossible when she felt so sick and afraid inside. "Not even by calling me names."

"No." Catarina seemed to be considering this. "No, Luce. Of course not. But I can make you suffer until you do."

"Or you know?" Luce's voice was suddenly just as bitter as Catarina's; it didn't even seem to belong to her anymore. It felt like a stranger was speaking there in the water with them, a stranger who'd appeared inside Luce's head. "I *could* just show you how to do it, Cat. Call the waves that way, I mean. I could *teach* you. Then you'll still be our greatest singer, and maybe you'll stop believing these horrible things about me!" *Maybe we'd be friends again,* Luce thought with a spasm of grief and longing, but a second later she wasn't sure about that. Did she still want to be friends with Cat now that she'd seen how hateful she could be?

A look of astonishment flurried over Catarina's face, but she hid it almost instantly behind the same smirking mask she'd worn ever since Luce had given into her pride and shown just what her voice could do now.

"And why would you want to do that?" This was an improvement in one way, Luce realized: it was the first time in days that Catarina seemed to be actually listening to anything Luce said at all.

"Because I'm your friend!" But Luce didn't really mean it, not anymore, and the dishonesty of her tone was obvious. Catarina bit her lip and watched Luce in a way that was both nasty and quizzical. "And, I mean, you're so much older than me, and you're so good at—at keeping the tribe together and keeping everyone safe. You always know what to do . . ." Catarina's look was still unyielding, and Luce stammered on with growing desperation. "And anyway, Cat, you *are* our best singer! Even if I can do that thing with the waves, I mean, I never sound as gorgeous as you do. I'm not even close . . ."

"Do you really believe that, Luce?" The tone was as slick and cold as ever; why was nothing she said ever enough? "Then challenge me. Sing your very best, in front of the whole tribe, and make them decide. What frightens you so much, little coward? The responsibility? Or—because you've decided, too late, to feel *guilty* . . ."

Luce was in a bind. Now, if she still refused it would sound either like she thought Catarina couldn't actually defeat her or else like she really was too afraid. Luce felt a surge of resentment at being manipulated this way.

"*No.*" Catarina's brows shot up, and Luce scrambled to come up with an excuse. "I don't want anyone to go around saying that I even *thought* I could beat you. And I'd just embarrass myself . . ." Catarina's strained smile ratcheted into a sudden grimace; she actually bared her teeth.

"We have no queen now, Luce. I know the truth, no matter what the others all think. Do you even realize—what that could mean?"

"You're my queen, Catarina." Luce heard that her tone sounded more resentful than loyal, though. "You always will be."

"I won't pretend for you, Luce." It came out in a dull hiss. Then there was a lashing of fins, a smear of silver light, and Catarina was gone. Luce kept heading toward the dining beach but slowly. Her movements were heavy, weighed down by sadness. She'd depleted her air supply by talking, and slipped up to breathe. She was in a blue bowl, ringed by soaring cliffs and even vaster distances.

* * *

Anais was talking, loudly, as Luce broke through the waves where they were all cracking mussels on the rocks. "Samantha and I went scouting this morning, and there's a pretty nice little cruise ship heading our way! They've stopped at some island, but in a few hours . . . Maybe the people on it aren't all *that* classy, really, not like the last one we got, but there might be some stuff worth checking out. I say we snag it!"

Catarina whacked a mussel. She was staring off into the distance, toward the island where the Coast Guard boat had sunk. Luce waited for her to tell Anais not to do it. Anais and her followers had taken down another yacht just two days before. It was insanely dangerous; if they kept on this way they'd attract more and more human investigators to their area, and soon enough they'd *all* get killed.

Instead Catarina just shot Luce a razor-sharp look, daring her to say something, and suddenly Luce understood what Catarina was telling her, although without words. *If you don't like it, Luce, then challenge me. You think you can do better? Take over as queen, and you can stop them from doing this . . .* Luce stared down at the wisps of seafoam curving out around her body. Was Catarina prepared to see her tribe destroyed simply to force Luce into a final confrontation?

Almost all the mermaids were wearing plundered clothes and jewelry now, in vivid colors that clashed with their shimmering tails and with the greenish silver of the water. Even Luce was still wearing the long pearl necklace, since she couldn't think of a way to get rid of it without hurting Dana's feelings. Only Catarina was still sleekly naked. She looked marvelously free beside the other mermaids, their arms now tangled in sodden spangled blouses that dragged haphazardly back and forth with the currents. The cave was getting so cluttered, too. Anais had finally talked a pack of girls into towing a large flat-screen TV back to the cave; it leaned forlornly against the craggy wall, its cord slopping around like the tail of a dead rat in the water.

"I think I'd rather go off for a swim by myself," Catarina finally announced in such an exaggeratedly lazy, dreamy way that Luce was sure she was really going hunting for a young man canoeing or sailing on his own.

"Wow, Cat!" Anais chirped; Luce flinched at the impudence in her voice. "You've been spending so much time alone! Are you sure it's, you know, healthy? I mean, you wouldn't want to turn into one of these weird loners, would you? Not like . . ." She darted a look at Luce—fast but not so fast that everyone wouldn't notice.

Samantha giggled in the toadying way that she used now whenever Anais insulted Luce. That was happening more often, too. If only she *were* queen, Luce thought, she'd find a reason to banish Anais, orcas or no. The girl was poison; she was ruining the whole tribe.

No, Luce realized. It wouldn't work. The rest of the girls were too taken in by Anais; the frequent attacks on ships seemed to affect them all like a drug. They didn't care at all how reckless it was. Luce was beginning to appreciate just how effectively Catarina had kept the tribe disciplined; she'd held their wildest, most destructive urges in check, but now . . .

If they were ever going to get rid of Anais, she and Catarina would definitely have to work together. And with the way things were between them now Luce didn't see how that could ever happen.

Catarina didn't respond. She just leaned out on top of the water in a drowsy way, her eyes half closed, then after a moment skimmed deeper, heading out to sea.

Luce hadn't been eating enough for days, and now her hunger was catching up with her. She sat methodically smacking mussels on the rocks. She'd made a terrible mistake, singing that way in front of Catarina, but she still couldn't understand why Catarina was refusing to get over it. Why couldn't they just forget it had ever happened?

"You know, I feel like I could use a little stretch, too," Anais said after a minute. "That cruise ship isn't going to be moving for a while. It's too boring just waiting around all the time."

"Can I come with you?" It seemed like Samantha couldn't stand to be away from Anais, not even for a few minutes. She followed her everywhere, clinging to her elbow, laughing at everything she said, and Anais seemed to take her adoration as the most natural thing in the world. Luce was surprised when Anais shook her head.

"God, Samantha, can't you ever let me have some private time? You just want to talk and talk all day. Maybe I want to go for a swim by myself!" Samantha's face fell, and Luce felt a fleeting chill, a kind of dark cloud slipping through her. Anais's body sliced like a bloodred shadow under the waves, the hem of her dress a pulsing silk jellyfish around her azure tail.

There was one good thing about Catarina being so furious with her: Luce could practice singing again, since it didn't seem like Cat could get any angrier. "I'm going back to my cave, if anyone wants to find me," Luce announced coolly. "I'm going to work on some new singing tricks I've discovered." Half the tribe stared at her with disoriented expressions, but, Luce thought, if the idea of practicing was so strange to them, wasn't that their problem?

And there was no point anymore in trying to suppress her new ability to call the waves either, not now that Catarina knew. She might as well try to get really good at it.

* * *

In the early evening she swam back to the main cave. Now the sunset came late, and the light would turn a milky twilight blue, but the sky never became completely dark. Instead the sunset would slowly roll around the edge of the horizon until it merged into dawn. Luce told herself that she shouldn't let it bother her that Catarina had called her a coward—hadn't she been braver than anyone in the tribe that time she'd crawled on shore and saved Violet? But the comment still rankled, and it would be unbearable to let Catarina think Luce was avoiding her out of fear.

The voices in the cave were loud, uproarious, like a human party. Luce wasn't particularly surprised to see that they'd stolen a few bottles of liquor from the cruise ship; girls were passing bottles of scotch and vodka from hand to hand, pitching drunkenly in the water, their tails swinging haphazardly and sending up salt spray everywhere. The slurred voices sent prickles of anxiety down her back. They reminded her too much of her uncle. Miriam lay alone in a dark corner, and Catarina was reclining with regal disinterest and a sleepy, satisfied look on her face, but everyone else was in tumult, squealing over the enormous heaps of clothes and trinkets on the beach, trying them on, sometimes ripping the tight dresses and tops as they thrashed into them with limbs sloppy from alcohol . . .

"No way!" Anais screamed, snatching something away from Violet. "No way! Those are so completely mine! I saw them first! God, who ever would have thought that those cheap losers on that ship would have had something this great!" Luce's eyes went wide; Anais was waving a pair of strappy, spike-heeled sandals around her head. The straps were dense with colored rhinestones glittering maniacally in the dimness. "Manolos! Real Manolos out in this crappy place! Oh, and I think they're even my size!"

Luce was flabbergasted. Why didn't anyone say anything?

"Can I just hold them for a minute, though?" Violet asked shyly. Anais just pouted and jerked the sandals farther back.

"Nobody is *touching* my Manolos! Everybody heard that, right? If I catch any of you putting even one sneaky finger on these . . ."

Luce couldn't restrain herself anymore. "Anais!" she yelled, almost before she'd realized what she was doing.

The ruckus in the cave collapsed into sudden quiet. Everyone was staring at her as if she were a stranger intruding on them. They obviously hadn't noticed her arrival.

"Yes, Luce?" Anais sneered after a moment. "That goes for you, too, naturally. If you even *breathe* on my Manolos—"

"Anais," Luce said quietly. "You have a *tail*." The silence only got thicker, and suddenly Luce was laughing bitterly. "Are you planning to wear those on your *head*?" A few mermaids laughed with her but only a few. Anais shot a contemptuous glance around at them.

"What part of 'Manolo Blahnik' don't you understand, Luce? My God, anybody would think you'd been living in a cave your whole life!" More girls laughed at this: Jenna and Samantha. But even they sounded a bit halfhearted. Luce could feel something unexpected swelling in her chest: a kind of dark, biting strength, a serene fury. The sneers didn't bother her at all, and she smiled.

"Actually," Luce said, "I grew up in a van." Her voice was still fairly quiet but very distinct. She knew everyone in the cave could hear her. There was a kind of flutter of consternation, and the silence grew like something alive. Even Catarina had raised her drowsy eyes to stare at Luce, and Miriam rolled over and sat up.

But as usual there was no silence so deep that Anais wouldn't break it. "Oh my God! You mean your parents were *homeless*, Luce?" She let out a piercing shriek of laughter. "You grew up as a *bum*? Well, I guess that explains some things."

Luce shook her head. "My mom died when I was four. I was mostly just with my father. And sometimes we got an apartment for a while, or we stayed in motels. But there were a lot of nights when we slept in the van. I didn't mind, though. I liked traveling. We almost always had fun." As Luce spoke, she could see it. The inside of the red van filled her eyes and the odd flitting lights cast by the mobile made from tiny round mirrors that hung in the back, and she breathed in the slightly musty scent of their sleeping bags spread out on the floor . . . There was the sound of her father's warm laughter as he taught her to cook chili and fried cornbread on a camping stove. All at once it was realer to her than the dark cave, the circle of mermaids staring and listening to her so intently that she could almost hear the hum of their concentration. "If that makes someone a bum, then I guess you could call us that. But really my dad was a repairman. And a thief."

Anais squealed with laughter again, but apart from that the cave was perfectly quiet. A single drop of water from a stalactite splashed down. The echoes persisted for a very long time.

"Well, Luce! Well, I guess this really shows the difference between you and me now, doesn't it?" Anais was sneering broadly, trying to make everyone crack up, but it didn't work. When Luce glanced around, the dimness of the cave shone with widened eyes.

"You're right, Anais," Luce agreed. She couldn't believe how powerful she sounded. Her speaking voice was never this strong; she had this kind of cutting force only when she sang! "It shows exactly the difference between us. You see, I *cared* when my father died." A few low gasps escaped in the shadows; of course everyone remembered what Anais had said when she'd first changed. Who could forget something like that? "I cared a lot. I still miss him every day." For the briefest of moments Luce saw Anais's face buckle, but then she mastered herself again. Her sneer became shriller.

"Poor little baby-waby misses her scumbag, crook, loser father! See, Luce, you're just the kind of girl who loves nobodies like that. Because you're a nobody yourself!" No one seemed to be paying much attention to Anais now, though. Violet let out an abrupt sob.

"Is that why you had to live with your uncle, Luce?" Violet didn't sound nearly as meek as usual. She was almost howling. "Your father died, so you had to live with that uncle who—who beat you and who tried . . . Like they did to my brother . . ."

"Yes," Luce agreed; she still felt bizarrely calm, even as Violet began rasping in hysteria. "That's why I was with my uncle." Dana splashed drunkenly over to Violet and pulled her into a hug. Violet struggled free. She was stretching her arms toward Luce, but not as if she wanted to embrace her; Luce was reminded more of the way a rock climber might reach, urgently trying to grasp a handhold just a little too far above.

"How did he die!" Violet yelled. "How did your father die? Luce, what *happened?*"

Luce's profound calm almost failed her now. Could she really say this? Violet's eyes were wild with need, Catarina's mouth was set in a hard line, and Luce saw the shining stripe of a tear on Miriam's cheek.

"He died in a shipwreck," Luce said at last. "He was working on a fishing boat, and they went down. Probably somewhere near here."

Not even Anais could speak in the silence that followed. Everyone was looking around at one another, except for Violet, whose face was hidden in her hands. They were all absorbing the implications, and all at once Luce's head ached as if it were about to split open. It was simply too much truth, too much . . .

A terrible sound wrenched the silence. It got louder, higher, tore at all of them, and Luce gaped around in confusion. Miriam was screaming at the top of her lungs. She threw herself across the water, her fists flying out, her tail slashing in all directions. Mermaids jerked out of her way, but Catarina and Dana lunged in the opposite direction, seizing Miriam by her arms. The midnight blue tail still swung and heaved, and blobs of seafoam flew through the dimness.

"Bring me some of those clothes!" Catarina commanded; suddenly all her intensity seemed to be back, her strength. "Miriam, I *won't* let you dishonor yourself. We need to tie her up before she hurts someone." There was a stunned pause, then a few girls rushed to obey her, binding Miriam's arms behind her with silk scarves and panty hose. Soon she was immobilized, her writhing tail wrapped in three pairs of arms, but she was still screaming.

"DON'T YOU SEE!" Miriam shrieked. "DON"T YOU SEE!" Violet was hyperventilating again, clinging to a crag, but everyone else was squeezed in around Miriam now, trying to calm her down. Luce swam closer, too. "Oh!" Miriam wailed. "Don't you see? All this time we've kept blaming the humans. But it's us! We're the ones who are responsible for what happened to Luce! If we hadn't killed her father, she would have been *safe*, she would have been *happy*, she could have grown *up* . . ."

Luce was embarrassed by this; it seemed so dramatic. But of course what Miriam was saying might be true. She couldn't honestly deny it.

"Oh, Luce!" Miriam had found her in the crowd, and she was fighting to free her arms. "Oh, Luce! I'm so *sorry* . . ."

"I don't blame you, Miriam," Luce said. But there was something cold in her heart as she spoke the words, and they didn't sound right. Miriam sobbed.

"But I suppose you blame *me*, Luce?" The voice was Catarina's; it was silky, patient, and ferocious. "Or should I call you Lucette? Lucette Gray Korchak, I believe you said? You blame me, and that's why you . . ." Catarina couldn't finish the sentence. The gray eyes flashed inside Luce's. It was like the moon gazing into her, swelling the pain in her head. An image of Catarina hungrily kissing her father's mouth in a rush of bubbles filled Luce's mind; she couldn't keep it out.

"*Should* I blame you, Cat?" Luce asked very softly. Everyone gaped, and in the corner of her eye Luce saw Anais again grinning viciously to herself.

Luce knew she shouldn't leave things this way. Anything that made Anais so happy must be terrible; it must be something she should try to stop at once. But the pain seared her mind with blasts of white heat, and Miriam was screaming again, making the ache leap in time with her voice. There were too many eyes all staring at Luce, driving into her like some kind of nightmarish rain . . .

Luce turned and swam away through the pale gray waters.

16

A Song for Miriam

It was at some point in that indeterminate, endless dawn when she heard it. It carried with immaculate clarity over the echoing surface of the water, rebounding from every wave. Luce wasn't really asleep, just in a kind of feverish daze, but that particular sound would have recalled her even from perfect unconsciousness.

A scream, but it was louder, and somehow paler, than a normal scream. Luce knew what it meant at once. She'd heard it before; it had even ripped from her own throat. The scream broke into strange pulsations of noise, a kind of gagging "HA, HA, HA," and then faltered, but an instant later it came back again at full force: a long, high note of purest agony. Luce was already out of the cave, her tail spiraling violently behind her; she was nothing but the movement of indigo waters. Unidentifiable shapes veered suddenly away from her head, but there was no time to worry about colliding with something. She had only moments left, moments . . . That scream was the sound of a mermaid out of the water. And as she raced closer Luce became sure of what she'd suspected from the first moment. It was Miriam.

As long as Luce could hear her there might still be time.

Soon some of the shapes had reaching arms and corkscrewing tails like hers, all of them converging on the voice. They ruptured the waves with their speed, and a harbor seal zigzagged in confusion at the onslaught of bodies. For a few seconds the scream fell away, and then there was only the blue-glowing water stirred into streaks of white by dozens of tails, the gush of racing foam in Luce's ears and the roar of her blood. Where was Miriam's voice?

It came back but more faintly now: she was on a different beach, one they never used because it was too broad and open, too easy to spot from passing boats. Had she deliberately chosen a beach where they wouldn't immediately think to look for her? There was no air in Luce's lungs, and no time to swing up to the surface for a breath. Instead she slashed out, driving herself faster, until the water blurred in her eyes and she was barely in control of her direction. It was all one vague onward thrust, a formless press for speed into the sudden, uncanny silence. Pebbles scraped across her belly before she even knew where she was, and then she saw the curls of amber morning dancing on top of the waves. Air poured into her lungs.

Miriam was there but at least twenty feet back. It was incredible that she'd managed to drag herself so far from the water. Luce bit her lip as she thought of the pain Miriam must have endured during that long crawl up the beach. She still had her tail, she was still trembling and exhaling a raspy, rattling hiss, but her scales were no longer their usual glossy blue-black. They looked disagreeably ashy, flaky: almost like dandruff or the shells of desiccated seeds. A dozen girls were around Luce now, all leaning on the shore, all reaching, but Miriam was far above them, almost at the line of black clotted seaweed that marked the highest tide. Even if someone miraculously managed to reach her, Luce thought, they'd never make it back to the sea in time. A quickly strobing vision possessed Luce's mind, just for a moment: now it wasn't Miriam lying there but her own mother. Alyssa was shaking from pain in the back of the red van, fighting to suppress her screams; she was dying all over again, while her small daughter clung to her chest. Then Luce's eyes cleared, and she realized that, while it would be impossible to pull Miriam back into the waves, she might still find a way to save her.

She could make the sea go to Miriam.

It would take a much bigger wave than she'd ever conjured before, but still she could try. Luce closed her eyes and concentrated on gathering every last bit of strength so she could pour it all into her voice. The note began to form, to spread . . .

"Miriam!" It was Violet shouting near her. "*Miriam!*" And then Luce heard a final, sharp groan like tearing flesh way up on the shore. The song she'd barely begun crumpled in her chest, and she looked up. It was already too late.

Miriam was silent, unmoving. Her scales were peeling off so quickly that it was hard to really see what was happening; they seemed to become like tissue paper, then like something even frailer, spiderwebs, old crumbled flecks of seashell, wandering smoke . . .

All at once Miriam had two long, bluish, naked human legs where her tail had been. Her toes were curled tight, like a new baby's. The skin on her legs looked raw and unused, traced by oddly dark purple veins, and her black hair lay in ropes along the tide line.

She was dead, lost beyond all doubt or hope. All that was left of the girl she had been was a grimace of stilted pain.

The tribe was still gathering. Stragglers were catching up to the mermaids gathered along the shore. Every time another head broke through the water, a fresh cry of shock shivered out across the sea. Luce was unnaturally aware of the rhythm of the surf against the pebbles, aware of the aching immensity of the sky above them all.

What she felt was a song, Luce realized. She'd failed Miriam, she'd wounded her beyond repair, she hadn't reached her in time, but she absolutely wouldn't leave her body there on the beach, stripped and sad and exposed to the view of anyone who came by. Miriam belonged to the sea. Luce could feel something strange entering her chest: the whole silky interface of ocean and wild sky. She could make the water bend, rise . . .

The noise that erupted from Luce was a mixture of song and scream. A wave with peculiarly vertical sides towered five yards into the air, knocking bewildered mermaids out of its path. It teetered for a moment, struggling for balance, then as Luce's voice ascended to a higher pitch it gained strength and raced far up the shore. They all saw Miriam's pale body lifted in the water's arms. She floated above their heads for a moment, stretched out peacefully at the top of a moving silver bier.

Then Luce gradually lowered her voice; it followed a velvety downward slope, carrying Miriam back home.

Miriam was in the mermaids' arms. They kissed her eyelids, and their hands swirled over her, caressed her cold wrinkled feet, then gently carried her out to the deep water. They were all singing at once, all swimming out into the spreading ocean, and their song was more uncontainable than it had ever been before. None of the anger, none of the bitterness mattered now; they were together in the song, united in one endless vibration. Luce saw Catarina in a rippling blaze beside her, her hair mingling with the molten gold of the dawn. None of that mattered. Fins sliced the blue depths with giddy speed. Anais's blond waves scrolled through the water, and Luce's voice merged with hers without the slightest resentment. They sang for Miriam, and no ocean could have been big enough to hold them.

The ship just got in their way.

It was huge, the biggest cruise ship Luce had ever seen in their territory, its sides as white and numb as an iceberg's. Luce dimly registered its bulk slicing the air in front of her. There had to be hundreds of passengers on a boat that size. It didn't matter. They didn't have any business coming here, anyway. This was a place where the sky crashed and dripped, liquefied in the howling of the mermaids for their dead. The elegy was half a scream, inhumanly sustained, and they would make the whole sea scream with them. None of them said a thing; they only sang. It had nothing to do with the humans, and it wasn't a song intended to enchant them. Luce let her voice rise into another sky-sweeping wave, and now she rode along the crest of the water-tower she'd raised, her mouth open around a shriek of unimaginable music.

She could see the people stumbling out onto the deck, still in their pajamas or sometimes just underwear. They were all driven insane by a sound that was at once intolerably beautiful and murderously sad; they were running into one another like ants, clawing their own foreheads until the blood dribbled down. Luce saw one man smearing yellow paint on his face then shoving his cheek against a wall, using his own head as a brush. The ship slowed, feinting from side to side as the pilot's mind reeled under the impact of that unearthly music. It wasn't a song made for humans to hear, and there was no way they could endure it. The world they lived in wasn't a *human* world, Luce thought. It was the humans' own fault if they were arrogant enough to believe that it was. If you were honest, if you were brave, you'd know that anything could happen: you might overhear a mermaids' funeral, their voices distended in frantic grief; you might die. She made the wave carrying her arch like a swan's neck, and she swept back under the water.

Catarina's voice was silkening now. It softened the air into floating kisses. Luce understood, of course. They hadn't wanted the ship, not at a time like this, but now that it was here it didn't stand a chance. Any human who heard the mermaids singing had to die; the timahk made that clear. Gently the mermaids let Miriam's body go. Then one by one they followed Catarina's lead, and the stupendous scream-song relaxed into a thrum. Only Luce was still shrieking, but finally even her voice jolted upward, higher and higher, until it floated like a single savage star. The star had appeared out of nowhere at the top of a worn farmhouse staircase, and it was poised to fall into the arms of the lovely dark-haired woman who waited at the bottom. Luce still sang for Miriam, but now for the first time she also sang her own mother's death from a ruptured appendix on the dirty floor of the red van. Her mother squeezed Luce's hand and tried to smile, but her smile kept knotting up from the pain . . .

The mermaids were spreading out, falling into formation around the ship. Catarina had turned it to the right. They were going back to the island, then, but approaching it this time from the other direction. There was no time to worry, no time even to think. Dana was swimming in the wake, so Luce let her voice carry her around the ship's left side. The note finally broke and tumbled down the stairs, and as it fell Luce thought of her mother. The song spelled Alyssa's name. A few blurred forms began to pitch from the deck, streaking past Luce as they plunged into the water. Luce's voice rose into another angelic scream, and she burst up through the waves and stared at the white hulk above her.

A boy of maybe fifteen leaned out directly above her. His dark blond hair was a tousled mess, blowing across his eyes. He stood proudly, his chest out and chin lifted as he gripped the railing. He stared right at her with a dark, sarcastic, open-mouthed grin on his face. Luce couldn't understand what was happening at first, then something hit her: the note of a singing voice that stood out in perfect isolation against the thrilling swarm of mermaids' voices.

It stood out because the voice was *human*. The boy above her wasn't enchanted at all. He stood there singing deliberately back at her, even as an overweight woman in a hot pink sweatshirt flung herself over the railing right next to him. If he wasn't enchanted, though, why didn't the chaos on all sides send him into a panic? Next a middle-aged man gaped down at Luce; he seemed astonished to discover that he was capable of such absolute love, and he clambered up the rails, beckoning Luce frantically with both hands. The boy barely glanced at the older man as he leaned out and then over, waving even as he fell.

The boy's voice rose, veering badly off-key as it reached for that soaring, impossible note. He held it anyway. Luce was silent now, gaping back in shock. The boy looked at her, and his coarse, unmagical human voice tumbled down a long staircase. Then at the bottom of the stairs it turned abruptly, running out into a sunny garden.

Luce was dumbstruck. It was unbelievable enough that a human boy was *singing* to her; it was even worse that he was bellowing a crude approximation of Luce's own song. But now, going even beyond that, he was *changing* it as if he could make it his own! It was inconceivably insulting, worse than insolence. But also, she had to admit, a bit impressive. Since when were humans so unafraid of the secrets rippling under the surface of their safe little lives?

The boat's engines were grating, snarling, its wake rising higher as it throttled forward. She had to get herself together, Luce realized. She couldn't let a human enchant *her*! She pressed her voice back up, driving it into the death song, staring at the blond boy and wrapping him in coils of trembling music. He didn't break. He stared at her with grim defiance, and his voice dueled with hers. It was only then that Luce noticed the cloud of dark shimmering that clung around him: the indication. He was a metaskaza, then. Was that why he was so brave and why he was able to resist her?

Metaskaza, except that he couldn't be. He'd drown instead of change, purely because he was a boy.

It was so *unfair*, Luce thought. And then the ship slammed headlong into the sharp crags of the island. Birds like splatters of snow-white blood sprayed out around the prow. The metal crunched, and the deck jerked up into a sudden slope. The boy's eyes left Luce's for the first time as he staggered, caught himself, and then glanced around; even now no fear was visible on his face, only curiosity and perhaps sadness. He turned his gaze back at Luce, daring her with his eyes—but daring her to do what?—and climbed onto the tilted railing, swaying for a second as he found his balance. Then he dove gracefully, and his body formed a long blue streak as it sailed past the white ship and down into the swells. It took Luce only a second to catch up with him.

Any human who heard the mermaids singing had to die; Luce knew that. There was much more than the timahk at stake. Their existence had to be kept secret from the humans forever, or Miriam's awful visions would almost certainly come true. The boy was a witness to the mermaids, to what they did to human ships, and Luce had a responsibility to make sure he didn't live to tell anyone what he'd seen. Her own feelings had nothing to do with it.

She hooked an arm around his waist and spiraled her tail, careful this time to compensate for the weight dragging her to the right. She lashed away from the carnage as fast as she could, hoping desperately that no one had noticed her leaving. He was already gagging a little, leaning back and prying at her arm to free himself, but Luce was stronger now than any human. She sliced so fast through the empty waves that all she could see was the greenish pale frothing water, the yellow of lingering dawn, and when the singing grew a little quieter behind her she angled sharply up, breaking the surface. A school of porpoises leaped around her and then scattered in alarm.

The blond boy coughed, spitting up gouts of salt water. Luce used her free arm to hold his head facedown just above the surface so he could disgorge the water without choking. She glanced behind her. They were still much too close to the fractured ship, the shrilling mermaids, for her to take the chance of swimming slowly along the top of the waves. She had to hurry; she had to be back before anyone realized that she'd vanished . . . The boy looked over at her wearily, stripes of wet, tan hair gripping his cheeks. He had unusually wide-set ocher eyes, a large nose; Luce got the impression of a certain ragged grandeur, and the kind of unyielding, open intelligence that could gaze at a mermaid with steady acceptance. He might be angry, she thought, but he wasn't even surprised by the uncanny turn his life had taken. He knew how the world could be.

"Take a really deep breath, okay?" Luce told him. "We have to dive under again."

She tried not to go too deep and to bring him up for air at reasonable intervals, but she was in a desperate hurry, and also she'd forgotten just how frail humans were. By the time they were close enough to glimpse the docks of the small village up the coast the boy was only half conscious, gagging up seawater every time she surfaced. His head rolled against her shoulder, and sometimes his hands groped feebly through the empty grayness in front of them. She'd bring him as close to the village as she dared. At least it was a warm morning, and once he was out of the water there wouldn't be any danger of hypothermia.

He had the indication, Luce told herself. He wouldn't tell anyone about the mermaids, and even if he did, he wasn't much older than she was. No one would take him seriously. Besides, whether he knew it or not, he was one of them. He was really a merman, only he couldn't get rid of his legs.

He had the indication, so in a way—if you just thought of it the right way—maybe it would have been a violation of the timahk *not* to save him.

She shoved him facedown onto a stony beach and then backed away, watching him for just one more moment. He seemed to regain a bleary awareness of his surroundings, dragging himself up until only his sneakers were still submerged in the splashing sea margin, then rolling awkwardly onto his side to gaze back at her. Water hacked up from his chest and poured down his chin. He was going to be okay, though; Luce could see that. She saw his yellow-brown eyes regarding her from beneath one up-flung arm in its drenched blue sweatshirt, but he didn't speak or even smile. It was such an interesting face, she thought; not exactly beautiful, but alive with quick-moving emotions . . .

She had to *go*, Luce knew. She had to get back to the shipwreck, hope that in the tumult of voices and drowning bodies no one had noticed that one especially powerful voice was missing from the chorus. She backed a bit farther out into the water, waves lifting her repetitively so that his returning stare rocked in her eyes. *Stop it right now, Lucette.* She had to squeeze her lids down tight before she could tear herself away. It was a windy day, and the water was rough and angry.

When Luce got back, she found Catarina and Dana just polishing off the last survivors. A few girls gave her strange looks, but no one said anything, and Luce didn't know if it was because she'd been away too long or because, now that they were calmer, they were thinking of her fight with Catarina, and of the wave she'd called to bring Miriam back to the water.

No one said anything. They'd sung themselves empty.

* * *

The magical communion of their grief was fading. Everyone remembered the events that had led up to Miriam's suicide, and they began to have trouble looking at one another. A pall of exhaustion and embarrassment spread over the tribe, all of them straggling weakly back to their cave. And now that she wasn't stupefied by the first shock of mourning and the exultation of their dark, shared song, Luce felt sick with guilt. Hadn't she sworn she'd never help kill humans again? Now a thousand fresh, cold bodies rolled in the surf, their outspread fingers trailing against the seafloor. Passing silver fish were reflected in their unseeing eyes . . .

And while she'd persuaded herself that it wasn't exactly a violation of the timahk to save the bronze-haired boy, Luce was vividly aware that no one there would agree with her. She was glad that she was too tired to think straight, too tired even to feel.

Everyone seemed equally depleted. They lay side by side all day; for the first time in weeks Luce took her old place beside Catarina. She knew this peacefulness between them couldn't last, but for now—just for now—Catarina smiled at her again with broken, tear-streaked eyes, and Luce let her head drop against Catarina's pale shoulder.

"Well done, Lucette," Catarina whispered. "My brave Queen Luce. You brought Miriam back to us. Oh, there's nothing more terrible than a mermaid left abandoned on the shore . . ." Luce wondered drowsily if Catarina was being sarcastic, but her voice sounded warm and gentle, traced with lulling half-song. Dimly Luce realized that Catarina was enchanting her, coaxing her into a deep and healing sleep.

17

Shame

"Boy, it's going to suck if Luce and Catarina get all friendsy-wiendsy again." It was Anais; she was keeping her voice down, but the words still trickled into Luce's half-dreaming mind; they smeared and coiled, hardly words at all for a moment, but then as consciousness rose in her she understood them. "Why is Catarina such a dope for her, anyway? I mean, she's just this stupid misfit freak . . ."

"Oh," Samantha whispered back dismissively. "Oh, Cat just always has a soft spot for girls where, like, they changed because of somebody molesting them. You know, she has a *thing* about it. Like Luce's uncle groping her makes her special or something . . ." Luce didn't feel like listening to this. She made a show of moaning and stretching, like someone about to wake up. "She's waking up. Shhh, okay?" Luce opened her eyes and saw Anais sitting much too close, staring at her with fixed curiosity—but with her head turned sideways so that she gazed from the corners of her sky blue eyes. Luce flinched. She didn't mind the other mermaids watching the images that winked in the dark sparkling around her, or at least she'd come to accept it, but having Anais look at her that way almost felt like having her uncle's hands sliding down her body all over again.

"Do you mind?" Luce snapped. She knew she'd slept for many hours, but she still felt utterly exhausted. Anais didn't change her position, but a smirk appeared on her face. Other mermaids were starting to wake up here and there in the cave. Jenna stared at Luce for a second like she couldn't understand what she was doing there then turned pointedly away.

"So, what was it about you, Luce?" Anais cooed, sickly sweet. "I mean, what were you doing to make your uncle think you were ready to go like that?" Luce felt nausea like a fist inside her stomach, but she forced herself to keep her eyes raised, gazing straight into Anais's leering face. "I mean, really. He wouldn't have tried anything unless he thought you wanted it, would he?"

Don't answer, Luce told herself with her nails digging into her palms. *Just don't answer.* She could feel Catarina stirring beside her, but she didn't let her eyes waver from Anais's face. Would it be possible to shame her into shutting up?

"Ooh, I guess so! You can admit it to *us,* Luce. I mean, we are your best, best friends," Anais lilted, and Samantha giggled.

"What's going on?" The voice was Catarina's, and Luce felt a flutter of hope. Would Anais really dare to keep talking this way with Catarina listening?

"Oh, we were just encouraging Luce to, you know, open up. Like, she'll feel better if she can finally talk about whatever it was she did to get her uncle so *excited* . . ." Catarina's tail arched sharply up out of the water, but Anais was out of range. "I mean, we all know Luce is a special girl, don't we?"

"You have *no* idea who Luce is!" Catarina was hissing; her eyes glinted with cold rage. "You! You're incapable of knowing someone like her, of recognizing—that heart! And for you to *dare* suggest . . ." Catarina suddenly seemed too angry to speak, and Luce stared over at her in amazement. How could Cat insult her one day and defend her so passionately the next? It was more than she could understand.

"Oh, Catarina, do you think so? But I don't see why you're upset. All I was doing was saying how wonderful Luce is!" Anais cocked her head sideways again, and Luce tensed as she realized that Anais was gazing brazenly into the sparkling around Catarina. Catarina's mouth opened in a snarl, but before she could speak Anais cut her off, with a sudden, trilling spurt of high-pitched laughter. The needling in Luce's skin turned into a wave of icy shivers, and for a minute Anais only laughed higher and faster, doubling at her waist so that she had to lean on one hand to keep herself from toppling into the water. Catarina's snarl stalled in place, her upper lip curled above her shining teeth.

"Oh boy oh boy oh boy!" Anais shrieked. "Wow, you must be a really, *really* special girl, Cat! For those guys to think they could do *that!* I mean, I guess we all already knew that you were . . . talented—"

"Shut up!" Luce was yelling now, queasy with disbelief. She never would have imagined anyone saying something like this, not even Anais. "Anais, just shut up! What happened to *you,* anyway?" Then Luce saw Catarina's face, and the shout died in her throat.

Catarina should have been in a fury. She should have been terrifying, a blaze of blanched skin and leaping flames.

Instead her face seemed to cave in on itself. She wasn't looking at Anais at all, but at her own knotted hands. *No!* Luce wanted to tell her. *Whatever you do, don't let her see you're ashamed.*

It was too late, though. Anais was grinning triumphantly.

"Well, maybe not everybody appreciates Cat's talents the way I do. I think I've seen more of her in action . . ."

Luce wobbled. This couldn't possibly mean what she thought! No, Luce tried to reassure herself. Anais was only talking about what she'd just seen of Catarina's human life, whatever it was that had changed her. After all, Anais was the only one there who'd ever had the nerve to infringe on Catarina's privacy that way.

Luce had to do something to make this stop. "ANAIS!"

It was better than nothing. At least those syrupy blue eyes swung toward her, away from Catarina's collapsed mouth and downcast gaze.

"Yes, Lucette?" Anais's voice dusted down like powdered sugar.

"Everyone else here, you can see what happened to them. I mean, if you're messed up enough that you'll go looking where it's none of your business . . ." Anais's smile didn't weaken at all. "You're the only mermaid here where there's nothing to see, really. So what happened to *you?*" When Luce glanced around for a second, she realized everyone was awake by now, gawking at them.

"You know, it's funny you ask me that, Lucette." Luce hated the phony maturity Anais was putting on now even more than she hated her fake sweetness or her fake tears. "Samantha and I have discussed that very thing. Nothing that bad ever happened to me, really. My parents both loved me very much. They always told me I was their princess, and they gave me anything I wanted." Disgust clogged Luce's mind as she listened, but somehow she knew Anais was telling the truth. But then why had she changed? "Isn't it interesting? If you think about it, everybody always seems to get exactly what they deserve . . ."

Luce thought that the rest of the mermaids might finally turn on Anais. After all, she was basically saying that Samantha *deserved* to be thrown from a moving car, that Jenna *deserved* to be trapped in a burning house. Luce looked around for support. Even if they couldn't actually expel Anais, couldn't they pressure her into leaving the tribe?

No one met Luce's eyes. After a second Luce understood why.

They actually believed what Anais was saying to them. At least they half believed it or they were afraid it was true: that their parents had left them or hurt them because of some deep, secret flaw in their own hearts. It didn't take much, just the smallest crack of self-doubt, and Anais's words could insinuate themselves through the gap and then drive it wider.

They were all ashamed. Just like Catarina. Even Samantha, who had insisted so loudly that no mermaid should ever allow herself to feel shame for one second. And Luce had never felt so sorry for them. "You shouldn't listen to her," Luce whispered. "None of you should." She waited a moment, and no one answered. "Cat? I mean, do you want to come back to my cave for a while?" But Catarina wouldn't even look at her. There was no point in staying with them, not now. If anyone wanted to talk to her, they could come and find her.

When Luce surfaced for air, she saw a man's body washed up against the beach where Miriam had died. He bobbled loosely, his head tapping at the rocks.

She would find a way—someday—that the mermaids could live without anything they had to be ashamed of.

She would find the song that showed how them how.

* * *

Luce stayed alone in her cave, only darting out occasionally for food. She was still strangely exhausted and slept long hours. When she woke she'd sing quietly to herself, calling tiny waves to come and dance around her while her mind filled with images of the dead: Tessa and Miriam, Tessa's mother, her own parents, the curly-haired Coast Guard boy. It was hard for her to think about anything else now. She knew that sometime she should try to straighten out all the confusion with Catarina, but she kept putting that off. It would almost surely be painful, and Luce had all the pain she could deal with for now. There were so many things she should have done differently, so many times when, if she'd just said the right words, there might have been one less body lolling in the deep gray water.

Luce sang. It was the only thing that made her grief bearable. As soon as she stopped, it felt like knives driving into her chest.

It had been a crazy thing to do. It might even have been wrong, selfish, irresponsible . . . but Luce was glad she'd saved the boy who sang back to her. His face was one image that she didn't have to see in that winking museum of lost faces.

Only four days after Miriam's death, Luce heard the mermaids singing. They sounded shrill, manic, completely out of control. They were taking down another boat, and it was much, much too soon, especially since the last one had been so huge. Helicopters rattled overhead all the time now. But Luce couldn't make herself care. In her mind's eye she was watching Tessa, who was sitting cross-legged at the bottom of the sea with a book spread on her knees, the tip of her tongue sticking out as she reached some particularly dramatic point in the narrative. Luce didn't know what book it was, but even so, she sang along with the story, with the rise and fall of the characters' thoughts. Then she saw that she'd actually made one small wave break free of the ocean's surface, and circle in midair . . . She wanted to call Tessa to look, but the wave plopped back into the water in a shower of droplets that glimmered like tears . . .

She could hear the mermaids singing, and the crunch of a boat hitting the cliffs very near her cave. Maybe Anais would get a new dress or something.

Luce sang to herself and to the dead. Other mermaids could sing for the living. Even if it was strange and awful to hear Catarina's voice tangled up with Anais's, not too far away. How could Cat possibly sing with Anais after the vile things she'd said? Then Luce realized what was wrong in the tone of the song licking over the sea now. The whole tribe was hopelessly drunk again, deranged by human liquor.

Luce found herself listening very intently in the minutes that followed the ship's crash, although she didn't know why it seemed so important to keep track of all the individual voices— or really, just of *one* voice. Luce was listening to make sure that

Catarina stayed up near the surface with the others and that she didn't take off alone on any mysterious dives. Luce realized that her heart was beating faster, that she was peculiarly cold. But no, it was okay. Luce could follow Catarina's voice the whole time. She never left the group. After a while the singing dropped away, replaced by the fainter but still distinct sounds of girls' voices squabbling over choice bits of plunder, and Luce finally relaxed. But what was she worrying about? Catarina could swim deep down without endangering herself, even as she gave her own reserves of air to some boy in her arms. Luce had seen her do it, after all, and Cat had been fine. For a while Luce went back to daydreaming, to scattering her voice in tiny flying notes like rising sparks. She was just so tired now; maybe she always would be.

Then Luce sat up abruptly. She'd realized what was bothering her.

She'd seen Catarina twined around a drowning human boy. But someone else had seen it, too, on a different occasion. Luce had suspected this before, but suddenly she was sure of it.

Much as she hated the idea, Luce realized she'd have to follow the tribe anytime they attacked a ship. Just in case . . . Luce couldn't stand to finish the thought, and for an instant her voice stabbed upward, bringing a small fountain of salt water with it.

* * *

Luce tried to time her forays out for food at hours when no one else would be around. She even tried eating at beaches besides the dining beach, but the other spots where the mussels were good were all too exposed, and with the new frequency of boats and helicopters in the area she was too nervous to spend time anywhere that wasn't underwater or in some particularly sheltered nook of coast. After a few days passed quietly, she slipped over to the dining beach in the long slur of sunset, probably close to midnight, when the tribe would usually have headed back to the main cave.

But on this particular evening, she found them all still there. Dana waved shyly, and Violet smiled, but everyone else ignored her. Even Catarina seemed to have given up her campaign of trying to provoke Luce into a contest; her old friend just sat talking to Jenna, pretending Luce wasn't there at all. So, she'd gone back to being invisible, Luce thought; that was manageable, even if it hurt her. She'd had a lot of practice at being a kind of living secret when she was human, and she could adapt to being one again: the dark eyes that gazed out of the water . . .

Anais cracked a mussel, but she didn't eat it. Instead she dangled it over the head of an iridescent, pinkish larva, which leaped and gibbered eagerly, trying to grab the treat. Anais just twitched the mussel higher then made a looping motion with her free hand. After a few more futile lunges, the larva seemed to comprehend; it turned a messy somersault in the water then bobbled up, begging and squeaking. Anais taunted it for another few moments, and as the larva started whimpering she popped the mussel in its gaping mouth. The tribe looked on, and Luce saw a confusing assortment of expressions on the watching faces: Kayley seemed disgusted, Violet pitying, others maliciously delighted.

"Who knew you could train these gross little things!" Anais shrilled. "I'm going to have to think of some, like, more useful stuff I could get them to do." She cracked another mussel, but this time she withheld it until the larva executed three flips in a row. It wobbled dizzily the third time, slapping sideways into a protruding rock. Anais laughed. Luce was terribly hungry, having made herself wait so long for dinner, but as she watched the eager little larva prancing in front of Anais she had trouble swallowing. The poor little things were so lonely, Luce thought, so eager for attention, that they didn't even mind being degraded in order to get the older girls to look at them. Now Anais was making the larva leap, though with its stubby, uncoordinated tail it couldn't go very high. A cluster of other larvae drifted closer, open-mouthed, emitting mewing sounds.

"Good one, Anais!" Samantha laughed as the larva belly-flopped back down with a frightened gurgle.

"No guys here," Anais explained lazily. "You really have to do, like, *whatever* to keep from getting bored." The moon was rising in the pale blue of the summer night, and Luce looked out to see its glow forming a trail of faint stripes across the distant waves: a trail that led into the deepening sea where the mermaids never swam.

"Totally," Samantha agreed. But what wouldn't she agree with if Anais said it?

"I mean, I keep hearing about that Coast Guard boat you guys sank, back before I got here." Anais's tone was still casual, but there was a hidden tension in it that made Luce look back at her again. She was just in time to see Anais darting a stealthy sideways glance at Catarina, and the glance was much faster, much sharper, than the sleepy drawl of her voice. "So, you know, I keep thinking we should be on the lookout for another boat like that. I mean one with a lot of hot guys. We'll at least get to have *some* fun with them, even if we're not allowed to keep them . . ."

Catarina was still talking to Jenna, seemingly oblivious, but from something subtle in the tilt of her fiery head Luce could tell she was listening.

Luce forced herself to keep eating. Otherwise she'd just wake up famished in the middle of the night. Besides, she had a feeling she should hang around a while longer, just in case any- one said anything important. But the subject of boys seemed exhausted. Now Anais had a new larva flapping hopefully in front of her. It was slower on the uptake than the pink one, though, and couldn't figure out that it was expected to turn a somersault before it could have the mussel. "Stupid thing," Anais cooed. "Stupid little bitch. You think I'm feeding you before you do what I want?"

Luce thought of bringing the larva a mussel, but she didn't feel like getting into another fight with Anais tonight. She was too drained.

Before she headed back to her own little cave, Luce swirled over to Catarina, who was seated on her favorite sofa-shaped rock. Luce could see her bronze-gold tail flaring and ebbing un- der the blanched water.

"Cat?" Catarina completely ignored her. Luce's voice could just as well have been a breeze passing by. "Hey, Cat!" Jenna was glaring now, leaning out past Catarina's shoulder, and finally Catarina glanced around.

"How nice of you to stop by, Lucette." She didn't sound unfriendly, but none of the unexpected warmth she'd shown af- ter Miriam's death was there either. Her tone was purely empty, the voice of someone chilled to the quick.

"Cat, I just want to ask you . . ." Catarina's eyebrows shot up; Luce knew she was waiting for the challenge to come at last. The look on her face was a mixture of apprehension and relief. Luce stared into Cat's gray eyes and raised one tentative hand, but then she didn't reach out, didn't touch her. "Just, *please* be careful." Catarina's expression returned to a perfect blank. She might have been looking at a patch of moonlight glinting off the sea.

* * *

Over the next few days Luce had trouble sleeping, and when she did everything around her seemed to have its own voice: the water hummed and purled, the rocks trilled in a wheezy soprano, and the faint moonlight fell like the broken notes produced by creatures that were half seal and half cello. The cliffs had two different voices: one for day and one for the blue, sun-streaked Alaskan night. Even when she was awake her mind was stained by the residue of dreamed music, until she sometimes wondered if she was hallucinating, and she sang to herself in the voices she heard pouring from the tides, the sun, the jagged cliffs . . .

The only song she never seemed to hear anymore was the mermaids'. She didn't run into them again, and no one came to see her. Maybe everything was okay after all, and she'd been worrying for nothing. Only once or twice Luce woke from a song like a trance with the aching sense that someone had been listening to her, just outside her cave.

Everything was music, even her. She didn't feel quite as lonely now that the whole world kept singing back to her, though she still missed Tessa, and Catarina, and Miriam. It was all her own fault, Luce realized, that she and Miriam hadn't become very good friends. Miriam had tried to get close to her, but Luce was so accustomed to isolation that she hadn't really responded. Miriam couldn't hear her, but Luce still sang to tell Miriam how sorry she was . . .

Her dream of changing the tribe was ridiculous, though. Luce knew that now. If she was ever going to realize her vision of belonging to a tribe that didn't kill, she'd have to start over fresh; she'd have to travel down the coast, maybe find brand new metaskazas who weren't already addicted to their songs of murder.

And, Luce realized, she'd have to be the queen. It was the only way. And since she couldn't imagine wielding so much power she stayed where she was, listening to the enchantment of pure being. Sometimes she floated down the coast, letting the currents control her body. It was a bit reckless with so many humans around now; Luce often heard their graceless voices carrying over the water, but she didn't quite care.

She lost track of time. (Sometimes she knew whether it was night or day only by the pitch of the cliffs in her ears, the blue or bright timbre of their song.)

* * *

Luce was stretched out on her back out in the open sea. She knew, of course, that it was reckless to drift that way, so far from the cliffs. If something leaped at her from below she wouldn't see it coming, and she'd have no chance to escape. She didn't care anymore. She floated, listening to the waves that gently lapped against her ears. Their song was a slow, percussive chant, a kind of moan. *Beautiful*, Luce thought. As she floated onward the music split into two sounds, gaining a very faint harmonic overlay, and Luce smiled appreciatively. It was like living warmth inside the wind, and it seemed to come from far, far away: the hum of distance itself. It brought heat rushing to her cheeks, made her blood run faster, and Luce suddenly thought of the boy with bronze-blond hair, the one she'd saved. She thought of his mouth sneaking up inside the waves next to her and then cresting onto her lips in a slow, smooth kiss . . .

Luce started from her daydream and rolled over, scanning the sea in all directions. The sound shattered and echoed off the water and off the cliffs, so that she couldn't be sure which direction it came from. Somewhere ahead, probably, and a bit to her right.

It wasn't some half-hallucinated song of the distance she was hearing at all. It was Catarina, singing in the soft, insinuating lull she used when she was just starting to lead a boat to its doom. And out on the horizon Luce caught sight of it, no more than a gray speck. She could tell that it was turning by the way the bright sunlight on its flank was gradually rotating into shadow. Luce could swim at terrific speed, of course, but she was many miles away.

The note rose, and the gray speck began to move faster. Luce knew what was coming, and a lump of shame almost choked her.

She'd been wasting her time on selfish dreams, and all the while Catarina was in danger.

18

Violation

The mermaids' voices were clearer underwater. Luce swum toward them so quickly that it felt as if she were plunging down a waterfall, thrusting the waves behind her. Her vision brimmed with bubbles, the undulating movements of jellyfish, then a gray seal's mouth clamping down on one thrashing, reddish fish. Pictures gathered in her eyes and scattered again, everything confused by speed. Luce could distinguish several of the mermaids now: Dana's loving, velvety caress of a voice, Rachel's excitable dread, the brutal joy of Anais's soprano.

She slashed her way forward. If trouble was coming, it would be when the voices stopped.

When she popped up to catch her breath the boat was much larger, and even though the distance made it appear to be traveling much more slowly than it actually was, Luce could make out the noise of throbbing engines pushed to their limit. She couldn't be sure, but she thought the ship had a military look to it. Incredibly, the mermaids were leading it back to the same island, even though a helicopter had buzzed overhead perhaps twenty minutes earlier. Luce shook her head; it was willful craziness, a drive toward their own destruction as well as the destruction of the humans. Luce dove again.

Even deep underwater she could hear the crash, broken into wavering echoes by the movement of the waves around her. The pulsation of mermaid songs reeled louder. Luce didn't want to picture it, but the image was unavoidable: young men and women in uniform, lunatic smiles on their faces, welcoming their own descent into the waves while the mermaids called them on. They'd be getting to the point soon where individual mermaids would break away from the group to target the few humans who had the strength of mind to try to pull free from the enchantment, and swim for it . . . The point where a mermaid might think she could slip deeper than the rest, unnoticed.

Luce threw herself into a violent forward trajectory. Her tail spun so quickly that the muscles cramped. She swam deeper, too, angling for the same spot where she'd seen Catarina take her prey before.

Hair as bright as an ember, gradually descending: Luce could see it, far away in the green deep. She was swimming so quickly that her vision smeared, but she was almost positive the sinking form she could make out ahead was too big to be Catarina alone. And, Luce realized, the ocean had slipped into silence; she couldn't hear the mermaids singing, not anymore. She hurled on, though her tail was burning from the effort.

A towering crag rose from the sea-bottom, not so far below Catarina now. And waiting just behind it—where Luce could see it but Catarina couldn't—a mass of something too soft and too colorful to be stone, a mass that hovered in place but with a slight disturbance of flicking tails at the bottom. Luce drove herself faster, but she could already see that there was no way she could make it there in time.

The tribe was waiting in ambush, and Catarina would float past them before Luce could get there. Luce was so sick with expectation that when it happened it seemed almost like it might be a movie of the thing she'd dreaded unspooling in front of her. It almost felt like it might not be entirely real, like by the time she arrived there'd be nothing there but some drifting seaweed. Luce was close enough now to see Catarina writhing urgently in the arms of a young dark-skinned man, close enough to hear the low, satiny whorls of her song as she kissed his hungry mouth. The couple sank, lost in the feeling of each other's bodies, until they were no more than ten feet away from the lurking tribe.

There was a momentary lull, and then a shout of vicious triumph from Anais. Luce was almost there now. She could see the young man abruptly ripped from Catarina's arms, and the huge silver bubble that stretched for an instant between their lips. Anais threw the boy aside, ignoring his sudden frantic flailing as the enchantment abandoned his mind. He sank deeper all alone.

A crowd of mermaids closed in on Catarina, all of them drunk and enraged, with a chorus of delirious shrieks.

Luce was only moments away now. She couldn't believe what she was seeing. She'd expected Catarina to be formally expelled, and she was prepared to go with her, but *this!* Fists swung dizzily into Catarina's sides, hands raked at her face. Already Luce could see a subtle taint of blood leaking through the water. Even Jenna was pounding Catarina as she cowered, trying to pro- tect her head; even *Rachel* . . . Water foamed around their whip- ping tails. Only Dana and Violet hung back, looks of appalled bewilderment on their faces, but even they didn't do anything to stop it. The tribe was going to murder Catarina right in front of them and they only gawked helplessly. Anais's hard voice was shrilling with excitement, egging the mermaids on.

Luce was swimming faster than she'd ever gone before, and she drove headfirst right into the middle of the mob, her own body pummeled by a confusion of fists and swinging tails. She was slightly higher than the others, dashing in at a downward angle, and she beat her own tail into their faces, shoving mer- maids apart with the full force of her long body. She had to clear a space, just enough that she could get in front of Catarina, block the others . . . If she could even separate her from her at- tackers for a moment . . .

Mermaids began to fall back. Some were still shaking with bloodlust, but others widened their eyes with looks of stunned recognition, as if they were shocked to realize what they'd been doing. Luce managed to drag Catarina's limp body a few feet back and slip down in front of her. Catarina was conscious enough to cling to Luce's shoulders; her face sagged against Luce's neck. There was a dreamlike pause, a hesitation, as Luce looked around at the faces of her former tribe.

"You're all breaking the timahk . . ." They were deep enough that everyone was low on air, squeezed uncomfortably

by the unaccustomed pressure of many thousands of tons of water above them. Speaking was difficult, and it would only hurry
the moment when even a mermaid would drown. There was a
brief silence, then Anais replied haughtily.

"I'm queen now, Lucette. And I say the timahk doesn't
count in a situation like this . . . where a mermaid was actually
kissing . . . If you don't get out of our way, we'll just have to kill
you, too." As Anais spoke Luce was gathering power in her
chest, pulling in the secret music that the ocean understood, and
that it would answer. Anais nodded to Jenna and Samantha, and
they reached to grab Luce.

Luce's song leaped up in one long, expansive, ear-splitting
cry. It joined with the water and made it into a wall, strong as
stone, slamming forward. A tangle of tails and struggling arms
were flung suddenly away from her, driven back at least ten yards,
and Luce could hear their yells of outrage, see the swirl of colors
as they pulled themselves apart, maybe getting ready to lunge at
her again. Luce knew she didn't have enough air to sing that
overwhelming note a second time, not if she was going to have
any hope of making it back to the surface. She pushed up, as fast
as her own sore muscles and Catarina's weight would let her.

Their pursuers would be exhausted after all their violence
and just as desperate for air as Luce was. And their shock at being hit by an underwater wave in that unexpected way might
cause some of them to think twice about taking Luce on; it
should buy Luce and Catarina some time. They broke the surface together, and Luce could hear the rush of air drawn deeply
into Catarina's lungs in unison with her own ravenous inhalation. Luce maneuvered Catarina around to her right side so that

she could tow her by her waist, just the way Catarina had done for her twice before.

There was blood on Catarina's forehead, on her chest, and she swayed in Luce's arm. Bruises mottled her pale skin, and Luce suddenly noticed the way her left wrist flopped. Cat was clearly in no shape to dive again; that was unlucky, since swimming on the surface would slow them down. They'd have to swim a long way, too, to reach some fairly remote cave where Anais wouldn't think to look for them. Luce's own cave was out of the question. There was nothing to do but head south and hope for the best. Luce began to make her way across the water, pulling Catarina with her. The fiery head wavered and tipped onto Luce's shoulder. For several minutes they swam in silence, slight tremors flowing now and then through Catarina's back.

"Luce?" The voice was very quiet.

"It's going to be okay, Cat." Luce glanced back. "I don't think they're chasing us. Not yet. I'll take you someplace where you can rest."

"You don't have to do this, Luce. You shouldn't. You should let them kill me." Somehow these words hurt Luce more than anything Catarina had ever said to her. She glanced over, but Catarina's eyes were closed tight, her lips swollen and plum-colored.

"Catarina?" The gray eyes opened very slightly, like a tiny leak of moonlight in the golden afternoon. "This is *exactly* what I have to do." And as she said it, even in her exhaustion, Luce felt a rush of sad, sweet pride.

* * *

Her strength was starting to fail her. It took at least two hours of painful, laborious swimming before Luce decided that they were far enough from the main cave to be safe. She'd towed Catarina farther than she'd ever gone before, out past the fishing village and down to another stretch of wild coast, where she finally found a small round cave with a perfect underwater entrance. It was situated in a crevice between two high cliffs, and it felt wonderfully peaceful after the horror of the morning. Luce collapsed on the shore, and when she looked over she saw that Catarina was already asleep. Maybe she'd been sleeping for a while, and Luce just hadn't realized it. As gently as she could, Luce washed the clotted blood from Catarina's dreaming face. They needed food, Luce thought; in just a few minutes she'd go out and search for some. She needed to find some driftwood, too, and maybe washed-up rags or fishing net: something she could use to set that broken bone in Cat's left wrist. Any moment now, she'd gather her willpower and go . . .

* * *

The cave didn't have any fissures. It was only by the pale blue glow hazing in through the entrance that Luce guessed it must be midnight. They'd slept for hours, then. She sat up, lightheaded and unsteady. Catarina seemed to be sleeping still, but she was clinging to Luce's hand with her own. Impulsively Luce leaned in and kissed her softly just above a green swell on her forehead. When she pulled herself back up Catarina was gazing at her.

"You have to go back, Luce. The sooner the better. It's a waste of time for you to worry about me. The way things are now . . . You have the tribe to think about."

"No!" Luce was surprised by the anger in her voice, the intensity. "Of course I won't leave you, Cat. I'm going to look after you until you're better, and then we can swim south together." Catarina glowered at her with a bewildering mixture of emotions; Luce wasn't sure if Cat was feeling tenderness, or fury, or shock, but her gray eyes flared and she tried to sit up. She couldn't do it, though.

"Absolutely not. You're queen now, Luce. You can't just leave. You have to accept your responsibility." Luce found herself grinning bitterly.

"Is that an order, Cat?" She still felt dizzy. Dots of green light flocked across her eyes; she saw Catarina grimace on the far side of a moving field of chartreuse. "And anyway, how can *anyone* be queen in a tribe where every single mermaid just broke the timahk? I'd have to expel everyone. I'd be the queen of a bunch of rocks and some larvae . . ." She heard herself laugh, but somehow she couldn't feel it. "Anais wants to be queen. She's the *perfect* queen for them. After what they did to you!"

"I deserved it." Luce opened her mouth to object, but Catarina waved her to silence; Luce was annoyed but also secretly glad to see Cat's old imperiousness coming back to her. "Luce, really. Did you see what I did? Anais can't be queen. She could never be the true queen, not if you were living within a thousand miles of her! But she's right, that I—am unworthy—to be protected by the timahk . . ." Luce just felt impatient now.

"You know what? I've seen you do that before, Cat. After the Coast Guard boat, when I was still metaskaza and you tricked me into singing with you? I saw you with that boy then, and I knew you were breaking the timahk. *Dishonoring* us." Luce looked straight into Catarina's eyes. She felt so weak, balanced precariously on a strange force of life that seemed to push up from somewhere below her. "I knew you were breaking the timahk, but I didn't *care*." There was a moment's silence.

"Luce!" It came out in a kind of howl. "Oh, you're too innocent, you don't understand . . ." Luce just stared at her. Catarina was beside herself, the words coming up as if she were gagging on them. "Luce, there are reasons why, why we can't ever permit ourselves to do—what I did, what I've kept doing! How long do you think it would have been before I gave in to temptation, and let one of them survive? Do you think I didn't *want* to? That I didn't fantasize about it? Saving a human boy, and having him as my own? Oh, Luce. *Everyone* in our tribe is disgraced. All except you! But you can—you can restore their honor. If you'll only do what you have to do, and lead them . . ."

Catarina was in hysterics, her eyes squeezed tight, so she didn't see the blood rush into Luce's face. She didn't see Luce bite her lip and turn suddenly away, didn't hear her heart drumming painfully. Shouldn't she tell Cat the truth and confess that she'd done the very thing Catarina hated herself for even daydreaming about?

"Even Marina . . ." Catarina was moaning. "Our great queen, our *voice* . . . There was a human boy, seventeen, with the sparkling all around him, in the wreckage of a ship we brought down. And even she succumbed, Luce! She carried him ashore. She started visiting him secretly. I was her lieutenant, her right hand, the way you were . . ." Catarina laughed horribly now, tears streaming from her closed eyes. Her words fell rhythmically, joined to the beat of the sea, and there was a trace of singing in them. "The way you were to me before I really understood that you'd made me into a false queen! I noticed that Marina was missing too often, and I followed her. *Now* do you understand?"

Luce was mesmerized by the story, and so weak that she tipped back down to lie on the rocks beside Catarina. But she couldn't tell where this was all going. She shook her head, and her dizziness slopped like water in a tipped basin.

"I don't think I do. Understand. Catarina . . ."

Cat's terrible laugh came again. "I followed her; I saw them together; I couldn't believe my eyes. If you realized—what she meant to me! I couldn't bring myself to denounce her, though I knew that I should. Instead I confronted her. I gave her an ultimatum. Her lover had the indication, after all. Why shouldn't he join us?" Luce remembered what Catarina had told them all on the day when Anais had first joined the tribe.

"You told her she had to change him into a merman. Or else you'd tell everyone?"

Catarina let out a long, droning sigh, a sigh that was half a sob. When she spoke again it was almost an incantation. Her accent was thicker than Luce had ever heard it.

"Change him or drown him. Yes. I told her there was no other choice. I told her I'd kill him for her if it hurt her too much to do it. She knew how wrong it was to fall in love with a human, of course. She was ashamed of herself, and she agreed that I was right to demand that of her. She agreed! When she swam off to meet him that night I persuaded myself that I'd done the right thing . . . You understand?"

"You told us she couldn't do it. You said it almost killed her . . ." Luce's voice merged with the rhythm of Catarina's now. Catarina's tears picked up the dusky glow from outside, reflecting it back in twin lines of blue neon.

"I found her the next morning, lying at the edge of a beach where humans came sometimes. Crazy, anyone could have seen her, but she was too weak to move. I carried her to a hidden cove. I didn't want the tribe to see the condition she was in, start asking questions. She was weeping, on and on. She said he hadn't changed. She'd sung until both their hearts were broken from the cruelty in her voice, but still he hadn't changed . . ." Luce could feel the hot seep of tears, but they didn't seem to be her own. The tears belonged to Marina.

"So she killed him?"

"I asked her that, of course. I thought she was weeping so terribly because he was dead, and I began to regret that I'd forced her . . . She told me not to worry. She told me it was all resolved. Those were her words but in Russian." There was silence and a dim phosphorescent pallor in the rocks above them. Luce had decided that must be the end of the story when Catarina spoke again.

"She crawled on shore that night. He was there, and he held her while she screamed, but he didn't bring her back to the water."

Luce thought she understood now. "You heard her, Catarina?"

"I heard her. I saw her in his arms at the very end. I shouted at him to carry her to the sea and he refused. He was in a rage. He said he was certain she'd survive the transformation back, that she belonged with him on land . . ." It was hard to know if the sound that came from Catarina now was laughter or sobs. "I could have enchanted him, made him walk into the water, but I didn't know how to make him bring her along. By the time he stopped yelling at me, she was dead. And I—I never saw my tribe again. I couldn't look at them."

There was a long silence. Luce wanted to know what Catarina had done to the man who'd kept Queen Marina out of the water, but after a moment's consideration she decided not to ask. Cat had told her enough.

"So, Luce . . ." She could hear Catarina straining to raise herself, and Luce opened her stinging eyes to see Catarina half smiling above her in the dimness. Still, Luce was astonished by what came next. "So, now you understand why I saved your life the night we met. Even though I knew perfectly from the first moment that you were a threat to me . . . That voice! Now you see why I needed you anyway."

Luce gaped at her in bewilderment. Was Catarina losing her mind?

"I—don't actually know what you're talking about, Cat. But I'm really not a threat. I *promise* . . ."

"I won't live as a false queen, Luce. How do you imagine I could bear to rule, knowing my place was rightfully yours? Although that's beside the point now." Catarina gazed searchingly down at her. "You really don't understand? Luce, when I heard your song it made me believe that Marina might have been able to forgive me for what I did to her. It gave me hope that in her last moments . . ." Catarina shook her head, and her hair brushed Luce's wet cheeks.

"I went after you, though I was endangering myself by doing it, though I had every reason to leave you where you were. I needed, more than anything, to keep hearing you sing, to keep feeling . . . that forgiveness. You remind me of Marina sometimes. Crazy but so brave . . . You'll be a very great queen, Luce, if you can just keep yourself from—from giving in to those desires, that longing, the way Marina and I both did. Every time I've ever looked at you I've wanted to warn you, but I couldn't, not without letting you see my own corruption. How could I possibly show that to someone so pure-hearted? But, maybe, since you're so young . . ."

Catarina didn't finish the sentence. She didn't have to. Luce understood all too well.

"Catarina . . ." This insistence that she would be a queen was ludicrous, anyway. Who would obey her? "I'll never be queen. Not of any tribe. I don't even want to, and I'm too weird for anyone to want me that way. You hear the stuff Anais says about me, like I'm just this complete loser freak . . ."

Catarina smiled, but when she tried to reach out and stroke Luce's hair her face abruptly contorted from pain. Luce was appalled with herself. How could she have forgotten that Cat's left wrist was broken?

"You still don't understand, Luce. You're such a child sometimes!" Catarina's voice was suddenly tight with agony, so Luce suppressed the urge to take offense at this. "I've been coming to your cave. I've been listening to you. And you're certainly the greatest singer I've heard since Marina died. I sometimes wonder if you might even be better than she was, and I never would have believed . . ."

Luce was embarrassed by this, and at the same time she hated to think that Catarina had been suffering for hours while she just slept and did nothing to help her.

"Um, Cat? I need to figure out a way to set your wrist. If I can find a couple of good pieces of driftwood and some net or something . . ." Luce's words came out too fast.

Catarina smiled, although her pain made it tighten into a grimace. "That would be very kind of you, Luce. And something to eat? We'll be able to talk—more calmly—once we've both had some dinner." Luce nodded.

"Wait here. Try to sleep. I'll be back as soon as I can." Luce felt nervous about leaving Catarina on her own, but there was no other way. They were both giddy from hunger.

* * *

It took longer than she'd hoped to find everything they needed. There were no mussels but plenty of oysters, so Luce found a plastic grocery bag strangling some seaweed and untangled it to carry them back. The seaweed looked good here, too, and the driftwood was easy enough, but for a long time she couldn't find anything that would work as a makeshift wrapping for the cast. This was one time when it would have been helpful to have Anais's piles of stolen clothes on hand. Eventually Luce decided that the snarled plastic grocery bags she saw here and there were the best thing she could find for now, and she tucked a few of them away with the oysters.

She had to tell Catarina the truth, Luce realized. If she could make Catarina accept that she'd already broken the timahk herself, in the worst possible way—that she'd actually rescued a boy, not just fantasized about it, that she was even guiltier than Cat was herself—then, just possibly, Catarina would get over her shame enough to let Luce travel south with her. She hated to think of how Catarina would look at her as she told the story, but still . . . it was the only decent thing she could do.

Before she swam back into the high crevice between the cliffs Luce paused to stare out at the sea—which was always so familiar even when it was strange but where she was always utterly lost even when she knew exactly where she was. In the faintly dusky sky she could just make out a pale scattering of stars. She listened to their buzzing voices, which sounded like tiny metallic wings whirring to hold them in place; she thought the stars might be like crickets, singing with the friction of their bodies instead of with their throats. She thought that, after dinner, she might try to describe the sound to Catarina, and she turned between the cliffs carried by a sudden feeling of elation. A clean stroke of freedom would carry them both away from here.

The cave was empty. Luce called again and again, although the space was so small that there was no corner where her friend could possibly be hiding.

Catarina was gone, and Luce was all alone.

After a while Luce curled up with her head leaning on a rock, wondering why she wasn't consumed by despair. Instead she felt an inexplicable sense of peace. She was cradled in music. The rocks around her chanted like slow, growling bells, and each curl of the water stroked her fins with silky notes. She'd been so afraid of leaving her tribe, but she understood that she never would have heard the music resonating out of every crook of the world if she hadn't taken so many risks. She'd opened her heart to that music in solitude, and it had come to her. And even now that her tribe was broken, her friends dead or vanished, Luce realized the world's voice sounded hopeful, vital, full of the soft vibrancy of pure being.

Gently she sang back, letting her voice glide into complex harmonies with all the inhuman voices humming around her. A crystalline sphere of water floated up between her hands, raised itself nearer—Luce almost wondered if it could see her—then stroked against her lips. It felt like a kiss.